MURDERING THE MESSENGER

MURDERING THE MESSENGER

Michael Jecks

SEVERN
HOUSE

First world edition published in Great Britain and the USA in 2023
by Severn House, an imprint of Canongate Books Ltd,
14 High Street, Edinburgh EH1 1TE.

severnhouse.com

British Library Cataloguing-in-Publication Data
A CIP catalogue record for this title is available from the British Library.

ISBN-13: 978-0-7278-2306-9 (cased)
ISBN-13: 978-1-4483-1228-3 (e-book)

All Severn House titles are printed on acid-free paper.

MIX
Paper from
responsible sources
FSC www.fsc.org   FSC® C013056

Typeset by Palimpsest Book Production Ltd.,
Falkirk, Stirlingshire, Scotland.
Printed and bound in Great Britain by
TJ Books Limited, Padstow, Cornwall.

Praise for Michael Jecks

"The comical hero provides an amusing instrument for
exploring the mores and history of the period"
Kirkus Reviews on *The Merchant Murderers*

"An amusing mystery replete with historical tidbits and
fascinating local descriptions"
Kirkus Reviews on *The Moorland Murderers*

"Plenty of historical detail, loads of twists and turns, and a
hilarious tale of criminal ineptitude"
Kirkus Reviews on *Death Comes Hot*

"Steeped in the rich, bawdy background of 16th-century
London . . . Enough suspects and red herrings to keep
mystery fans intrigued"
Booklist on *The Dead Don't Wait*

"An enjoyable jaunt through mid-16th-century England . . .
The novel's energetic pace never flags"
Publishers Weekly on *The Dead Don't Wait*

"Entertaining . . . Jecks brings the seamy side of Tudor
London to life through rich, atmospheric descriptions of its
taverns, brothels and streets"
Publishers Weekly on *A Missed Murder*

About the author

Michael Jecks is the author of forty-seven novels, including the acclaimed Last Templar medieval mystery series, modern spy thriller *Act of Vengeance*, and seven previous Bloody Mary mysteries. A former Chairman of the Crime Writers' Association, and founder of Medieval Murderers, he lives in northern Dartmoor.

www.michaeljecks.co.uk

PROLOGUE

Monday 29th March, 1557

When I first saw the body, I thought I must be mistaken. Rachel should not have been there, she should have been packing, preparing herself for the journey, for in the next few hours she was supposed to travel to France – which was important to me, since she intended I should accompany her all the way to Paris. It was my task, I had been informed, to protect her at all costs on that journey. And *at all costs* had a horribly familiar and dangerous ring to the words. It meant I should throw my life away, if it meant she was saved from danger. That was not an appealing prospect.

It was all because Rachel Nailor meant to carry out a vital mission. My Lady Elizabeth had decided to send her to speak with the King of France's officials, begging for his aid in her present – which means her latest – crisis. Rachel should have been resting before undertaking her journey over the water. And I was determined to escape this mission and the risks it involved.

Yet here she was, amidst mess and destruction, a sad huddle of clothing, her blood staining the flags all around. I confess, it made me tearful. I am no soft-hearted fool, but until only the day before I had thought that . . . but no. I won't think of that. There is no point clinging to dreams when you waken to the grim truth of life. And the reality was, she was not interested in a coupling. Later I would learn how disinterested in me she was.

Life is there to be lived, unfettered by remorse for what might have been.

Besides, I had other matters on my mind. Such as, I was being accused of her murder.

ONE

After enduring a lengthy and troublesome sojourn in the wild and dangerous west of the kingdom, living amongst tin miners, peasants and felons of the worst sort, it had been a relief to return to civilization the previous year. I need only say that it was a matter of considerable satisfaction to find myself once more inside the protective cocoon of London's walls. Never again, I swore, would I wander so far west. The peasants there were the most unappealing, grim, violent hardheads I have ever met, while the merchants made London's thieving mercenaries look like paragons of virtue by comparison.

Not that I could return to my old home. There were two problems there: Pudge and Saul. Saul Appleby was troublesome, for I had developed a rather close acquaintanceship with the delightful Susan, his wife. Saul was a niggardly, sour old fellow in his middle years, with less life in him than a candlestick; she was a buxom hussy of near thirty, with the sort of wandering eye that makes a man feel his codpiece could do with enlargement.

All was well, but after one of our assignations was broken up by his returning home early, necessitating a swift exit on my part, it was clear that our ability to meet for a little mattress-walloping would be considerably facilitated were we to have a little distance between our homes. We did not wish our pleasant exercises to be interrupted by her husband, and it wasn't possible to send all the servants away whenever he was gone from home.

Then again, there were other incentives for removing to a new home, such as the repellent Pudge. He was one of those fellows who considered that he should have access to my purse, and ideally my interior organs; he knew where I lived, and I was keen to make his interview with me as difficult as possible, especially since Pudge, this foul tavern-keeper, seemed to believe he had the right to take all my money in exchange for a small party other people had organized in my house. I had, of course, tried to explain to the bovine brogger that it was not me whom he sought. Others had fooled him into providing the ale and wine for the party, but Pudge was not of a mind to allow bygones to be bygones, and even now, I heard, he was seeking my new accommodation, and ideally my neck.

So I had moved from my old address to the parish of St Helen's. It was only a short walk from my old haunts, which had the advantage of proximity to Susan, while being far enough to confuse Saul and the more foolish dolts seeking my money.

However, there was one large and unavoidable distraction in my new parish.

His name was Peter: Father Peter.

I was early into Mass that first day, grumpy with a grumbling belly. I dislike Lent, and this was the third week. Kicking my lazy and shiftless servant, Raphe, from his cot, I dressed in my finest, with black doublet and hose, both decorated with fine silver threads to give a subtle ostentation to my appearance; the cloak to set it all off was lined and embroidered with black silk, matching my cap. All in all, I looked the picture of a successful, wealthy merchant, which was distinctly preferable to exhibiting my actual career as an assassin. People tend to grow anxious around men of my profession, or so I imagine. I have never taken the risk of informing them.

It was not to impress the women that I dressed so carefully, but to reassure the good priest, Father Peter. This was my first appearance in his church since I had arrived in the parish, and I believe it is important to make a good impression. That was even more vital at that time, with the disputes between the different styles of religious observance.

As it was, this did not turn out be the calm introduction I had hoped for.

*   *   *

Father Peter was a short, plump man of some five-and-thir. summers, with hair that was receding from his scalp like piss running down a wall. His eyes were too close together, his lips thin and mean, his chin weak, and overall he was not a picture of saintly generosity. In short, he was ugly. With a face such as his, his hair had good reason to withdraw. His expression was that of a man with acute piles, whose backside was giving him constant pain. When he saw me, if anything his expression soured still more. He had nasty little rat-like eyes of a particularly dark blue, and he stared at me in the venomous way a lord might view a leprous beggar. Of course the church itself was menacing with its Lenten decorations, the linen veil over the altar, the curtain about the lectern and so on. It made the church feel sombre, so perhaps he was just reflecting the mood of the period.

I was determined not to feel intimidated, and strode to him with a broad smile to indicate my pleasure at meeting him, but he continued to view me with every sign of black suspicion.

There have been so many changes in the Church in recent years, of course. Many priests still aren't sure whether they should be reciting prayers in Latin or English, and the loyalty of many to either Rome or to Henry's new church has led to more than a few disputes. Some priests have been evicted from their own parishes, and members of congregations forced to move because of disagreements with their priests. Perhaps Peter viewed me as suspicious, a foreigner who might hold any number of dangerous beliefs. A man who might hold opinions that were the opposite of those the good father propounded.

'Father, I am pleased to meet you. I have recently moved into the parish, and was hoping to join your congregation.'

'Oh?'

Not the most effusive welcome, perhaps, but at least there was a slight lessening of tension about his features.

I explained that I had moved to the house only a short way down the street alongside the churchyard's wall, and he nodded as if in acceptance. And then the bell tolled overhead as the service began.

If there was a challenge put down for the priest who was most likely to bore a parishioner to death, I would have wagered a good sum on him. His service, such as it was, was miserable. I was forced to sit at the side with other unattached men, there being no pews to spare, and there I must endure the lash of the priest's scowl as he glanced about the church. Every time he looked at me, it felt as though I was stung by a wasp, his gaze was so virulent.

In self-defence I cast about at other members of the congregation. Near me was a thin, sallow-faced man of perhaps forty years, although from the look of his hair, he might have been a lot younger. He had the sort of leathery skin and gauntness that spoke of a life of poverty and hardship. I nodded and gave him a welcoming grin; he scowled at me. I looked away hurriedly, only to find myself speared by the stern gaze of the priest once more. Perhaps it was Lent making him grim. Many who fast become grumpy.

It was a large church. At the front of the main pews, a little to the left of the altar, was the most notable fellow in the parish, a judge, sitting in his own pew with his wife. This was Sir Gerald Marbod and his wife Eleanor. I had heard of them from my master, John Blount. Marbod was one of those who was a supporter of our Lady Elizabeth rather than her half-sister the queen. At the very front of the main pews in the nave were an alderman, Master William Kirk, and his wife Agnes, who both sat with noses in the air, as if a rat had crawled under their seat to die some time ago. There was another small family group behind them, and then the run-of-the-mill parishioners, with women and men generally segregated. Occasionally a man could be seen with a woman, but that was commonly a widow with her son. In short, it was much like any other church in London, apart from the vehement denunciations of one and all by the priest at the front, who seemed to believe that the only way to inspire his congregation was by accusing them all of lewdness and lust . . . and gluttony, but mostly lewdness and lust.

The only saving grace of this, my first, service at St Helen's was the pair of small, slim figures sitting modestly and chastely among the women. The younger of the two was clearly a maid of some sort, perhaps a cook's assistant; but the other, she merited some study.

Her bent head showed off a marvellous slender neck, and the tunic and cloak did not disguise the ripeness of her figure. She was a refreshing sight, and it was a relief to know that there could be alternative diversions in this new locality. I reflected that she alone justified the cost of my new house. Just as I was thinking that after the sermon I might speak with her with a view to investing in a pot or two of wine that might, with good fortune, help persuade her to visit my home, I became aware that the priest was bellowing still more loudly – and it was invective aimed directly at me.

I don't know what sort of man he thought I was. No, that isn't true, he made his impressions about me abundantly clear. He appeared to deprecate my roving eye, as if a man should not admire a young filly while in his church. He gave me, and the rest of the congregation, to understand that I was no better than a whoremonger for studying the woman in such detail. Admittedly, I had allowed my eyes to wander even as my mind did, but I don't know why he came to the conclusion that I was a mere wastrel. That was a little unfair, but that he did was plain enough from the way he pointed at me, giving everyone in the church to understand that I was precisely the sort of man who should be avoided by those who sought to preserve their souls.

In all likelihood his belly was grumbling from fasting. That was the best excuse for his rudeness.

It was humiliating, but I was rewarded by a flash of dark eyes from the woman in the pews, and I saw that she was smiling. Plainly not everyone was convinced of the priest's exhortations.

There was still hope, then.

It was annoying to be thus upbraided in front of everyone, when my only crime, so far as I could see, was to be the best-dressed fellow in the area. I was glad when, at long last, the service was ended and I could withdraw to the sunshine outside. Happily, the two young women were waiting in the churchyard, the maid standing back while her mistress chatted to another woman.

From closer to, she was yet more appealing. Slim but

buxom, with broad hips, she was a delight to the eyes. She had a confident air which argued against her being a mere servant girl. Her companion from the pew was pretty enough, and may well have been maid to a wealthy merchant, I guessed, but if I knew women at all, this confident woman must be wife to the merchant at least. Her face was pleasingly regular, with full lips that begged for a kiss, and eyes that were prone to narrowing in laughter, from the look of the little creases at the corners. She was the sort of woman who would delight in pleasant surroundings, good company, laughter and gaiety. There was something about her that told me she would be a difficult quarry, but one who, when snared, would make for a thrilling bedchamber gallop. Yet overall, there was a watchfulness about her that spoke of intelligence and experience. This would not be an easy wench to persuade into my bed, but if I could, I was sure that she would be a rewarding wrestling companion. She and her companions ceased talking as I approached, all watching me almost warily.

Her friend was a matronly soul of middling height, with a round, cheerful face and reddish blonde hair poking from beneath her wimple. She had the sort of laugh that could clear six inches of rust from armour in one blast but, while deafening, she was a happy, kindly-looking woman. The sort whom a fellow would find warm to snuggle up to on a chill winter's night. Her ruddy face spoke of experience and, if my guess was accurate, she had plenty of knowledge of the pleasures of men. She had that sort of twinkle in her eye as she watched me approach.

'You are new here,' she said. 'I am Mistress Spink. Who are you?'

'I am called Lucky Jack,' I said, and turned my broad smile to the other maid. 'And who are you?'

'Mistress Nailor,' she said, almost as if reluctantly. It was plain that I would have to work hard to win her approval, but that it would be worthwhile was never in any doubt.

It was good to chat with them, but I was to be disappointed. Soon it became clear that they had other business, and Mistress Nailor made her apologies and strode off towards a pair of men standing at the church's gate with the little maid hurrying a few paces behind her. Nailor clearly knew the two at the gate, and it struck me that both bowed to her, but she barely acknowledged them – so my estimate was right. This was no maid. Mistress Nailor must be a woman of some importance to command the respect of two bully boys like them.

I say that as a fellow who has some experience of men of the tougher forms. In my time I have been a pickpocket, a thief, and now I have a reputation as an accomplished assassin. I have come into contact with many men of dubious character who gained their ill-repute solely for their violence. These two gave me the feeling that they were of a similar mould.

'You like her, then?'

Mistress 'Call me Gawtheren' Spink was still standing at my side, and I cast an eye over her attributes. They were extensive, it has to be said. No slim lightweight, yet she had a build designed for comfort.

'She is appealing enough,' I said, and gave her a quick Honest Jack leer, which was wasted since she was staring after Mistress Nailor.

'All the men adore her,' she said, with a half-wistful tone in her voice. 'Yet she barely notices them.'

'Ah, but they wouldn't think to look at her when with you,' I said gallantly.

'You're quite a one, aren't you?' she said, and now encountered my lustiest grin. Her face creased into a reciprocal smile. 'You dare suggest a tumble here in the churchyard?' She suddenly grabbed my codpiece.

I was terrified that she might pull it free, and expose me to ridicule under the stern gaze of the priest, but as I squawked she let me go and laughed, and leaned against me. 'Mayhap soon we'll get to have some fun together, eh?'

Truth be told, it was some little while since my last encounter with a woman quite so eager for a quick bedchamber fumble, and I confess that I found her rather intimidating. I was relieved when she left me to join a young fellow, who stood glowering at me from the gate to the road. He reluctantly, as I thought, joined her walking towards the road.

It is surely unnecessary to say that these women gave me

pause for thought as I meandered homewards. Once there, I
bellowed for my servant and demanded a pint of wine as I set
my backside on my favourite chair and held my feet to the
fire. Lent be damned! I would fast on Friday and Wednesday,
but if I starved all week, I'd expire in a matter of hours. I
needed that wine.

It was unseasonably cool still, and I was pensive as I sat
warming my toes. After all, I had plenty to consider. I had an
entertainment planned with Susan already, but there was something entrancing about the young Mistress Nailor. She was
most appealing. In fact, there was no denying that I could be
tempted to consider her as a welcome replacement to Susan.

Oh, I know. This sounds like maudlin nonsense from a man
of the world such as me but, you see, I was by this time some
three-and-twenty years old (if the drunken sot who considered
himself my father could be trusted), and it was perhaps time
that even a well-made fellow-about-town like me should
consider a more permanent arrangement, rather than occasional dalliances with other men's wives. Not that this maid
would give me more than a quick glance, I felt sure. Especially
after that blowhard priest's comments about me.

It was sad to contemplate, but I decided that there was little
to be done about her. She was a lost cause to me. Plainly she
was a woman of some importance and standing. The two men
waiting for her was proof of that. Tangling with characters of
their sort was not conducive to a restful life. I was safer with
the arrangement of mutual pleasure contracted with Mistress
Susan, with the possible addition of the enthusiastic Gawtheren
Spink.

At least with either one, I knew I could be assured of a
happy outcome without the concomitant expense of a woman
in the house.

TWO

A week passed before I saw her again. I was once more relegated to the side pews, and this time I studiously avoided watching the women, but that was no help. Father Peter had plainly decided that I was some sort of bad apple sent to infect his congregation, and he was not going to let me enjoy a quiet seat in his church. Or it was his determined fasting that was making him so belligerent.

'There are some who only ever think of *pleasure*!' he ranted, and I could see the spray gush from his mouth. It made me glad to be sitting farther away from him than the wealthy folk in the front pews. Alderman Kirk flinched at the spume flying towards him. At the very front Sir Gerald Marbod sat with his wife, both studiously ignoring the rest of the congregation. I suppose it was the natural response of a rich man to the scruffier elements, trying to ignore them all, but to my eye it made him look like a guilty felon standing in court, a thieving man who knew he was complicit in some larceny, and dare not meet the eye of the jury.

'Ye are all sinners,' the incensed priest continued, jabbing with an imperious finger at the air. Somehow it felt as though every stab of that digit was aimed at my heart. 'But some are worse than others, some can never cure the tainted soul within their filthy breasts! There are some who spend their whole lives contemplating the pleasures of the flesh, rather than setting their sight on the marvellous, the life of abstinence and the protection of their souls for the life to come!' As he spoke he stared directly at me, and – just for a moment – I thought he was begging me for my salvation, that he wanted me to go and kneel and pray with him.

Well, I have to admit, there were plenty of considerably more appealing distractions. First and foremost, the women I had seen the week before. When I casually glanced in their direction, I met the knowing grin of Gawtheren Spink. She was sitting with the youth I had seen with her the previous week. I looked away quickly, but not fast enough. The priest subjected me, and the congregation, to another furious tirade about the male element and our promiscuity.

Afterwards it was a relief to escape the ranting priest. It was an unseasonably bright day, and I stood surveying the church grounds as the congregation milled about. Few hurried away, most preferring to loiter and chat, and I saw Mistress Nailor talking with two other women near the parish well. Mistress Spink was not with them, but instead stood at some distance apart from them, watching the other two with a look of keen attention on her face as she spoke with Mistress Nailor's maid.

I made my way over to Mistress Nailor and her companions, and was rewarded with a sidelong glance from Nailor, but no welcoming smile. It was disappointing, but I was sure that with my charming ways I should soon win her over. Few women can refuse my grin and courtesy. They try to steel themselves against me, but when a fellow has the favour of a clean complexion, good manners and all the trappings of wealth . . . well! Which woman could resist?

The sun was out, as I mentioned, and it lent a soft warmth to her features. A few stray strands of hair had slipped free of her coif, and they glowed in the sun. I was entranced to see copper and gold tints in them.

'Mistress,' I said with a bow. If I say so myself, it was a good bow, the sort of bow that would instantly have told anyone that I was a man of elegance and breeding.

She appeared to appreciate the respect I showed her, and inclined her head politely in her turn. The other women included Eleanor Marbod. She was a tall and stately lady given to a certain coolness in her manner, as though she doubted I was of quite the correct status to speak with her. There was another, shorter woman who was introduced to me as Mistress Croke. An uncommonly ugly name for a woman with a pleasing smile and rather a wayward eye.

I was soon to understand that the three women were among the least respectful to the priest in the whole congregation.

My favourite, Mistress Nailor, was the swiftest to let me know that she had little if any respect for the man. 'He is a most insulting priest. The way he looks at women is surely a proof that he has no understanding of our sex,' she said with a little toss of her head that set the auburn strands dancing.

'I was only aware of his barbs directed to me,' I said.

'He must have some cause for his disdain of you,' Mistress Croke said.

'I fail to understand why,' I admitted. After all, it was unlikely that he was aware of my profession.

'He imagines you a bad influence on the poor, impressionable young women of the parish,' Mistress Croke said with a deep chuckle. It was the sort of chuckle I would have expected in a brothel like the Cardinal's Hat, rather than the environs of a parish church, and I warmed to her still more.

Mistress Marbod announced that she must leave to see her husband, and looked keenly at Mistress Nailor, but her departure did not halt the conversation.

'The way he looks at me, one would think he was condemning me at the throne of Our Lord,' Mistress Nailor said. 'The arrogance of the man! Just because he can speak a little Latin and he considers all of us too ignorant to comprehend!'

'He is merely jealous of your beauty,' I said, and I was sincere. She was a truly wonderful picture to contemplate.

Mistress Nailor smiled, and I was delighted to see two dimples appear, although an eyebrow arched cynically. 'You must have a profession that is deeply disreputable, Master Blackjack, for him to have gained such an unfavourable impression of you so swiftly.'

'It is my sad fate,' I said.

'Is your profession so disreputable?' Mistress Nailor pressed.

'Deeply so. Were I to confess it to you, I would instantly have to leave the area, you would be so mortified,' I laughed. I have a good laugh. It has won over many a young maid's heart.

'Really? Do tell,' Mistress Croke said. There was a glint in her eye which I didn't like. It looked as though she did not trust me. Women of a certain type are often harder to convince.

She was slightly older, perhaps, and more experienced in the sword and buckler play of words between the sexes. Such women can be more prone to suspicion of innocent men like me, assuming the worst of a fellow, when in reality a fellow is perfectly safe. It is the entrancing, slimmer, prettier maids who need to be more cautious. After all, a woman like this Nailor or even Mistress Spink should be constantly alert for a man of dubious intent. I could easily see myself making a play for either – but not Mistress Croke.

But before I could answer, she was beckoned by a man with a haughty appearance who stood a little away from us. Mistress Croke immediately bent her head and left us to join him.

Mistress Nailor did not smile at Mistress Croke's pleasantry, but stared after her. 'I would love to leave this parish.' And then, more quietly, she added, 'Far from that household.'

It was a curious comment, and I was unsure for a moment whether I had misheard her, and would have asked what made the parish so uncongenial to her, but only a short while later Mistress Nailor glanced towards the gate and saw her two men waiting again. She immediately broke off the conversation and strode briskly to meet them, the young maid leaving Gawtheren and scurrying behind her.

'Wait, mistress,' I called, and wanted to suggest that we could all repair to a local inn, to continue our pleasing conversation, but she was already striding out to the street beyond with the men.

I ambled off after her. At the road, I was in time to see the trio marching down the roadway, the maid scampering behind like a puppy following her pack, and then they turned into Bishopsgate.

This is a good moment to describe the area. After all, now I live here, it will aid you to understand what the place was like.

Originally St Helen's was a nun's convent. The parish church in which the priest glared at me so ferociously had been the conventual church, with the nuns hidden away to one side, hidden by screens from the prying eyes of the secular world. The seats on which I sat in the nave were some of those used by the nuns before the dissolution when King Henry stole the silver and lead from all the Catholic churches to pay off his debts.

On the left-hand side would have been the nuns in their quire, while the scruffy local tradesmen were permitted to stand in the second chamber to the right of the screen. Their fortune lay in the fact that they were permitted to listen to the nuns singing, but of course they were not allowed to *see* the brides of Christ. Only the nun's own celebrant was rewarded with that pleasure.

As I say, in Henry's time the convent was taken and broken up. I don't know who was given which plot of land – or rather which parcels they were forced to buy from the ever-impecunious king – but by the time I took up residence, the Worshipful Company of Leather Sellers had taken up the north-east section of the conventual lands. They had almshouses, a large garden, and their livery hall, which had once been the nuns' dormitory. The large house that had housed the prioress was now taken over by a large, sweaty man called Stephen Anderson, who claimed to be successful leather seller himself. Personally, from the little I had seen of him, I thought him too bland and foolish to be successful at anything, other than consuming the vast quantities of sack and brandy which were his constant companions in the tavern.

As for the rest, there were small houses at the north of the priory which were now owned by more leather sellers. Meanwhile the Marbods lived in a large hall a short walk away, and the Kirks in a second a little beyond them. Mistress Nailor was heading in the direction of their homes.

When I left the churchyard, in front of me here was the row of ten buildings, all of which were owned by moderately well-to-do people – including me with my own little house. I had imagined that Mistress Nailor occupied one of these, but as I gazed towards Bishopsgate Street, I could see her striding into the roadway. She was plainly in a hurry, but I could see that her two men were working together, each surveying the roadway ahead and eyeing the alleys as they passed, holding her back somewhat. I was struck with the conviction that this was no ordinary lady. Such attentiveness in servants spoke of a woman who was aware of her own danger.

It was enough to give me pause for thought. Then, when I turned, I saw the young lad with Mistress Spink. Now I could study him, I thought he was perhaps sixteen or seventeen, the sort of age when a fellow is still skinny and gangling, before he musters the muscles of maturity. He stared with contempt at Father Peter, who stood at the church door bidding farewell to his congregation. The priest looked up, and his eyes met mine, and again I was struck with a certain look in his eyes, as though he was determined to battle for my soul. He had little idea what a fight that would be.

While I stood gathering my thoughts, Mistress Croke joined me with some others, one of whom she introduced as her husband. I recognized him from the previous week: a tall, serious-looking man with cadaverous cheeks and bright, unblinking eyes. He studied me silently for a moment before offering me his hand. 'I am happy to make your acquaintance,' he said.

'The pleasure is mine,' I said without conviction. I could understand why his wife was so friendly. Anything to bring a little life and happiness into her marriage would be welcomed. He was a most tedious man.

'It is always good to find new members of our congregation,' he said. 'We have a good, strong, royalist and Catholic parish. I am sure you will fit in well.'

He was more convinced than I was. From the sincerity in his voice, I guessed that he would be one of those likely to be keen to judge and burn anyone who had had the temerity to attend one of King Henry's church services in the last years. There were many unreconstructed Catholics in those days.

The others in our little band were the Anderson family. Stephen, the father, who I mentioned had an impressive capacity for wine and brandy, was a large man in his fortieth year, I would guess. He had the sort of round face that made the innocent think of pleasant, humorous fellows, the sort who would merrily invite another to share a welcoming bowl of wine or two in a tavern, a man who would be first to call for another mess of dinner or be first to start singing cheerily in a tavern.

His was not that sort of character. ...ad coal-black eye... small and deep-set like those of a ho...d from the way he could consume ale and meat pies, as...as about to learn, he was little better than a glutton. And ...a pleasant one. He was one of those who considered himsel... above any others in the parish, even as the grease dribbled on his chin.

His wife, Kate, was a slender whip of a ...rch who looked as though the faintest gust of wind from the ri...er would send her flying into the air. She doted on her son, John. This was a tallish, chunkily-built lad of some twenty summers, who dressed with over-ostentatious showiness. I like a man to have a sense of style and taste, but this fellow seemed to think that the best form of dress involved only additional silk and rich fabrics. He looked too foppish and gaudy for my taste.

As you can imagine I felt little sympathy with them. Still, when Croke invited me to join them in a visit to the Bull Inn, I was happy to agree. It was a good idea to get to know my new neighbours, after all. And the Bull Inn brewed a tempting beer and cooked pies which were hard to fault, and I was by this time feeling the need of a little sustenance. The good priest could fast if he wanted; I was hungry.

Entering from Bishopsgate, it was clear we were not the only members of St Helen's parish, nor St Ethelburga's, the parish adjacent to ours, who felt the need to recover after a lengthy and probably over-pointed sermon or two. I knew that I was in desperate need of a good draught of ale to calm my troubled breast after enduring Father Peter's vitriolic gaze. It would not have been so bad had I knowingly given him offence – or if I thought he knew of my occupation.

I was eager to put such thoughts aside in the interests of a jug of ale, and soon I was sitting with the rest of them in a comfortable little parlour with a fire smoking fitfully on the hearth and threatening to warm us unnecessarily. It was so close that I felt the urge to open my jack and allow the fine lining to be displayed. Not for any petty reasons of showing off, but purely because it was particularly warm. I was glad to see young John Anderson's eyes widen at the sight. It made me feel more rel to have demonstrated my position and worth so clearly.

Croke sat to right, the young Anderson on my left, his mother between and his father, and Mistress Croke between her own husband and Anderson. At first, all seemed moderately conial. And then things changed subtly.

'So, Master Blackjack, I hear you are a gentleman of leisure,' the old Anderson said, wiping a little drool of grease from his chin. He sat back to gaze at me, his chins wobbling.

'I have little need of work,' I said smoothly. It's always best to let men know your quality.

Croke sniffed. 'Some fellows think little of those who work; they consider such men are beneath them.'

'Not I,' I said. 'I believe that all men should be considered by their own worth. Whether they be a lord or a peasant labourer, each has his value.' Pure hogwash, of course, but it sounded good.

'That priest is a fool,' Anderson said haughtily, once he had absorbed my words. 'He insults all in his congregation. The man will go too far one day. When he does, he will regret it.'

'I thought it was only me,' I said.

'No,' Croke said. He looked judgemental as he pulled the corners of his mouth down into a moue. 'He insults anyone he suspects of lustful feelings, and rails against those who might have sympathy for Henry's religion. It is a wonder that his congregation returns. But he only annoys his own parishioners. Who among us would think to go to a clandestine church when the queen has decreed our true religion is returned?' he added quickly. Any man would be cautious while discussing religion. Too many had been invited to view the queen's chambers in the Tower and the paraphernalia of whips, tongs and hammers that could be used to persuade men that the only kind and gentle religion was the Church of Rome.

It sounded much like so many others I have heard declaring their religious commitment. There were always pyres flaming at the back of many people's minds. Once seen, it is very difficult to forget the sight of a man being enveloped by flames – or to forget the smells and sounds. I shuddered at the memory.

'Was he brought back when the queen changed the law, or

was he always here?' I asked. He didn't seem particularly keen on the folk he was supposed to shepherd.

'Oh, he was here, right enough. And as happily married as a man could be,' Mistress Anderson said primly. 'He ain't no better than he ought to be. And comes into church staring at us all as though *we* were full of guilt! If the truth were told, he was worse than any. He *deserted* his poor wife. She came back here to ask for his help, and he turned her away at the door of the church! It was other, better fellows who took care of her. She's had to leave the city,' she said. 'She lives outside the walls now, with the other homeless folk, her and her boy.'

'Very sad,' I said.

'Besides,' said young John Anderson, 'the priest hasn't changed his own behaviour. He's not as celibate as a priest should be.'

'Really?' I felt a spark of interest. It might be useful to have some ammunition to aim at Father Peter, if he continued to rant at me.

'Oh, yes,' John said. 'It's said he offers his own form of communion to most of the women in the parish.'

His mother pursed her lips. 'John! That will be enough!'

'I only say what everyone knows. He's been—'

'John, be silent!' his mother snapped.

He hung his head a little. 'Sorry, Mother.'

'With many women?' I asked. 'Women like Mistress Nailor?'

It was Croke who snorted at that, and while his wife laughed shortly, he enlightened me. 'Her? She wouldn't take her skirts up for a mere priest! Oh, no. She considers herself too high and mighty for that – she would expect a merchant with money and a title, ideally. We should feel privileged she deigns to join us in St Helen's church; that's what she thinks.'

'She seems a pleasant enough woman,' I said, but I couldn't miss the sidelong glance Anderson threw at his wife.

'She wouldn't piss on any of us if we were on fire,' his wife said.

'Why should she consider herself superior?' I asked. 'Is she of noble birth?'

'Hah! She was to marry the Marquess of Northampton, but

he had been married before, and although he divorced his first
wife, Queen Mary refused to accept it. So Rachel Nailor is
no longer a marchioness. She's only a stale,' Emilia Croke
said with an unbecoming satisfaction. 'Though she thinks she's
more important than us. Hardly even gave a good morning to
us here when she first appeared, although she is a little more
neighbourly now. Still, Master Marbod sends two men with
her wherever she goes. Doesn't trust her not to misbehave,
I'll be bound!'

That won a round of nods with all grimly satisfied at the
rudeness of this incomer to their close-knit community. I
feigned disinterest.

'She has lived here long, then?'

'Nay,' Emilia Croke said. 'She just appeared some months
ago and moved in with the Marbods. I'd bet she earned her
money like many women.' She gave a long, slow nod at that,
as though it was self-evident what she meant.

Which it was, of course. A widow or young woman desperate
for money in London would often resort to the last possession
to earn a crust, and that possession was at least negotiable.
Sometimes a maid would be fortunate, and would snare a man
who would pay for a chamber and servants, for as long as his
actual wife did not discover his stratagem. Others would go
to a bawdy house where there were at least some defences
against the more violent clients. My friend Piers was the apple
squire at the Cardinal's Hat, a noted house of ill-repute in
Southwark, where he served as the bully boy to remove the
more violent visitors when necessary. The women all adored
him, and much of his pay was in kind, as he boasted to me
regularly enough. When he was sober, anyway. Perhaps that
was why the girls liked him. They could offer him a knee-
trembler when they wanted a chance to relax, and leave him
snoring while they dozed between clients.

However, I have met with many women who have taken
that route to riches – or, more often, poverty – and none has
struck me in the same way as Mistress Nailor. I learned today
that her name was Rachel, a strangely lovely name that suited
her perfectly, in my estimation. I was not persuaded that Rachel
Nailor could be a woman who had sold her body for money

even if the value placed on it was a king's ransom. No, I was convinced that this was mere malicious tattle-telling. After all, I could read and understand women. It has been a key strength of mine, and one reason for my success with women. I have always had a knack with them.

It was interesting, however, to see how Kate's words affected her husband, who became suddenly sheepish, and fiddled with the sleeve of his jack, where a loose thread dangled. If I had to guess, I would think that Master Anderson had once enjoyed another woman's favours, and his wife was not the sort to ever let him forget it.

If Rachel was living with Sir Gerald Marbod, I wondered, was she related to him?

My question left my companions staring into their ales. There was a lot of blowing from inflated cheeks, reminding me of the sound of a horse having sniffed a dandelion, before Stephen admitted that Sir Gerald and his wife were not related, but kindly looking after her. His attitude surprised me, until I reflected that Master Anderson was newly wealthy, from his appearance. His son was dressed gaudily as if to impress, and it struck me that Stephen Anderson had a chip on his shoulder. He might have money, but that didn't make him a gentleman. An aristocrat would not respect his wealth. Marbod, however, was a knight and judge, an important position in the City. Perhaps Anderson had been snubbed by Marbod – or even by Rachel Nailor. Had Anderson tried to seduce her and been rejected with some force? It amused me to see how embarrassed he was, and how he attempted to change the subject.

But it also left me fascinated with her, and desiring further talk with her.

You will know by now that it is enormously difficult to catch me unawares, and harder still to so surprise me that I lose the power of speech. Of course, that is particularly the case in the presence of beautiful women. I am known for my good looks, the slight scar that gives me that devil-take-you appearance that all women find attractive, and my confidence with the opposite sex. I have an easy ability with women that they always appreciate. It is, as you might say, the brand mark of my masculinity.

To return to my parlour that afternoon and find the object of so many of my thoughts over the last week – particularly the more lustful ones – sitting there (very prettily it must be said) with her little maid standing near the window, was the source of a deal of mental agitation. I stood somewhat bemused.

'Close your mouth; you look like a hooked fish,' Rachel Nailor said, a little severely, I would say.

'But of course, Mistress Rachel. I . . . well, I . . .'

'Yes. Quite. Meanwhile, I have been advised to visit you, much against my better judgement, and I have been waiting here for some little while. Where have you been?' She gave an elegant sniff and curled her lip. 'Oh. An alehouse. Moll, you can leave us. Go to the kitchen and enquire about some wine.'

'Not an alehouse, not at all,' I said defensively. 'The Bull Inn. A pleasant hostelry for a lunch, and I —'

'I am sure,' she said as her maid walked from the room. 'But we don't have time for that right now.'

'No?' I gave her my slow smile then. It always produced the right result.

Not this time.

'Why are you leering? I was assured you were competent and moderately intelligent, but I begin to doubt his words.'

'Whose words?' I said, rather piqued by her attitude and sharp manner.

'Our confederate: John Blount,' she said, and I felt my cods shrivel.

Some of my friends reading this may find this a surprise. After all, most men, when talking about their own master, would likely feel more pride than terror. However, in my own case matters were a little different.

John Blount, I had come to learn, was the chief political strongman for Lady Elizabeth, the daughter of Anne Boleyn and King Henry. Since Mary, Elizabeth's sister, had taken the throne, Mary had declared that Anne and Henry could not have been married, since her own mother's divorce was illegal.

Thus Elizabeth was no longer to be considered a princess, since she was born out of wedlock. Yes, it's complicated. But John Blount, and therefore I as well, was a servant to Elizabeth, and a part of his duties involved getting me to remove certain obstacles to the smooth running machinery of Elizabeth's household. That meant disposing of those men or women who might cause the Lady Elizabeth embarrassment or danger. And since danger to Elizabeth inevitably meant danger to her household – in other words John Blount and, by association, me as well – whenever I heard that he had suggested somebody should speak with me, I felt the same shrinking anxiety. All too often the result was a demand that I should murder someone, and I am not, by nature, a violent man.

'I . . . er . . .'

'Do you have any wine? Your servant offered me some this half hour past, but I have not seen him as yet. Now Moll has disappeared too.'

'He's probably drunk it all, or smashed the last of the jugs,' I muttered. Then: 'How do you know John Blount?'

She gave me a long, hard stare. I have to confess, it made her look all the more attractive. There was measuring in her gaze, and I felt as though she was stripping me bare, but not with a view to bedding me, it was more a thoughtful look as if she was peering into my soul.

'I have known him for many months past,' she said after a pause of reflection. 'I am servant to the same superior as he. And our superior is now in danger.'

She didn't have to tell me that. The fact was that Lady Elizabeth was permanently in difficulty. Her sister knew that only Elizabeth had a rival claim to the throne, and it was only the fact of the dubious divorce of Mary's mother that gave Elizabeth that claim. Furthermore, Mary was as aware as I that Elizabeth was a most lively, devious and competent politician, and was availing herself of every opportunity to disrupt Queen Mary's reign and strengthen her own position. Her schemes had already led to her being imprisoned in the Tower, held under guard at remote palaces, and seen the arrest of her households. The main reason for my own fleeing from

London in the previous few months was caused by the fear that I would be one of the next of her servants to be arrested. Fortunately that occasion had been driven more by fear than reality, but it was plain enough that my position would be somewhat equivocal, were my position as executioner-in-chief to the queen's rival to become widely known. The fact that I had never intentionally committed homicide would not save me.

But most recently, the queen and her Spanish husband had hit upon a brilliant scheme to neuter Lady Elizabeth, as I was about to learn.

However, being vigilant and intelligent as well as beautiful, my guest placed a finger to her lips, and then darted to the door on light feet. She pulled it wide, staring out. I half expected to see a shocked Raphe crouched at the keyhole, as did she, but to her mild chagrin, there was no sign of him or her servant, little Moll. She closed the door quietly, took my hand and led me to the far corner of the room, where it would be difficult for anyone to overhear our speech.

'King Philip is determined to ensure that England will not ally herself to France. The Spanish are determined to have the support of the English army in their wars with France. To do that, they must force Elizabeth to renounce her religion and bind her to the Catholic church.' If ever a voice dripped with vitriol, it was hers now. I dare not look down in case I saw the acid eating into the floor. 'He has set his heart on ensuring that the princess marries Emmanuel Philibert, Prince of Piedmont. He is Catholic, and a sworn ally to the Spanish crown. Even now he is the Lieutenant of the Spanish Netherlands and fights the French.'

'And Lady Elizabeth does not wish to marry him,' I said. I wished her to understand that I fully appreciated the situation.

'Of course not! He is a Catholic, and were the *Princess* Elizabeth' – here she added a certain emphasis to the title – 'to marry him, he would wield all power in the kingdom! My lady could not submit to such a political marriage to benefit the Spanish at the expense of the English crown!'

I nodded, ignoring the slight insult. 'So what will she do?'

'Much. First, she seeks to send a message to the French, to procure safe passage to Paris, where she will seek refuge.'

My jaw dropped. 'To France? But . . . if she does so, her sister will not be pleased!'

The Lady Rachel seemed to suffer some gastric anguish or something. She closed her eyes briefly and when she opened them once more, she was recovered. I felt as though I was pierced by the intensity of her glare. 'What choice does the princess have? To remain here and be wedded to a man of little importance or fortune against her will, to be forced to renounce her faith and hand away all her authority? It would be unbearable. That is why we must aid her.'

'Aid?' I said.

'Don't squeak! We have to send to Paris to ensure the safe passage of the princess and guarantee her security on arrival. That is why Blount suggested that you should go there with me to be my bodyguard.'

'He suggested what?'

'Keep your voice down!'

I clenched my jaw. 'I cannot leave England. I do not speak French – what good would I be, adrift in a foreign land, knowing nothing of the customs, the —'

'You would have a companion who could advise you,' she said.

'Ah . . . you would join me?'

'I did say you would be my bodyguard.'

This did not endear the journey to me entirely, but it did at least have the merit that I might be able to enjoy her companionship. With close proximity, my charms surely could not fail to win her over.

And then the full horror of the situation struck me again. To be sent to a foreign land, to have no understanding of their culture and manners – I had heard terrible things about French behaviour and their treatment of foreigners – and no comprehension of their language . . . It was terrifying. Added to that, I would be in the company of this politicking woman, Rachel, which meant I was begging for misunderstandings, and potentially arrest, and who could tell what kind of punishment I might receive? In barbarous lands like France, I felt sure that a man of my elegance and position would be sure to suffer at the hands of rude foreign peasants.

I hurried to think of good reasons for not joining her. Fortunately, one occurred immediately. 'It is impossible, I fear. Were I to join you, I would be failing in my duties to Master Blount and our principal.'

'He has already released you. That is why he sent me here to explain to you,' she said.

'But the Lady Elizabeth could be in danger; I must remain here to be near her and defend her.'

'You can protect her better by ensuring her safe conduct to Paris. To do that we must smooth the way for her. You are needed with me, to ensure my survival. I will carry the message to the French king, and you must serve me in any way necessary to guarantee that I reach him with the message. You know what that means.'

I felt my stomach tighten at those words. It was not stated, but it was plain to me that when she said I must 'serve' her in 'any way necessary', that did not mean shaking the sheets with her. It might well entail my giving my life in order that she might continue securely. She meant I may have to lay down my life in a foreign land, at the hand of foreign brigands, after a journey of hardship and stress. I wanted to point out that I could just as easily expire by making a journey to York, and at least the footpads on the way would be comprehensible and might show a little regard for another Englishman's life, whereas those in detestable foreign countries would savour the opportunity of making an Englishman beg for mercy.

'I shall have to speak with Master Blount before I make any firm decision,' I said loftily.

'He said you might take that attitude,' she said, and there was that sharp edge to her voice again. We were standing close together near the window, and as she spoke she stepped away and peered at me in the light like a woman studying a particularly poor piece of needlework. 'He said to tell you that if you refused to accept the commission, he would personally ensure that your name and address would be given to certain men from whom you would prefer to remain concealed.'

I swallowed. That dunghill rat! That foggy, hard-headed, lubberly drunkard son of a whore! He knew that I had good reason to maintain a certain privacy, that to bruit my location to all and sundry could easily cause me a degree of embarrassment . . . let alone pain.

'I do not refuse,' I said with hauteur. 'However, a gentleman like me must consider all ramifications of a situation like this. I have responsibilities of which you are not aware.'

'I doubt that,' she said smartly. 'Be sure to consider your *responsibilities* speedily. We shall be leaving in two days. We have little time to waste. Your princess demands haste!'

And with that parting shot, she called her maid to her and left.

I have to confess, I had not given thought to wine until she departed. The fact that my poor imitation of a servant had not brought her even a glass of drink, nor had come to enquire of my needs, suddenly broke upon me. '*Raphe!*'

That damned woman was no longer the source of my admiration. Yes, her face was appealing, and yes, her figure was entrancing, and yes, I would have liked to have danced the palliasse pavane with her, because that haughty expression of hers would have made the wrestling still more enjoyable, but the sight of her cold, contemptuous expression when she heard I was thinking to refuse her demand that I accompany her, was enough to kill off any desire. As was the thought of the long, arduous journey to Paris. It did not bear thinking of.

'*Raphe!*'

If there was one thing I was certain of, it was that I did not wish to travel to Paris. If there was a second thing I was certain of, it was that John Blount would certainly carry through his threat to expose me if I did not. I was caught in a cleft stick: I could not remain in London and I did not wish to risk the journey.

There was no sign of Raphe. Disgruntled to have to suffer so incompetent a servant, I gave up, walked out to the buttery and found a pint of wine that was ready decanted. I carried it back with me and sat. Should I remain and run the risk of being uncovered by my faithless master, or endure the hardship of the journey? Both choices seemed certain to end in the same unpleasant manner, with my suffering pain, hardship and probably death. At least if I chose to stay here in London, I would be comfortable. For a little while longer.

I wandered back to my parlour with my wine and a jug holding another two pints. This was a problem that required deep thought. And while it was a problem with two solutions, I could not pick the better of the two. So I deferred the decision by drinking until the problem floated away on the fumes of good claret.

I think there was something wrong with that claret. It had tasted all right on the way down, but now I had emptied both cup and jug, it seemed to have turned to acid in my belly, and my stomach was recoiling from it.

I shifted in my seat. My purse had moved to my side, and it was digging into my hip. The laces were loose, too. I retied them, feeling oddly sweaty and uncomfortable.

Perhaps I was unwell. My body had a touch of shiveriness, and when I tried to stand, I experienced much the same discomfort as I had when sent from Exeter on a ship. The ground roiled as though floating on a stormy sea, and when I tried to grab for a pillar to support myself, my hand all but passed through it like a ghost's. Or perhaps I missed my mark. In any case, I was poorly. Glancing at the window, I saw that it was gathering dusk already, and I scowled to have heard nothing from my servants.

'Raphe!' I called, but not too loudly. Shouting seemed an unconscionably foolish idea. I closed my eyes and focused on the doorway, making my way shufflingly towards it, reaching to walls and pillars all the way. It took some little while.

My servant was sitting at the table in the kitchen, while Cecily bustled about. On seeing me, she gave me a flatly disapproving glare and then ignored me, as if I was unwelcome in my own kitchen.

'What?' I demanded.

'You've been snoring like a hog in a midden,' Raphe said coldly.

'I have had a deeply unpleasant surprise today,' I said. 'And where were you, when I needed you to help serve me and . . . and a guest?'

'Helping Cecily and visiting church with her,' Raphe said. I am not sure, but I think that there was a slight colouring in his cheeks as he spoke. It was probably the cold.

'It is Lent,' the young harridan said, clattering a pan or two unmercifully. 'Some folk pay attention to the observances.'

'What?' I demanded. This benighted wench may be a competent cook, but such a pietist and killjoy in my house was more than I could stomach just now. Rather than engage in debate that could only demean her, I glared at Raphe. 'Well, in future, let me know when you're going to church or leaving the house unattended,' I snapped sharply. 'You left the lady here all alone. What if she was a thief?'

'She didn't look like one,' he said, now grown surly.

'I suppose you would know what a thief looks like?'

'As well as most,' he said.

I didn't continue, partly due to the roiling in my belly, and in truth the room was a little over bright for my head just then. I had to narrow my eyes to focus on his features. I was almost ready to make my way upstairs to my bedchamber, when there came a peremptory knocking at my door. Jerking my head impetuously at my servant, I had to close my eyes at the sudden shock to my system. The movement almost caused my skull to leave my shoulders. In genuine anguish I motioned more carefully with my hand to indicate that my so-called servant should go and see who was visiting us, and made my way to my parlour and the comfort of my favourite seat.

I had only been resting there for a few moments when the door was thrust wide, and in came my master, John Blount.

He is a tall, thickset man with the sort of square face that inspires a fellow to keep a hand near his sword or dagger. Marching in like a vengeful fury, he stood in the doorway peering around the room before entering fully. Behind him I could see Raphe's glower. It looked as if he was as resentful of Master John's appearance as I was, not that it should concern him what I, his master, and Blount, his uncle, should want to discuss.

Yes, his uncle. You comprehend now the reason for my not having dismissed the useless knave from my service?

I indicated that I craved some strong wine – mostly to settle my stomach – but Blount waved Raphe away with a 'Leave us, boy!' and studied me like a man peering at a beetle preparatory to squashing it. 'What form of dissipation have you enjoyed today? You look like a rat who's fallen into a vat of brandy. You smell like one too,' he added, unnecessarily, I felt.

'I have,' I answered loftily, 'been engaged in discussions with my new neighbours.'

'Aye, well, let us hope they'll remain friendly once they hear you're an assassin,' he said.

'There's no need for them to know,' I said, a hand going to my brow. His voice was as subtle as the blast of a soldier's trumpet. It seemed to sear my brain like a red-hot brand as it entered my ears, and I was put to considerable discomfort by the noise.

'Not if you behave,' he said, and took his rest sitting on the settle beside the fireplace.

'I don't know what you mean.'

'Let me explain in simple words for you,' he said. 'Your mission – and this is not an optional or voluntary task, there is no decision to make because that's been made for you – is to travel with Mistress Rachel Nailor to Paris, and there to protect her to the best of your ability, no matter what.'

'Eh?' I accepted with relief the jug that Raphe passed to me. I filled my goblet with wine and drank deeply. It helped my stomach, although I was aware of a sort of lightness in my head, which was not at all unpleasant, but a little strange. I wanted to giggle at the serious expression on Master Blount's face as he ushered Raphe through the door again and closed it firmly.

'Are you listening?'

I gave him a wide grin and moved my hand emphatically. Wine slopped out, and I swore mildly.

'Christ's Cods, you're as beastly drunk as a boy-bishop at the feast of Holy Innocents,' he muttered. 'Can you understand me?'

'Of course, of course,' I said, and took another slurp of wine.

'You will go with her, protect her to your utmost, remove any two-legged obstacles to her mission, even at risk to yourself, you understand? Her task is vital for Lady Elizabeth and our nation. Lady Elizabeth has to escape before she can be forced by the Spanish into a marriage that would hand the crown to the Spanish empire and deprive us of all authority to direct our own future. If she fails, and is forced to marry that thong-cutting rogue, Emmanuel Philibert, our kingdom is lost forever. You understand?'

I gave a fresh, airy wave of my hand and expansive smile.

Suddenly I was gripped by the jack and pulled towards his black features. I squeaked as the goblet upended and I felt the wine trickling down my hosen.

'*Listen* to me, you sotten lummox,' he snarled. 'You leave the day after tomorrow. You will go with her, and you will ensure the success of her embassy to the King of France. Any failing and I will take it out on you personally. Do you understand me now?'

I gazed into his black eyes and nodded disconsolately

THREE

A s a gay fellow about town, I know full well that there are mornings – and then again, there are *mornings*.

On the first, I will waken with the birds, and lie in my bed listening to their cheery twittering. The weather will be calm and warm, and I will rise slowly, in a leisurely manner, while thinking of the eggs and slices of ham or beef that will break my fast, and amble downstairs with a feeling of vague interest wondering what the day might hold, before wandering to a tavern to partake of a measure of good cheer in a glass of sack or brandy.

But then there were the other days.

On those days, all is ill. Those are the days when every hair in my head dragged at my brain; when every movement made a tidal wave of nausea crash through my body; when standing caused the entire world to whirl about me; when merely opening my eyes was itself a dreadful hardship.

This was one of those days. I woke with my mouth dry and rough. It tasted like some species of incontinent rat had made use of it during the night. I could barely open my eyes, they were so gummed, and when I stood and tottered to the corner of the room, I could see that while trying to piss in my pot the previous evening, my aim had been sadly inaccurate. Leaving that sight till later, I pulled my jack on and stood swaying gently, eyes closed, as I waited for the world to right itself once more. It took a longish time, as though the whole earth was watching my suffering with amusement.

And then my eyes snapped wide with horror as I recalled the previous evening. Had I dreamt John Blount's appearance? In God's name, I hoped so. After all, I could not leave the country – what? Take ship to France with that arrogant scold Rachel Nailor, and willingly threaten all those who would stand in her path with instant death? Blount may consider me a willing and cold-hearted murderer, but he was sadly mistaken, and I was incapable of taking on that kind of responsibility. I couldn't even speak French. What, was I supposed to guess when a peasant was muttering at me, whether or not he was promising a short and painful future for the wench, or offering us lunch? If he was anything like the peasants I had met while in Dartmoor and Exeter, it was more than likely that his use of language would be all but incomprehensible even to fluent French speakers. The likelihood of my being able to understand him was remote in the extreme.

I had no other option: I must escape this mission. I would have to speak to John Blount urgently and make it clear that this was a task which was outside my sphere of ability.

With that resolve, I closed my eyes again, swallowed hard to keep the bile at bay, and grasped the corner of my cupboard. I was attempting to keep the vision of John Blount's face, red and furious, bellowing at me as he gripped my jack, from intruding. It was a failed exercise. His features could be fearsome when he felt that a servant was failing him. For me to refuse to accept his instructions could well make him plan to remove me from Lady Elizabeth's household. Were she to learn that I had failed her, she would herself be likely to seek redress, and I was aware that her pleasant, kindly and innocent features concealed a heart as cold and calculating as Caligula's. The thought of telling her that I would not go was enough to send me back to the pisspot.

Downstairs I found Raphe sitting in the kitchen once more while Cecily bustled, warming ale for him, presenting him with a plate of bread and some cheese. I took one look at their domestic environment, and left them to it.

Departing from the front door, I let my feet guide me out to the Bull Inn. I had a feeling that I would need some liquid courage before visiting my master with my refusal to assist our mistress.

Before long I was inside the inn sipping a weak ale in the vain hope that it might settle my stomach and cure my general sense of being in urgent need of St Helen's sexton, a shovel and a grave marker. It really felt as though I was destined to soon be laid out ready for my plot. And that was before speaking to John Blount. I had only drunk a normal few pints at lunch, and then the half jug of wine. I couldn't understand why I felt so poorly. It must be an illness.

A cup or two of ale, and I felt a little refreshed – enough to be able to think of visiting John Blount at his home, but even as I drained the second cup and threw some coins on the table, I was aware of a general hubbub from outside the inn.

Urged by a sense of mild enquiry, I stood and caught a glimpse of the people outside. Several little groups were standing and gesticulating, men and women clotting the thoroughfare. Most were pointing up the road towards St Helen's church and, intrigued, I meandered out, in an amiable, two ales fug of mind. I allowed myself to be drawn along the street towards the church. It was not as though I had a lot of choice in the matter. Everyone seemed to be heading that way, and I was like a small fish caught in the eddies of the tide, pulled with the waters. At least now my head was feeling a little better, and my stomach was settled.

The crowd's focus was the church, and as I entered the little parish churchyard, I was surprised to see how the people stood at the door and peered inside. I could not understand, until I reached it myself and gazed in.

I have witnessed some messes in my life. When I was a child, growing up with a drunk whose idea of cleaning a room was to throw everything into the street and set it ablaze while capering with a jug of ale in his hand, if in a good mood, and to sit sullenly and glare at the fire and the world when he was not in a good frame of mind. Then again, the destruction wrought on the London Bridge during the short-lived Wyatt Rebellion springs to mind as well. The number of times I have seen places broken and all the goods inside devastated, I could barely count. At least once a month or so a fellow would witness a little brawl in a tavern, and be given an opportunity to survey the result: broken chairs and tables as well as heads.

But of course that kind of result is normal. A man expects the occasional fight in an alehouse. To see this was somehow much worse, even though it was not as extensive.

The altar had been cleared. Those items which had usually rested on the great slab of stone were now scattered, the communion cup dented on the floor, the cross and plate knocked to the side. The altar's veil had been dragged from its moorings and left scrundled in a heap on the floor, along with the curtain from the lectern and the altar cloth. It was not so much the amount of damage done, but more the deliberate way the church had been desecrated. I thought that to myself, peering inside. There were plenty of people who would look at this and immediately be certain that someone had deliberately caused as much damage as possible. Perhaps it was the work of the devil himself, I heard an elderly woman murmuring fearfully. Even the rood screen had been broken, the slender tracery of delicately carved swirls and loops snapped and broken away where a stool had been flung at it.

That was cause for surprise. Who would bother? I mean, I could understand a fellow breaking into the church and pinching the cross or the cup and seeing if he could sell them. There was usually some itinerant traveller of one sort or another who might try his luck in a new town, and even churches weren't safe from their depredations. I have seen that kind of behaviour before, and when I was younger, and before I acquired a certain status and reputation, I had once or twice considered a similar venture myself. Not since my position as assassin to Lady Elizabeth, of course. I wouldn't demean myself now.

However, there were some firebrands about still. They would look at a church recently rededicated to the Catholic faith, and see in that a hideous heresy that deserved to be wiped clean and returned to the true religion, as they saw it. Returning to the old Catholic ways was a certain way to offend a number of the new religious adherents.

I entered, because although many of the other viewers seemed anxious at the sight of the destruction wrought on the church's interior, I was not one to shrink from duty owing to mere superstition. After all, with my position, I am a gentleman.

Walking to the altar stone, I picked up the dented communion cup. Once, of course, the church would have had a highly decorated chalice, all made of silver and gilt, I expect. I daresay it was taken by Henry VIII's men and melted down to create this simple goblet. And I have no doubts whatever that whoever melted down the old chalice would have shaved off an eighth of the total weight of silver and pocketed it, because this size of cup was much smaller than other chalices I have seen.

There was a lid to the cup, and I reunited them, placing them on the altar. Then I picked up the altar cloth, and it was while I did so that I noticed the vestry door was open. Well, such things happen. If a man were to scatter all the silverware and cloth from the altar, it was hardly surprising if he took it upon himself to investigate the other recesses of the church with the hope of finding something of interest inside. A chest full of gold, perhaps, or a plate full of collected tithes? I had never been inside a vestry, so wasn't sure what might be there, but my imagination was fully as competent as any thief's, and it was working at full spate.

After setting the items back on the altar in the positions I considered they should be placed, I was about to go to the vestry when there came a loud cry. Looking towards the porch, I saw the figure of our priest.

Peter stood in the doorway like a madman, his hair dishevelled, his face a picture of horror and woe as he pointed at me and gesticulated as though incapable of speech. I was forced to reflect that I hoped he might remain thus incapacitated for his next sermon.

Sadly, my wish was not granted.

'You *desecrate* my altar! You heathen scum! Leave my chancel at once! You will be punished for your trespass!'

Now, I am no superstitious fool, but I confess that being berated in such a manner, with a priest calling on God to punish me, was unsettling. I raised both hands in a gesture of innocence. 'I only came here to pick up the altar cloth and—'

'Remove yourself!' he shouted, and I really think he was partly mad. It was the sight of the damage. As he walked down the nave and peered at the rood screen and the broken carvings, he paused, and there were tears in his eyes at the sight. Then his eyes moved back to me, and again he took on the appearance of a vengeful devil determined to exact full punishment for my past indiscretions.

I retreated before him.

He stared about him like an archbishop witnessing a witches' convivial gathering in a wood, and then his attention was caught by the vestry door. He gibbered at himself a little, and I walked to it to show I was at least innocent of any misbehaviour there. And it was when I reached the door and could see in, that I saw her.

I don't know whether you have ever had one of those odd sensations. For some time I stood goggling at the sight inside that little room. I know that my jaw dropped wide, and while I remained fixed to the spot, nothing much went through my mind, apart from the obvious consideration that there was nothing left in there to be stolen. There were some candles on a shelf, admittedly, and a book or two, well-thumbed, and a small pack such as a man might wear when visiting the baker or butcher, but very little else. It was a small room, with a chest for the parish records, and a body. That was all. Well, apart from the pool of blood around her gaping throat.

I stared, appalled, and felt the beginnings of a choking, heaving horror begin to stir in my belly.

'You . . . You *murderer*!'

That was my companion, the drunken patch of a priest, who was now pointing at me with a shaking finger, his mouth a perfect 'O' of horror as he denounced me as a killer. Which was rather ironic, when you consider how I was supposed to earn my living. All I knew was that I was in the presence of poor Rachel Nailor. Someone had almost decapitated her.

'Murderer!'

But that was not something I was prepared to discuss just now. I shook my head, and would have protested my innocence, but instead my stomach gave a convulsive heave and I threw up over his feet.

He stared down at the vomit over his cassock and blenched. When he looked up at me again, his eyes were filled with a kind of wondering hatred.

'Murderer! Murderer! Where is the constable? Call the coroner!'

*   *   *

There is no doubt that being accused of murder first thing in the morning, before breakfast and after only two pints of ale, is neither reassuring or relaxing. The demented priest was dancing about like a child at his first bonfire, while the gawking audience seemed to swallow his words whole, as though the imbeciles believed him. Ignorant fools that they were, they had all forgotten the fact that I arrived after most of them!

I tried to explain that, of course, but you try explaining something of such complexity to a gathering of hawkers, urchins and leather sellers. I can assure you it is no easy task.

Fortunately there was one fellow there who appeared to have a larger brain capacity than all the rest put together, and he ambled in, looked me up and down, and declared that I was 'no murderer nor church destroyer'.

I could have kissed him, were it not for the fact that he looked like he had just spent the week drowning in a vat of beer, and smelled the same. However, his sudden arrival did make others start to use their heads, and I was very grateful to hear another fellow, this time Gawtheren Spink's son, shout that it was the priest, that he was a foul murderer, and he had slain the woman. Someone else took up the shout, and soon the crowd was baying for blood, but this time it was not mine.

Alderman Kirk appeared just as the crush began to move forward as if to lay hands on Peter. I was trying to take my leave of this unedifying spectacle, and save myself from the need to explain myself further, but the people pushing in held me in place.

The alderman was a big fellow, broad in the shoulder and stern in appearance, but I have spent much of my life studying other people, and with my professional gaze, I assessed this fellow as weakly. He was the sort who could belabour others, but who would crumble at the first sight of resistance. Committees love this kind of man. He can look impressive in his finery, but place him in front of a group of his betters, and he would dissolve like piss on snow. He would, in short, bend to the circumstances, and to me he looked like little less than a miracle.

'I am glad to see you,' I said.

'What has happened here?' Kirk demanded of my companion. (I will not call the priest a friend.)

'Desecration, foul destruction and the felonious devastation of St Helen's church!'

He was close to gibbering again, and I sought to assist him. 'And murder. There is a poor woman in the vestry. She has been slain.'

'Anyone important?' the good alderman asked, showing the quality of his mind.

'Yes. Very important,' I said, perhaps a little hotly. He sent me a look that felt barbed.

'Who was she?'

'She was a lady, I think; a woman called Rachel Nailor.'

As I spoke, I could see the cogs and wheels of an ungainly intellect gradually slurring into motion. 'What was her name, again?'

Before I could answer, he had bounded towards the door and was peering inside. What he saw was not to his liking, from the way that he retreated at speed, almost knocking the unfortunate priest to the ground in his hurry.

'What happened?' he asked, and now his tone was less that of a senior alderman in the city, and more the tone of a child who, having enjoyed the fire enormously, had now become aware that the fuel used was all his favourite toys.

It was a sight to give me pause for thought. After all, only a man who knew of Mistress Nailor's importance to Lady Elizabeth would have reacted in such a manner. There was little shock and horror at the sight of a woman needlessly slaughtered, and much more calculation about how to ensure that he did not become tainted in some way.

It gave me some satisfaction to see that someone else was aware of the potential of difficulties over this woman's death, but I confess that I had little desire to remain there and chat about it. I was more keen to escape the church and seek a little calmness in a cup, if for no other reason than to settle my stomach. The sight of Rachel in the vestry had been enough to reinforce all the unsettled feelings I had experienced the moment I had first heard that I must join her in her journey to Paris. I felt very queasy.

Now I was pleased to hear Gawtheren Spink's boy again. He had appeared in the vestry doorway, and now he pointed at the priest and began his ranting again. As I began to shove my way through the press towards the doorway, this scrawny runt shouted, 'It was *him*! Look at him! It was Father Peter! He tried it on with all the women here, everyone knows that! She rejected his advances, so he killed her, and trashed the church to hide his own guilt!'

'How dare you!' the priest shouted, his face purple.

'You have women come and visit you here, don't you, old fool! We've seen them. And now you found one who wouldn't submit, so you murdered her!'

Yes, far-fetched as an outline of guilt, I think you'll agree. All I knew was, that this lad had distracted the crowd from me and my potential involvement, and that was a great relief. I gave him a mental blessing as I passed the three burly gentlemen who gripped him and held him back so he couldn't launch himself at Peter, who stood glaring with every sign of encroaching apoplexy. It was tempting to wait a little and see whether the priest collapsed with a sudden burst heart, but it struck me that I was better occupied far away, before anyone could recall that I had been seen with Mistress Rachel after church a couple of times.

Leaving the church, I found myself pondering the attitude of the alderman as I crossed the yard. Aldermen held senior positions in the city, of course, but that did not mean that William Kirk would necessarily have realized that the woman in there was important. It was, after all, an essential element of her secret mission that she should be unknown, and the reasons for her travelling to France must remain concealed. If this alderman knew of her, that fact showed that she had not been able to keep her status quiet. Had someone working for Queen Mary decided to rid her of Elizabeth, and decided that the best route to defang Elizabeth lay in removing any chance of her escaping to France? It was certainly possible. And if that was the case, anyone who knew her and could be considered a friend or ally might also be in danger. That meant a fellow such as me.

It was a thoroughly pensive Jack who slipped from the churchyard and made his way to the Bull.

But even there I was to find no peace.

I entered the inn and sat at a chair not far from the fireplace, calling to the maid for a large ale and mulling over the morning's excitement.

Such destruction in a church was not unheard of, but the sight of the broken rood screen and the poor body inside the vestry had both shocked me more than I would have anticipated. I mean, I have seen plenty of dead bodies in my time. Yet there was something about that woman's sudden death that truly struck me. She was not exactly a soul mate for me, but she was an appealing woman in the prime of her life, and to see her slaughtered in that unwholesome manner and discarded on the floor of the vestry, was upsetting. Especially when the memory of that enormous gash at her throat came back to my mind. The thought that she might have been killed because of her position and her mission to France was especially disturbing. Particularly considering that I was associated with her and that journey. I might also be in danger.

It was enough to make my stomach lurch again.

Sitting at my table, I attempted to engage the maid in light conversation, but she appeared a dullard, and my witty comments inspired only a surly look of disdain. She was plainly not experienced in dealing with a gentleman's dalliances. Instead, I drained my pot and was about to leave, when a voice hailed me.

It was young John Anderson, who wandered over to me, winking at the maid and receiving in response a beaming smile that lit up the room. It left me feeling less than enamoured of him – and her.

'Master Blackjack, how do I find you today? Isn't it terrible about poor Rachel Nailor? I heard about her murder. Dreadful! Shocking to think we could have such a callous murder committed here in our little parish. It hardly bears thinking about, that a woman like her could be slaughtered in the church and the whole building desecrated.'

'She could have been killed anywhere and left there,' I said to puncture his smugness.

He cast a sharp look at me. 'If that was so, surely her blood would have dropped all over the church's floor. No, she must have died there in the vestry. I heard you were one of the first in there. Was it you found her?'

'I found her with the priest,' I said a little shortly, thinking again, queasily, of all that blood.

'With Father Peter? Ah, well that's hard. I daresay you found the sight distressing, eh? I know what you were thinking about her,' he said with all the knowingness of a boy who could hardly grow a beard.

'I barely knew her.'

He chuckled, the smug popinjay. 'But you would have liked to, wouldn't you? Even the fool Father Peter couldn't help but see how you were paying more attention to her slender neck than his sermons! And when we left church, your eyes followed her all the way to the gate, and you would have pursued her beyond, I'd wager.'

'Would you, indeed?' I burst, and would have continued, had he not overridden my words.

'Aye, and what man with blood in his veins would not? I admit it, and I admire you for your forthrightness. You dared to seek her out, when most men in the parish . . . well! They might as well have been castrated for all the good they can do. Not many would dare to try their luck with her while their wives are watching.'

'I daresay not,' I said, and would have continued, but again his flow was not to be suppressed or dammed.

'No, I cannot blame you. Any man would have tried his luck with her.'

'You too? Where were you last evening?' I said, hoping to still his constant flow.

'I? Why, I was in the Green Dragon most of the evening, with Elias Spink.' He smiled. 'I am innocent of this. But the culprit will soon be discovered, I am sure. A heretic, a vandal and a murderer. That is a rare combination.'

I nodded gloomily. 'I need to discover whether anyone else was about the church last evening who could have killed her.'

'I and Elias passed up the road to the Dragon, and there was one man.'

'Who?'

'Only William Kirk. He was outside the church looking as melancholy and miserable as only he can,' the spark said.

'I see.' No, I didn't. After all, a man standing still outside a church was not proof of murderous intent.

'Your own position is troubling, of course,' he added thoughtfully. 'You are new to this parish, and you were seen to want to speak with her. Of course, a man of quality such as yourself would hardly be suspected . . . And yet people might form the unfortunate impression that you had reason to kill her. You might have felt that she was rejecting you unreasonably, or that she was passing her favours to another.'

'I had no such concern,' I said.

'Ah, well, perhaps not. But it is the way some men's minds will work, isn't it? I know my father said he saw you talking to her the Sunday before last. He thought you forward.'

'Surely not!' I said, and there was a chuckle at the back of my throat. After all, I was sure that the gross man was simply jealous. Not that he could consider himself any kind of competitor to my charms.

'You scoff, Master Blackjack, but he is a man of influence and position. Only a few men in the city can compete with him.'

'Besides I barely knew her. Others here must have had reason to dislike her,' I said, thinking of the sour comments in the Bull on Sunday.

The young fool nodded to himself as if sadly, before continuing, 'True enough! The miserable lurden, Richard Croke considers himself everything a woman could desire, and his wife has a terrible, jealous anger. It leaps from her eyes every time he tries to speak with another woman . . . it is like watching darts fly at their target. You could easily imagine that, were she to find him in conversation with another woman, Mistress Emilia would be likely to commit murder. There is no horror on God's earth that a jealous woman would not inflict on a competitor for her husband's affections. Or so I am told,' he added smugly.

It was truly tempting to push my fist into the arrogant puppy's face, but I have a dislike of violence. And he was younger, stronger and faster than me, so it might have proved a short-lived pleasure. Instead I yawned and gazed about me at the other visitors.

'Like your mother?' I said, just to wipe the smile from his face.

'She is a mild, kind woman,' he said.

He could say so, but I remembered how cowed his father had been when we discussed Rachel Nailor in the Bull.

'Mistress Nailor did seem to favour you,' the talkative imp continued. 'She was asking about your home on Sunday, and she seemed to want to pursue some conversation with you, no matter how inappropriate it would be for a woman like her to visit a man like you. A bachelor, I mean,' he added with a snide grin.

'Many people are keen to visit me at my house,' I said weakly. If I was convinced of one thing, it was that I did not want news of her visit to me, and any matters we had discussed, to become common knowledge. There was always the risk that her activities had become known to intelligencers for Queen Mary, and I had no wish to be invited to stay at the queen's leisure in one of the chambers in the Tower of London in the company of red-hot brands and chains, or any of the other rumoured devices used to elicit information from recalcitrant subjects.

'Yes, but she was most determined. In fact,' he added pensively taking a pull at his ale, 'I am not sure that anybody saw her after she was asking about you.'

I eyed the little wen with some disgust. 'What exactly is your interest here?' I asked.

He leaned back comfortably in his seat, peering at me, beaming. 'Ah, well, I want to learn who was responsible for this murder. I wanted to show you that I might be able to help you.'

'What makes you think I have any interest in the matter?'

'I don't know,' he admitted. 'But, seeing how close you were to her – or how close you wanted to be to her – I thought you would have an interest in finding her murderer, and it struck me I could help. After all, if you wanted to find out who the killer was, I am certain to be able to assist you.'

I looked at the little monster with disdain, but he continued, ignoring my obvious disgust.

'Oh, you have knowledge of other parishes, I am sure, and you are a man of the world, I perceive. But I know *this* parish. I have lived here all my life. I know all the people here.'

He looked so smug, leaning back in his seat, that it was tempting to discard him immediately. I had no need of his assistance seeking a murderer. What, did he think me a thief-taker or glorified coroner? There were attractions to his idea: if there were a killer loose in the parish, all of us could be at risk. A murderer might choose to attack someone else. After all, many were quite mad. If there was a lunatic murderer walking the streets, having a henchman of my own at my side was appealing. As for hunting down such a man, that would be in the interests of all – so long as I was not expected to get involved. I have been friends with too many felons to wish to be responsible for making one dance the Tyburn jig. Others might take umbrage and decide to wreak revenge on my person. No, better by far to leave such investigations to those who had the responsibility.

'I believe you have the wrong idea about me,' I said at last. 'I am new here, but I have no skills as an investigator of crimes. I am a mere businessman. To hunt down a murderer, that would take skills that others possess.'

He looked downcast. 'If you are sure,' he said, and then attempted to persuade me again that it would be in my own best interests to seek this killer, and that he could help. It grew tedious, and I ended the conversation by explaining that I had no interest in his suggestion, upon which he took his leave, while I sat and reflected on the strange dealings of fate.

I mean to say, here I was. Only the day before I had been threatened with making a hideous journey; this morning I had been accused of murder; and now? Now I was free once more, safe in my favourite metropolis, and free to continue enjoying life to the full.

With that, I called for another ale to celebrate.

* * *

It is no surprise, surely, that I was glad to see the pampered excrescence depart. However, as soon as my ale arrived, I was forced to consider my next activity for the day. Because it was clear enough that I had to tell my master about Rachel Nailor's demise. Accordingly, I sipped my ale slowly. This was not an interview to which I looked forward with enthusiasm. That I must let him know was clear enough, but I feared that his response would likely be to put into my care some other harpy – or even declare that I should undertake the mission on my own.

That was almost enough to prevent me draining my pot. My stomach was becoming queasy once more. It was strange how my belly was reacting today.

I was preparing to attempt to swallow the remainder and demand another, before making my way to his house, but before I placed my order, I realized I was being watched.

John Blount always tended to have one or two men with him. It was a sensible precaution when striding about London's streets. He had many enemies, and it was a matter of common sense to try to avoid confrontations without at least one henchman at his side.

Today, in the tavern, I saw one of them.

He was a man I had seen many times out and about with Blount. I had named him, not affectionately, the gorilla. He was the sort of man to wear his jaw pugnaciously outthrust as though pleading that someone might attempt to break his fist against it. In terms of intellect, the fellow was one of those whose brain must be remarkably valuable. He had never, to my knowledge, exercised it in any manner whatsoever.

If a man could buy a brain like that, he would be rewarded with a good many years of use, I would wager.

For now I merely threw him a nod of recognition as I called to the serving wench. The gorilla rose and walked to my table, where a space had recently been vacated by young Anderson.

My drink arrived moments after him. He took his seat at the table with me, and sat for a long pause, staring at me with chin jutting.

I essayed a nonchalant air, sipping as though unaware of his presence.

'Our master wants to see you,' he said at last.

'Our master, eh?' I said with a haughty curl of my lip. And he deserved it. He was merely a functionary whose job involved looking after John Blount and beating up those to whom he was pointed, all for a pittance. Whereas I was paid a good retainer and a fresh suit of clothes every year. It is astonishing how much more superior little details like that will make a man feel, in comparison to a mere rogue like him. Besides, one attraction of my position was that Blount's men all tended to know that I was highly valued, and that my main function involved removing those fellows who fell into the category of annoyances to Blount. Which was good, because knowing that they tended to treat me with a certain deferential respect.

Not that this gorilla was bright enough to realize it, of course.

'He said *now!*' he rumbled.

These two sentences must have ranked as some of the longest speeches he had ever been capable of. He sat back as if expecting me to rise instantly – or perhaps it was pride at getting the words out in the correct order? But then a small frown cracked the granite of his features when he realized that I was not moving.

After two enquiring grunts from him, I set my drink aside and leaned forward with hands clasped and both elbows on the tabletop. 'I will come,' I said, and sat back, calmly taking up my drink again. 'When I am ready.'

Of course this only led to a further fracturing of his face as he brought to bear his most ferocious glower, but since I knew I was safe in my own status, I ignored him, taking my time over my drink. When I was done, and my stomach felt less jittery, I stood, stretched, and allowed him to lead the way to Blount's house.

Leaving, I saw Gawtheren Spink with her son. He had not recovered from accusing Father Peter, and looked red-faced and sulky, I thought, while the woman berated him. It was apparent from the way that he averted his face from her, his face set in stone, just like any other young man unreasonably berated by his mother, that he was not enjoying the attention.

It was enough to make me smile to myself as the gorilla led the way, and I was feeling almost relaxed when we reached John Blount's house.

Here I found the door blocked by another of Blount's henchmen. This fellow nodded to the gorilla and rapped on the timbers sharply. There was a loud rasping as the bolts were drawn and I walked into his small hall. There, I was made more aware of the serious nature of affairs when I observed two more men in his screens passage.

'Get him in here!' was the barked invitation at his door. I guessed that Master Blount had already been informed of Mistress Nailor's demise.

'So you deign to visit me?' Blount said.

He was sitting at his table at the farther end of his hall. I had been ushered in, and now the gorilla was outside the door, while the two men whom I had seen outside his door stood disconcertingly close. That meant if I were to run, I would meet with these two before the gorilla could engage himself in the enjoyable pastime of removing my arm and using it to beat me about the head.

'I was about to come here when I met your fellow,' I said with a degree of asperity. After all, it was true. I would have been here some while ago, had the gorilla not made it clear that I was expected to drop everything and hurry here. Not that I felt that would be a particularly diplomatic response – it was a minor detail with which I need not trouble Master Blount.

He ignored my words, glaring at me. 'She's dead,' he said flatly. It was not a question.

'I fear so. I was in the church and—'

'Save your damned excuses! I don't want them!' he roared, his fist slamming on the desk.

I was perplexed. Yes, perplexed. I was, admittedly, a little late to respond to his summons, but that surely did not deserve such rudeness. 'But I—'

'Yes, you told me. You said you didn't want to go to France, and I ignored your words, didn't I? But that did not justify *murdering* her! In Christ's name, you slaughtered an ally of your mistress, just to save yourself the trouble of a journey to

Paris? Are you so set on murder that you'll kill off your allies. What the devil is—'

'*Eh?*'

There was considerably more. All the while Blount was pacing back and forth beside his table, expostulating and gesticulating with real rage. I don't think I've ever seen him like that before. I would have interrupted his flow, but there were two problems that assailed me. One, of course, was the fact that his flow of invective was truly unstoppable; the second was that for the moment the power of speech eluded me.

I suppose you will have heard the expression that the man's chin hit the floor? I have heard it often enough, but this was the first time I saw, or felt, the genuine impact of the words. It felt as though my entire jaw was dislocated as it fell wide.

'Don't put on that look of stupidity – it may convince some wench you want to tempt into bed, but it holds no water with me,' Blount snapped. 'I've seen you kill, and I know how competent you are when the victim is weaker than you! You may blench before trying to hurt a man as large as you, but when it's a woman or a fool, you can kill without compunction, can't you? Someone who stands in your way must die, is that it? I have guards with me all day and night now, so don't think you can remove me as well.'

'But I—' I tried, but he was into his stride now.

'You couldn't bear to think of travelling to Paris, could you? You saw only one way to save yourself, didn't you? There was only the one obstacle to your continued ease, so you decided to get rid of her, and thus there would be no need to go to Paris at all!'

'No! That isn't what—'

I would have continued, but he was standing right before me now, his face thrust into mine until it was only an inch away.

'Did you *really* think I wouldn't guess? Did you *believe* you could hold the wool over my eyes? Did you seriously consider yourself superior to me, with all my intelligencers about the city? I knew you had met with her, and I knew you were aware of the importance of the mission she was to undertake, and yet you decided to slay her. Not anywhere, but in a

damned *church*!' he added with rather a dampening emphasis
as his spittle struck my cheeks.

I wiped them defiantly. 'Master, I had nothing to do with
her death,' I stated firmly.

'You tremble like a lily. Even your voice is shaking,' he
said. 'If you did nothing, I suppose you have witnesses to say
you were elsewhere in the city when she was killed? What,
no ready prepared alibi? This must be a first instance for you!
Usually every execution you can prove you were at least two
parishes away from the scene of the death. Was there no time
to plan this killing? You launched yourself at her at the first
opportunity? You waited until the church was assaulted, and
then slew her?'

'No, of course not,' I said. But here I was getting into
dangerous waters. After all, I could hardly explain that I never
killed any of my supposed victims. Blount was certain that I
had a heart of stone and had slaughtered all those to whom
he had directed me. In reality, I had taken the infinitely easier
option of meeting with a certain friend, Humfrie, who would,
for a small consideration, undertake to remove those people
whom John Blount considered superfluous, if you take my
meaning. I could no more murder someone than fly. It isn't
in my nature. However, to confess that might run the risk of
exposing to my master that I was entirely disposable. After
all, a man like him, regularly commanding that others must
be killed, would naturally prefer to have as few others involved
as possible. Executing me and instructing Humfrie in my place
would naturally occur to him to be both cost-effective and
more secure.

So I simply stated, calmly and clearly, 'I didn't kill her.'

'Don't whimper, you pathetic worm! What did you mean
by it? I know you met her there.'

'I did not!'

'You sent her a message to meet you there last evening.'

'No, I didn't!'

'She sent to me to let me know. She was seeing you there
after nightfall.'

'You mean she was one of those involved in the destruction
of the church interior?' I said.

He scowled at that. 'Do not try to confuse me with your stories! You told her to meet you there, and murdered her, and for that our mistress is likely to demand your head. And I see no reason not to hand it to her, on a silver platter, if I can. Why should I listen to you? You can lie with all the conviction of a drunk in a nunnery! I should not . . .'

He continued again at some length, but as he ground to a halt, I tried to make him see sense. I held up my hand and shook my head. 'Master, I will say this only once more. I did not kill Rachel. I sent no message. After you left my house last night, I remained indoors. You can verify that with Raphe, if you so wish. I was not likely to go carousing after you issued me with your instructions. I had consumed too much wine and fell asleep.'

'No doubt you were ghastly and besotten,' he grated. 'Why should I believe that?'

'Because it is true and you can easily confirm it. You know that I was reluctant to undertake the task you set out for me, but you also know that I have never failed you before. When you have instructed me, I have always achieved the result you desired. Is that not so?'

He was scowling slightly less viciously now, and held his head aslant as though considering me afresh. 'You continue to deny it? Then how do you explain her saying that you told her to meet you there?'

'I have no explanation. I was asleep.'

'How very convenient,' he said. He returned to the other side of his table and dropped into his seat, toying with a fine-bladed dagger. 'However, it is out of my hands. The Lady Elizabeth will soon be aware that Rachel is dead. I expect that she will issue an order to see to it that the guilty man is punished for it.'

'But you must tell her it wasn't me!' I said.

'You think your excuse will save you? "Ooh, no, mistress, I didn't do it. I was beastly drunk at the time. I couldn't raise a smile, let alone a dagger. I was too drunk to commit murder!" Do you think that would work for your defence? No, nor do I. I see nothing for it, but that you should leave the city and hide. It may take her agents some little while to trace you.'

'But I did nothing!'

'Prove it! Find the man who did commit this murder and bring him to justice. Perhaps then, if you are lucky and the lady feels in a kindly mood, you may save your life. But, man, if you value your pelt, you should hurry, because her men will be coming to find you very soon. And when they do, your life won't be worth a clipped penny.'

Back at home, I barred the door behind me and stood with my back to it, shaking and feeling more than a little sickly.

There was no doubt that Blount considered me the most likely candidate for the crime, and if he believed that, why so must Lady Elizabeth and her advisors. If the hardhead was to go to them and tell them he thought I could be responsible, as far as my value went, a clipped penny was significantly more than I would have offered for my chances of survival. I had to escape this trap somehow.

The question was, how, exactly?

I mean, the woman was definitely attractive. It wasn't only me who thought that, as young Anderson had said. His own father had cast a covetous eye over her, as had Croke, according to the lad. And from his words, he had held a candle for her too. Then there were the women, who may well have hated her for the impact she had on their men: Mistress Anderson, Mistress Croke, not to mention the other woman: Gawtheren Spink. She had looked rather upset with Rachel yesterday, when we had been outside the church after the service. It had struck me at the time that she had looked highly attentive of the two other women chatting. Perhaps she had some reason to distrust Rachel too?

How should a man make sense of all this? I put my hand to my head in despair. So far I had suspicions about the Andersons, all three, the Crokes, Spink, and of course there was always the suspicious behaviour of the alderman. What had he been doing outside the church on the evening Rachel was murdered?

The alderman. I suddenly felt a bolt of clarity strike me between the eyes. The man had been anxious when he recognized the body. Why should he recognize her? Either he was seeking an affair with her, which might lead to embarrassment – but if that was so, her death would be a relief before his wife could learn of his infidelity. No, it was more likely that he was aware of her loyalties. Perhaps he knew of her mission to France. And if he was a supporter of Queen Mary, the sight of Rachel's death must surely be a relief. It would mean that the mission to save Lady Elizabeth must fail, and Queen Mary successfully marry her off to the Spanish ally, Emmanuel Philibert. That way Elizabeth would be removed as an irritant and Mary could ignore her and her plotting.

I was happy with my logic here. If he was Queen Mary's supporter, William Kirk would not have been so shocked and anxious. If anything, he would be concealing his glee at the removal of his queen's rival. Yet I was convinced he had been shocked to see Rachel's body. That meant he must surely be a supporter of Lady Elizabeth – perhaps even aware of Rachel's mission. And since he was not happy to find her body, that must mean he was in favour of it.

The man was a supporter of my mistress, Lady Elizabeth, I decided.

After a short stiffener of brandy to recover my *sang froid*, I felt sufficiently refreshed to be able to cope with the walk to the alderman's house. It wasn't far.

I opened my door and stepped out into the street, barely caring to look about me, until I happened to glance to my right. You can imagine my feelings on seeing the harsh-hewn features of the gorilla.

He was standing at a doorway only some few yards away from me, and on seeing me, his features creased into a deeply unpleasant expression. I would like to say it was gleeful, but it was one of those looks that indicated he was anticipating something in the future, and I could imagine exactly what that was: my demise and his potential elevation to my position. All he need do was prove my guilt, or perhaps remove me as a demonstration of his skills. It was enough to bring back the queasiness in the pit of my belly. He smiled. That was almost enough to make my bowels open there and then.

With an effort I pulled myself together and set off along

the busiest part of the road, where it would be difficult for a man to launch an attack on my back. As it was, my back felt like it was contracting, as if clenching all my muscles could force a knife or sword to miss its mark. I knew well how unlikely that was.

The alderman lived in a great house south of the Bull, and only a short distance from the church, right in the middle of the parish, and I repaired there as swiftly as I may, showing courage with every footstep. No one could have guessed that I was in fear of my life, excepting perhaps the manner of my walking, with an alert expectation of danger that led to my being forced to keep glancing over my shoulder. Not in a nervous manner, you understand, merely a sensible, cautious way, as a fellow would when worried about the attack of a footpad.

To my considerable relief, he barely approached closer than five yards during the entire journey, and I reached the alderman's hall safely, shutting the iron gate behind me as I entered the yard area. The gorilla stood beyond the gates, baring his teeth like an unhappy bloodhound deprived of his meal as I spoke with the porter. Once my visit was approved, I went to the door and knocked loudly.

Soon I was standing in the hall before a great fire and only now did it occur to me that I had no idea how to proceed.

Perhaps you have known a similar experience. After all, it is one thing to gaily approach a man and enquire of him whether he is a bachelor or married fellow. Usually the response will be curt, perhaps, but other than a few miserable folks, in the main an answer will be given. Who would feel a need to conceal his wedded status?

In a similar way, asking a man whether he has children, or whether he has a pack of hounds, or whether he enjoys visiting the bull-baiting pits, or a cock fight, will elicit a generally positive response. But when you stand in a man's front hall and look him in the eye and ask him whether he is a traitor to the queen or not, that is somewhat more difficult. It is broaching the subject, I mean to say, which can cause an element of annoyance. Some people are apt to take such a suggestion in a rather negative manner. An alderman of the City of London is a man with some power and authority, and making a statement which could be considered an allegation of treachery may well be cause of an element of danger. It is best, I have always found, not to insult the rich. They have a habit of allowing their disgruntlement to become all too apparent, leading to bodies found in the Thames or in cess pits. I certainly felt some anxiety, looking at the man approaching me from the private chamber.

'Yes?' he demanded.

He was one of those who clearly considered himself far too important to cross the floor to meet a relative stranger. Instead, he stood imperiously beside his chair and glared at me as if I was a mere beggar at his door.

'I saw you today at St Helen's,' I said suavely. I mean to say, if he couldn't tell from my suit that I was a gentleman much like him, my tone of voice would have done.

'And?'

'When you saw the body of Rachel Nailor,' I said. 'Um . . . What was she to you?'

His face reddened. It may be that it was the flush of embarrassment, but it looked more like the flush of rage, and I almost took a step backwards at the sight. 'What do you mean by this? Eh? Coming to my house and suggesting . . . what are you suggesting? Eh? *Out with it!*'

This was one of those moments when I considered that I might have bitten off a little more than I could chew. I had the choice, of course, of making my apologies and fleeing the place, but as the thought came to me, I was reminded of the face of the gorilla waiting for me outside, and then the memory of John Blount accusing me of murdering the woman, and my resolve was stiffened.

'I am suggesting nothing. I am saying that you clearly knew her, and knew her well, for I saw your reaction to discovering her body. You were upset, that was plain. Now, some suggest that I might have been involved in her death, purely because of gossip, and I feel a certain loyalty to the poor thing, and I wish to discover who is responsible for her murder. So I hope you will be able to help me to discover who could have killed her. Since you knew her, do you have any idea who might have wanted her dead?'

It was quite a speech, I'm sure you will agree, and as I finished, I felt a certain pounding in my breast. I had carefully avoided the matter of her loyalty to Princess Elizabeth and her mission to spoil the queen's plan of marrying her off, but that didn't mean I hadn't exposed myself to some danger. It all depended on his response as to how I might continue.

'That is a job for the coroner, not for you!' He stepped closer, and I saw his fists clench, and then he burst out, 'Damn your soul, who are you? What do you wish in here? Eh?'

This was not, to my mind, an unequivocal confirmation of his knowing her, but neither was it a denial. Not that it mattered. Because at that moment the door to his private chambers opened and his wife appeared.

I had not met her before, but I had seen her in church, of course. Not that she would have mixed with men like me. Agnes Kirk slid in like a snake, all sinuous and swift. Her feet could not be seen under her voluminous skirts, and she was clad in the highest fashion with her hair carefully arranged under her coif. She was a very elegant lady, as her carriage declared.

'Good day,' she said, and it sounded like a curse. Her husband's anger dissolved like mist in a bright sun. 'Who is this, husband?'

'This is Master Blackjack, my dear,' he said in the most servile manner imaginable. It was shameful to see how he cringed like a dog waiting to be beaten. 'He came to see me about that poor women found dead today.'

'I hardly think she was a "poor woman",' she said. 'She was surely a flibbertigibbet . . . well, one should not speak ill of the dead, but if truth be told, she set the hackles to rise on *all* the wives in the parish.' She set her lips primly. 'After all, every husband in the parish was besotted with her. Every one of them,' she repeated with a long, bitter stare at her husband.

He winced. So did I in sympathy.

'No, my dear, she was merely a poor young thing in need of some help, that is all,' the alderman replied with a singular lack of conviction. He looked as happy as a mouse seeing the cat, petrified under her gaze.

'She was a woman of known reputation,' his wife declared. 'And she was ever looking for the next man to snare. Marchioness, indeed! She behaved like a common trull from Southwark!'

I tried to calm what appeared to be a growing discomfort in the room. 'Surely not. She seemed a pleasant and reserved lady.'

'Yes. Well, we all saw how you leered at her through the Mass,' she said, and swept from the room.

I think it is fair to say that both of us needed to repair to a hostelry where there would be a more welcoming response. Any antagonism Master Kirk felt at my suggestion he might have known Rachel was forgotten in his terror of his wife. And not without reason, I have to confess. If I had been wedded to that tartar, I would have sought a tavern every day, ideally many leagues from her and London.

We repaired to the Green Dragon, which was a short distance further away than the Bull. It was less frequented by the parishioners, and seemed a little safer for private conversation. Clearly the alderman felt the same. For the nonce, we felt a comradely sympathy, much like brothers-in-arms who have experienced the same hardships in battle. We sought a calm, peaceful tavern in which to recover.

I was glad to see that the gorilla was discomfited to discover I was not alone. Perhaps he had intended to waylay me on my way from the Kirk household. For my part, I felt happy to know that I was less likely to be attacked while in the presence of a prominent city official.

At the inn I attempted to lighten the mood a little. 'Have you been an alderman for long? It must be a very trying job.'

'Not terribly long, a year or so. Another fellow, Adam Bonner, had the position before me, but when he died I was invited to fill his seat.'

'Oh.'

'It is not a terribly demanding position, but it can be, as you say "trying". There are so many conflicting demands from people who want help. It can be exhausting at times.'

'I see.'

He darted a glance at me. 'Agnes is not usually quite so . . . direct,' he said pensively once we had goblets of sack before us. He concentrated on his wine as though speaking to it. 'She felt that many men in the parish, even perhaps me, might have attempted to . . . to . . .'

'I feel sure Rachel does not deserve a reputation of that sort,' I said in agreement. I studied my own drink. We both sipped together.

'Agnes used to be a sweet-natured little thing,' he continued as if I had not spoken. 'When I first met her, she would barely say boo to a goose. Such a slim, shy, quiet girl. I thought myself the luckiest man alive when her father agreed to let me have her as wife.' He went quiet again. We both sipped again.

'I have known women who seemed perfectly sensible and sweet-natured who later turned into shrews,' I said.

'A shrew is a delightful small animal,' he said dolefully.

'Why should she harbour such feelings towards Rachel?' I wondered. 'It hardly seems reasonable, especially now that the woman is dead.'

'She . . . saw me talking with her,' he said.

This, I could tell, was the crux of the matter. If he was aware of Rachel's business in France, he must support Lady Elizabeth. Else he would have reported Rachel and the plot to the queen's intelligencers. That would have led to Rachel being arrested and questioned, surely. There would be little benefit to the queen in seeing Rachel murdered without confessing her involvement, if the actual ambition was to remove Lady Elizabeth as a threat. Most of Queen Mary's advisers would be determined to see Lady Elizabeth implicated in any plot so that she could be imprisoned and executed. Unless Queen Mary simply wanted Lady Elizabeth's determination to escape to France foiled so that she knew her only hope of survival was to accede to the queen's demand that she must marry whomsoever the queen determined – even this curiously named Emmanuel Philibert.

But I inclined to the view that my companion in vino was in truth, or veritas, a supporter of Lady Elizabeth. He had the appearance of a man so appalled by the sight of Rachel's body that he must have been either her lover, or he was fully informed of her mission and was therefore aware of its importance.

However, he could not come straight out and tell me, a relative stranger, that he was supporting the Lady Elizabeth, because that would mean confessing to treason. And in the same manner, it was impossible for me to admit to my own position in her household. Not only that I was a paid assassin, I mean, but also that I was intended to be sent as guardian of the woman, Rachel, who was being sent to Paris to negotiate Elizabeth's escape.

I sought some means of raising the matter of Lady Elizabeth without giving away my own position. 'Um . . . talking to her? When was that?'

'A week or two ago,' he said dully. He looked at me, and I knew he was lying.

'Surely that would not be a breach of etiquette?'

'We were . . .' He hesitated. 'In a rather private space.'

Well, naturally. If he was to discuss matters such as her passage to France, it would be conducted with caution and the utmost care and secrecy. He could not, sensibly, put himself at risk of execution by holding forth in a tavern or the street when discussing treason. 'Of course,' I said.

He threw me a look at last, and it was plain that he appreciated my understanding. 'We were in the churchyard after dark. I had no idea anyone would see us. My wife, I fear, heard of our assignation and believed the worst, and as a result she considered that I . . . and that Mistress Nailor . . . well, she thought . . .'

'Was this meeting to discuss matters of an intimate nature?' I hazarded.

He winced. 'My wife believed so, but no. We had a little business together.'

I felt sure he meant he knew that Rachel was engaged on political business in Paris. 'Did Mistress Nailor tell you that she intended to leave soon?'

'Yes. I don't think it was concealed,' he said. He glanced about him. 'Of course, she would hardly bruit such information abroad. There was a need for a degree of circumspection. But she told you?'

I had little idea what he meant by that, but I was prepared to adopt a knowing expression. 'Of course. We did not know each other intimately, you understand, but she gave me to understand that she must soon be gone from here.'

'She would have been supported. I would have supported her. But Agnes – well, she took the view that Mistress Nailor . . . that is to say . . .'

The tide in my goblet was rapidly going out and I was growing impatient. I had to learn what I could urgently for John Blount. I tried the direct approach. 'I know you were outside the church that evening when she died. Did you see her?'

His expression took on a still more haunted appearance. 'Me? Why, what would I have been doing there?'

It was a perfect non-answer. It didn't deny meeting her, but didn't admit that he had either. 'Do you know of anyone who would have tried to kill her?' I sighed.

'What? Me? No, of course not. Unless it was a matter of jealousy,' he said. 'Oh, poor Rachel! Poor child!'

Which struck me as a rather overblown description of a woman in her late twenties or so.

Outside, the sky had become overcast, and when I gazed about me, I saw that it was not only the sky. A few yards away was the gorilla, who had a face like a simian thunderstorm.

He stepped forward, but as he did so, Alderman Kirk joined me. I smiled at the gorilla as he withdrew, his demeanour that of a cat thinking to attack a mouse only to discover the prey was a wolfhound's tail.

I walked back with the alderman, considering his words. It meant he did not think her death was caused by politics, but by a more simple, human motive. That would, of course, be a great benefit to me, as an explanation. If I could demonstrate that her murder was caused by someone who was merely jealous or driven by lust, and seized an opportunity to slay her, I should be safe.

Neither of us spoke. The alderman was involved with his thoughts, and I was engaged with alternative narratives about why Rachel might have been killed. I was just conceiving an outline tale of her coming across a group of violently destructive thieves who had broken into the church and were in the process of destroying it, when I noticed young John Anderson on the other side of the street. He was staring at me with some intensity, and although I tried to ignore him, he waved urgently.

'I think John Anderson wishes to speak with you,' Alderman Kirk said unnecessarily.

'I am sure it is nothing,' I said, but even as I did so, the young fellow risked his life by darting across the road, almost under the hooves of a pair of mounts thundering past. One rider snarled a curse at him, trying to cut him with his riding crop, but missed.

As he approached, Kirk made a mumbled excuse and hurried to his hall.

'Master Blackjack,' Anderson called. 'I trust you are well? Did you know you are being followed?'

He pointed behind me to the gorilla, who suddenly halted and showed a great interest in the jettied ceiling over his head.

'Am I?' I said.

'That is the man you saw in the Bull after I left you, I think? I saw him leave and trail after you when I had left the inn, and a short while ago I saw him follow you and the alderman to the Green Dragon and out again. Do you know him? He must be a footpad, from his appearance. Shall we confront him?'

I was tempted to pat him on the back. 'No, no. He is just some unfortunate without a brain. Let us merely stand our ground here for a short time, and see if he desires to remain. If he is a footpad, the fact that you have spotted him will drive him away soon enough, I am sure.'

'If you say so. However, I think he ought to be forced to answer what he is doing here,' the boy said, and demonstrating an excess of zeal over intellect, suddenly dashed forward to speak with the man. For my part, I was more than content to pull my hat lower over my pate, duck down out of sight from the crowds, and slip away. Thus I did not witness the results of the interview.

It was not my concern if the young fool had got it into his head to commit suicide, after all.

*　　*　　*

There are few sensations so gratifying as escaping danger; even better, to do so at the intervention of a fool who fails to recognize his own error. This headlong rush into danger was all very well for those of youth and energy, but it would not do for a man of my standing. It would be unseemly for a gentleman to become engaged in a brawl in the street, after all. So in preference I trotted quietly to a side street, ran up that at full-tilt, taking the first right turn, down along that, then left, and kept on going until I realized I was close to my old haunt. And that meant I was near to Susan Appleby.

I have described my once-neighbour before, in an earlier adventure. Mistress Susan was a full-figured woman with a wayward eye and refreshing lack of inhibition, who had made her interest in me perfectly clear some little while before. She had many advantages, and I do not refer only to the physical attractions; rather, I mean that she was married, more or less happily, to a grasping, mean-spirited man called Saul, who was ever keen to keep his wife under close supervision. I suppose by reason of his suspicion that she might be behaving exactly as she was with other men such as I.

Be that as it may, I was not one to complain. For as often as was possible, she and I would meet, now that I had a new house a little farther from her doors, and Saul had the cost of maintaining her. Today, what could be more natural than that an old friend and neighbour should visit her, finding myself near her doors? It struck me as the perfect excuse. And since I had no desire to return immediately to my own home, since to do so would give the gorilla an excellent opportunity of finding me again, I immediately bent my steps to her front door.

It was a rather lovely building. Saul was successful in his business (Susan had told me his trade, but at the time she had ensured that my mind was otherwise concerned, and I did not note the details), from the appearance of the place. His timbers were freshly limed, the daub whitewashed, the glass of the panes clean. It looked the sort of house a richer merchant would aspire to. And he had the enormous advantage of being regularly away from home.

The door was opened by the family bottler. He stood with

that vaguely supercilious expression that said as clearly as words that he remembered me, but took my introduction and swore he would soon be with me again. A few moments later I was ushered into the hall where Susan sat at needlework.

She stood up, carefully setting down her work, and gave me the cool look of a matron welcoming her husband's friend, whom she recalled as being the drunk who missed the piss pot on his last visit.

'Master Blackjack. What a surprise.'

Of course, I knew that she could scarcely be more effusive, with her bottler hovering and no doubt absorbing every word for future use when he saw his master, so I wasn't surprised or upset. Instead I assumed a lofty manner as I asked about her husband and her health. No man who saw us could possibly have guessed that I had been enjoying her favours only a week ago when she managed to escape the house briefly and came to enjoy a little mattress-walloping with me. Soon her bottler was sent out to fetch wine, and I was almost ready to leap on her, when she held up an admonitory finger, turning her head slightly and listening intently.

'So, Master Blackjack,' she said, all haughty like Queen Mary receiving the French ambassador. 'To what do I owe the pleasure of your visit?'

'Ah, Madam Appleby, it is always a joy to see you again,' I said in my most obsequious tone of voice. 'How could I not visit when I discovered myself near my old door? The memory of waking in my bed there brought so many happy memories of this road.'

Ah, indeed it did. The number of times I had woken to see, through my bedroom window and into her bedroom, the sight of her in various stages of undress, had been the initial cause of my devoting my attention on her. The boundless beauty of her features was only excelled by her excellent figure, which promised much to a man who could persuade her to share them.

I smiled at the memory.

'I am sure,' she replied. 'And it is always very pleasant to see an old friend and neighbour. However, I fear my husband is away just now, but if you can wait, he will soon return. He was only visiting a shipmaster briefly. I hope you will stay in order to see him?'

I shuddered at the thought. 'Nay, I fear I must shortly be returning to my own home. My business about here has been conducted already. But no doubt I will see him again soon.'

The bottler finally returned. Since the buttery was, I know, only a short step from the screens passage, it was obvious to me that she knew he was listening in to her conversations from outside the doorway. Which was itself interesting, because assuredly that meant her husband did not trust her, and had set the bottler on her as a spy. It is terribly sad when all trust between spouses has fled.

At least the quality of the wine was good. I enjoyed one cup, chatting inconsequentially of this and that and the people in the parish here, while the bottler stood looking rather uncomfortable, staring into the middle distance as if he could not hear a word we were saying, and all was supremely unimportant in any case. With his bulbous eyes, he looked like a bear who had just felt the surprising thrust of a stuffing expert who wasn't aware his subject was still alive.

After sending the servant away for one refill of wine, I decided I must get home before Saul returned. I had no desire to experience his studied rudeness, having received it before often enough. He seemed to suspect that I was better acquainted with his wife than he would have liked, which only served to show that he was not such a blockhead as he liked to make out.

I took my leave of her reluctantly, my eyes dropping to her two most prominent attributes with regret, and she thrust them at me like twin reproaches. It was difficult to leave, but leave I must with that blasted servant still standing in the room, mute and condemning, or so I felt.

The street outside was empty, bar a few children and youngsters hawking their wares, and I strolled along full of thoughts concerning Mistress Appleby that would have made Father Peter's ears burn. I really should confess before long, I thought, with a view to seeing how my admissions of more or less frankness would make him react.

It was only a short distance to my new home, a quarter-mile

if that, and it took only a matter of minutes to cover the way, and when I reached my door, I was somewhat surprised to see that John Anderson stood waiting for me.

He greeted me with a smile and a flourish. 'I am glad to see you well, Master Blackjack,' he said. 'I had feared that some other footpad had knocked you on the pate. At least it was not the man I saw. I perceived that you needed some freedom from the fellow, and engaged him in conversation for a period, but he evaded me after a while, and I had thought he might follow you here, so I came to protect you.'

'I am indeed grateful,' I said, and entered my door.

To my annoyance the young pustule followed me inside, looking about him like a prospective buyer. 'Not unpleasant, but you should have more in the way of decoration,' he said, as if he had any right to an opinion.

'I like it as it is,' I said firmly.

He followed me into my parlour, where I reluctantly accepted fate and bellowed for Raphe, who was soon despatched for wine.

'Who was that fellow? Was he a mere footpad, or is he known to you?' Anderson asked.

'I have met the fellow before, but I have no desire to renew his acquaintance,' I said. I saw no need to elaborate.

'In your place I would be careful,' he said. He took a gulp of wine – these youngsters, they have no idea how to appreciate good wine – and continued, 'I mean, after what happened in the church, with the rood screen broken, the altar desecrated, and the poor woman murdered, it's obvious that our streets are dangerous. An older man like you should take care when walking abroad.'

I bridled. *In my place*? An *older man*? I was scarcely four, perhaps five years older than this puppy! 'I have my own defences. No robber will get the better of me,' I declared, and resolved from that moment to ensure that my wheel-lock pistol remained with me at all times.

'For certain you are,' he said, giving me the sort of tolerant look a man might give an ancient grandfather. 'But I do think you should remain vigilant. If a man dares desecrate a church, who knows what else he might attempt?'

I shuddered at that thought, and at the memory of Rachel's throat. So slender, so lovely, and now so gaping. I gulped wine quickly.

To change the subject and bring a different picture to my mind, I said, 'I was talking to Alderman Kirk earlier. He was saying that he has only been an alderman for a little while.'

'Yes. Before that he was a successful man of business, but when Adam Bonner was waylaid and slain, Kirk was asked to fill his place. I think he was surprised, but keen. After all, an alderman can easily make a lot of money.'

'He mentioned that Bonner had died.'

'Oh, yes. He was found with his throat cut in the alley up near Leather-maker's Hall. A year or so past.'

'Really?' I mused on that. There were many footpads in London, and cutting a man's throat was a quick and sure way to kill your victim. Better by far than stabbing in the back, as I have learned. Humfrie says it's too easy to miss the mark and find that your victim irritated at being stabbed, shouting and bringing onlookers, as well as returning the favour with a sword or long dagger.

The two deaths were surely not related.

Not long afterwards I managed to dissuade him from remaining, and saw to it that he was ushered from the house. Yet he had given me much to reflect on. In the sudden shock of being accused of the murder of Rachel, I had entirely forgotten about the damage done to the church.

Was that vandalism somehow connected to her death, or was it inflicted merely in order to confuse any who tried to investigate her demise? It was quite a conundrum. In desperation I even considered using the services of my recent visitor. Anderson was a pimple that needed pricking, but at least he had an alibi for the night when Rachel Nailor was murdered. I should confirm his story and learn whether he was truly in the Green Dragon and with Elias Spink, as he had claimed. Although, if he had seen Croke there, it meant he was near the church too – he could be the guilty man himself. If so, perhaps he might be useful. He had certainly saved me from the gorilla's attention. With that thought crossing my brain, I dozed.

Waking abruptly, I had a horrible conviction that the gorilla was gripping my head and seeing how easily it could be removed from my shoulders, but it was only Raphe's damned dog, Hector, who was scrabbling from behind me, his paws on my shoulders and his tongue on my ear.

'Get off me, you damned devil!'

I sprang to my feet, heart pounding at the sudden waking. I repaired to the kitchen to remonstrate with Raphe.

There, Cecily gave me a slightly anxious, frosty stare, as though she was keen to criticize me for my enjoyment of the day, but lacked the conviction. I gave her a steady glare which persuaded her to relent, and I asked where Raphe was, and why his hound had been allowed to disturb my rest.

'He'm outside. He'm keeping an eye open for ye.'

I could make little sense of that, but then again, I rarely could. Cecily was not a Londoner as such. She had come to the city from the far east, near the coast, I believe, but her family were unable to support her on their peasant income, so they had sold her, or simply kicked her from home, to find her own way in the world. She had learned her craft in a merchant's house working under a senior cook, and when I heard of her, through Raphe, and discovered that she was ambitious for her own kitchen, it seemed worthwhile to hire her, since Raphe was so utterly incompetent. He could not boil an egg without burning it.

Having been pointed towards the door at the rear of my house, I walked out. Raphe was at the gate to the church close. This was the passageway that gave access to my garden from the road past the church itself, and he stood peering through a gap in the slats of the gate.

'That dog of yours almost ruined me just now, and if you can't keep it under—'

I stopped. He had lifted his hand to me as though to indicate I should hold my tongue, and I was so incensed to be treated thus by my own servant, that I took a deep breath ready to blast him to the Indies and beyond, but before the words formed, he turned to me and something in his eyes stopped my mouth.

'What is it?' I hissed, and that quietly.

'There's a man been standing out here all afternoon since you returned, watching the house.'

I tutted to myself. 'It's just the gorilla,' I said. 'I know him. He won't break in.'

'Why call him that?'

'He's built like one.'

'Not this fellow. He's lean and scrawny,' Raphe said, and I pushed him aside to have a look.

When you peer through a gate's slats at a figure some little distance away, it is not always easy to discern features. The splinters which the joiner forgot to adze away from the planks that made up the gate detracted from a clear view, and they appeared as broad smudges in my vision. I tried to study the figure, and I have to confess, it did not look like the gorilla. He was unlike any man I knew. He appeared moderately well-clad, with plain hosen and jerkin, nothing elegant or valuable enough to mark him as a rich man, but not poverty-struck either. I placed him as a groom or similar servant to a wealthy man. But he was plainly staring at my front door with dedication.

'Have you seen him before?' I hissed at Raphe.

'No. I saw him a little after you returned, and he's been there since.'

At least I had managed to refresh myself, I thought. If need be, I could elude this latest spy. It was a surprise that John Blount should have hired such an obvious watcher. He was usually more careful in the type of men he took on. I mean to say, he employed me, which does give an indication of the sort of sensible decision of which he was capable.

Then again, on reflection, it occurred to me that he had also made use of others, like the gorilla. No man was forever infallible.

I whispered instructions to Raphe that he should watch the fellow, and then follow him when he finally departed, to find out where he lived. From that I might be able to discover more about him.

Meanwhile, I had more urgent business.

My garden had a second gate at the rear of my little yard. I made my exit from that, and thence along the rear alley to

Bishopsgate, and along the great thoroughfare to the hall where Rachel Nailor had lived. There, I knocked firmly on the door, stood back, and waited.

It was growing dark. It was many hours since my last real meal. Cecily would be pleased to learn of my Lenten moderation. It was time I had some solid ballast to the belly. I must visit the Bull later, I decided, and select one of their pies.

As I reached this conclusion, I heard the bolts being drawn, and was soon confronted by the young woman who had accompanied Rachel Nailor at the church and in my house. I smiled at her, and she gave me a rather tearful response, her face pale and fretful. I could almost think she was scared of me. She was quite pretty, with a round face and large brown eyes. Her hair was dark and curling, from the ringlets dangling from her coif. She might justify a little effort later, were I to have the opportunity.

On hearing my name and my reason for visiting, to offer my condolences to the household where Mistress Nailor had been living, I was ushered into the hall, a large and pleasant chamber with a small dais bearing a long table, and the walls all lined with heavy tapestries. This was obviously not a room in which secret conversations would be held – there were too many heavy draperies; they could conceal an army of spies. No, this was a pleasant family room in which a lord and his family would eat and converse in confidence that nothing they said was remotely interesting to the queen or her rivals.

I was left to stand near a large fireplace and the child departed the room to fetch her master, Gerald Marbod.

He was soon with me. A tall, stooped man with a hat to cover an elegantly fringed tonsure that left his pate and brow completely devoid of all hair. He had piercing grey eyes that took in my attire and appearance at a glance, but before speaking even to welcome me, he strode past me, waving the young maid away. 'Leave us, Moll.' He seated himself in a high-backed seat to the right of the fire and studied me with a frowning demeanour. 'I understand you came to offer condolences.'

'Yes, I was most sad to hear of Mistress Nailor's death. A sad loss, I am sure.'

The judge nodded and continued to survey me with eyes narrowed. 'You were not a friend to her, I believe.'

'No, I only met her briefly twice after church.'

'You are new to the area,' he said.

I was beginning to feel that I was being interrogated, which was confusing since my intention had been to question him. 'Um, yes. But tell me, she—'

'I suppose you met her in the church. She would not have been keen to speak with someone in the street.'

'Eh? Oh, no. Yes, I mean. I met her in St Helen's, and we spoke in the churchyard afterwards. So, was—'

'I daresay she was abrupt with you. She tended to be with strangers.'

'Oh, yes. She was most short with me, but I managed to win her round.'

'Next you will tell me that she invited you to visit her?'

'No, she visited me,' I said with some warmth. This interrogation was passing beyond the seemly, and I was aware of a degree of irritation. 'I discovered her when I—'

Once more he interrupted me in mid-flow. It really was annoying. 'So you say she discovered your home and arrived at your door without warning?'

I bridled. 'I do not see what this has to do with my offering sympathy.'

'Very little, but it might have much to do with your visit from her, and possibly your true reasons for visiting me today.'

'I—'

'You and she were engaged in the same plans. One could almost call it a conspiracy.'

I felt the cold, clammy claws of fate grip my bowels. I would have grabbed for my pistol, but unfortunately, although I had determined that I would load and prepare it for just such an occasion as this when John Anderson advised me against risks, for some reason I had entirely forgotten to bring it. 'I . . . I don't think—'

'Sit!' he commanded, and since my legs had become wobbly, I obeyed.

'She told me she was going to meet you. She wanted me to know in case anything happened to her. As it did. I know of her mission and her desire to leave tomorrow, but it never occurred to me – or her – that danger lurked so close to home. Tell me all.'

I was about to open my mouth, but then caution took hold of me, and I was struck dumb at the thought that this man could well be a fraud, set to trap me. I smiled and shook my head. 'No, I have no idea what . . . um . . .'

'Your name is Jack Blackjack. You are employed by Master John Blount to help with the household of Lady Elizabeth. Your duties are foremost to protect her and her companions, a task to which you have proved singularly capable. Yes, I know of you, your occupation and your present situation. Now, speak!'

I looked about me at the walls of hanging tapestries and heavy fabric. Any number of men could be concealed behind them, and even with this plain-speaking man, I was left feeling decidedly exposed. You may think me overly anxious, and that I should have trusted this fellow, but in truth I was alarmed to think that he knew so much about me. And that he knew of the mission to Paris.

He saved my embarrassment. 'I quite understand, Master Blackjack. Follow me. We shall go to my garden. There is a bench there which is some distance from the garden walls, and we can speak in solitude without the risk of eavesdroppers.'

Rising, he made his way to a door behind the dais. From here we walked to a rear door from his parlour out through a small dairy, and thence into the yard. There was, as he had promised, a small quadrangle of grass with flower and herb beds to left and right, and salad leaves and other greenery in the other half of the beds.

In the centre of all the profusion, there stood a comfortable looking bench. He led the way to it, waved me to my seat, and joined me on the hard boards.

'Tell me all,' he said.

I confess I was reluctant, but since there were no witnesses to overhear us, and because he had already demonstrated a

degree of knowledge, I gradually told him of Mistress Nailor
and her visit to my house.

'She was determined to go, then?' he said.

'Very, and she demanded my attendance.'

'For your *special* skills – yes, I can understand that,' he
murmured, peering at a group of flower buds on the nearest
plant. 'She would need to be able to rely on a consort on her
way. Else the queen's men, or the king's, might try to waylay
her. As, it would seem, they did.'

'I don't understand that,' I said. 'Why should they damage
the church? What would lead them to break the rood screen,
pull off the veils and altar cloth, to damage the communion
cup – and why kill her in there?'

'I would wager it was to throw suspicion on to a stranger,
a thief who was set on the destruction inside the church, and
who was confronted by the woman walking in. The robber set
upon her, killed her and fled. That would be the tale he would
expect the coroner to tell.'

'But it wasn't true?'

'If my guess doesn't miss the mark too widely, I would
imagine that she was murdered, and her body taken to the
church so that she could be concealed there. Either that, or
she entered the church and was slain, and then the murderer
set about creating a scene that would explain her death.'

I swallowed. 'From the blood, I would think she was killed
in there. There was so much.'

'Were there drips or smears on the floor of the church?'

'No.'

'Then you must be right. Her throat was cut, so much of
the blood would have left her as her heart kept pumping. I
have seen such deaths. Who ever did this must have been
smothered in blood himself. So, then, she entered the church
and came across the murderer involved in his destruction. He
killed her to silence her, and then fled.'

'Which would mean she knew him. The murderer was known
to her,' I said.

'Yes.'

I recalled John Blount's expression as he told me that she
had received a message purportedly from me, calling her to

the church. It made me shiver, and I asked whether Marbod knew of such a message.

'I had not thought of that. Yes, a messenger brought it for her. I did not know what was in the message, though. So someone was attempting to use you. You were to take the blame.' He frowned. And then he looked at me, and I felt that clenching at my guts again. His eyes narrowed. 'Whoever it was had conceived a firm idea whom he could blame for the murder.'

'Really?' I said, and then slowly my mouth fell open. Yes, I gaped.

He nodded. 'Yes. The one man who was known to her, whom others had seen her talk with, and who was new to the area, that one man might be expected to try to conceal his involvement. Someone tried to fit you as the culprit, Master Blackjack.'

I left him and made my way to the Bull. Terror was gripping me now. I have seen the pyres burning alleged heretics and traitors, I've heard of those hanged, drawn and quartered for their betrayal of the crown, and the way things stood, I could imagine myself being the main figure in such a street theatre.

It was plain that I must leave London. I had to fly to some part of the country where I was unknown, where I would be safe from being uncovered, and where the false, treacherous knaves who were trying to nail me to the guilt of the murder of Rachel could not find me. Yes, escape beckoned.

Quickly I began to assess the items I would need to take with me. Powder, shot, my wheel-lock pistol, food . . . *food*! That was a thought. The inn offered a thick pottage with sausage and plenty of barley and greens bubbling away in a copper. I could smell it from the parlour, and soon I was sitting with a large bowl, a half small loaf of bread, and shovelling food into my mouth like an orphan beggar after a week's starvation.

And as I ate, the fear and danger receded somewhat. It was less that the risks were minimized, and more that I was reminded of recent events. When I had taken myself to Devonshire to escape London, I had been prey to thieves, vagabonds, outlaws and disreputable fellows of business, all in the first few days. Were I to return, I would be sure to run the risk of being assaulted yet again. That was not an appealing consideration.

Then again, were I to make my way to some other corner of the realm, who could say but that the dangers would not be increased? I was not a traveller by nature; I was a gentleman of London, a civilized fellow, who was at home in the great metropolis. What did I know of the wilder parts of the kingdom? If I were to make my way to the marches of Wales or Scotland, who was to say that I would not end up murdered by some of the rebellious and violent, uncouth men of those places? News of the mad Armstrongs, Elliots, Fenwicks and Nixons of the Scottish wilds were often relayed to us down here in London. It did not make sense for me to try to go there. But then, York was no safer. The Scottish had oftentimes invaded and attacked all the way to the city. Nearer home? I had heard stories of murder and mayhem from St Albans to Chepstow. The fact was, the queen's reign had seen dissatisfaction and rebellion since she had first taken the throne from poor Lady Jane Grey, and all the more since she had seen the child executed.

I was surely safer here in London. Especially if I could show someone else was guilty of the murder.

Who could have tried to post this unjust accusation against me? The poor woman was barely cold in her grave, and now I had learned that someone had planned to accuse me before inviting her to the church, before murdering her. It must be someone jealous of my position, I thought. But the idea intruded on me that the facts seemed to go against that. Surely, it was more likely that it was my position in the service of Lady Elizabeth, and therefore my mission to France had become known to someone who had a foul desire to implicate me and thus weaken the Lady's household. After all, if they could destroy one mission to France, there was still an opportunity for Lady Elizabeth or one of her entourage to arrange for a second, and again to try to send me to protect the ambassador selected. If they could remove Rachel and emasculate me at the same time, making it impossible for me to go on future journeys, that might make Lady Elizabeth's plan just that little bit too precarious. She might resolve not to make the attempt, and merely lie down and accept her fate.

No, not she. Others may look on her as a weak and feeble woman with the stomach of a puppy, if they knew her not, but I knew her better. She was a ruthless, determined daughter of King Henry. I would put little past her, once she was convinced of the path she must take.

I finished my meal and felt better for it. No, I would not flee the city. Here I was safer. But I must discover who was responsible for Rachel Nailor's death if I was to be truly secure.

It was as I was considering making my way homewards, that I saw the Anderson family enter.

Young John Anderson saw me before I could conceal myself behind my hat or one of the other patrons, and although I was determined to rise and escape, the trio joined me at my table, and Stephen Anderson thrust wine upon me. It was impossible to refuse him. I resolved to make good my escape as soon as possible, but for now I was forced to accept their hospitality.

And soon I was glad that I had, although their news was hardly of the sort to ease matters.

'What did you say?' I demanded.

It was John who had spoken, and he glanced at me with surprise, so it seemed. His mother shook her head, an eyebrow raised as she looked across the table at me. Her husband had his nose deep in a cup of strong wine at the time, and I could not see his face.

'Yes, it is true,' John said. He was embracing a pot of mulled ale that steamed like a damp fire, and he was obviously enjoying his position as narrator of this new information. 'She was pregnant.'

'The wench was plainly no better than a common street walker,' his mother pronounced. 'To think that we had the mother of a foundling here in our parish. She deserved all she got.'

'That's hardly fair, Mother!' John declared. 'What if the poor woman was raped?'

'Raped! These women deserve all they get! What, you think she was not responsible for her own behaviour? Dressing as she did, behaving as she did, she knew what she was about. Women like her are no better than they should be! She called it upon herself by her behaviour and lewd speech with men,' his wife said hotly.

Her husband said nothing, but up-ended his pot and reached for the jug to refill it. He looked like a man who had drunk spirits of vitriol.

'Who says this?' I said.

'The queen's crowner came to view the body earlier,' John said, ever the master of details. 'He held inquest over the corpse, and when they undressed her for the jury, it was suspected that she was with child. A midwife was called, and she confirmed it.'

'I am astonished,' I said. Of course, it did explain her lack of interest in my own special attributes. I have only ever known my charms to be ignored when there was good reason. 'Who could have been the father, I wonder?'

It was merely a mild rhetorical enquiry, but it was interesting to see how the trio responded. Mistress Anderson pursed her lips as though they were sewn together firmly, and she sat primly stiff-backed as though determined to add nothing to her earlier comments on Rachel's character and behaviour. Her husband said nothing, but kept his eyes downcast, and I was sure that it was not the darkness, but that there was a rising tide of redness that suffused his cheeks. I felt sure he was embarrassed by his wife's rudeness about the victim of the murder. Meanwhile their son looked about the room with studied nonchalance. I was sure that he knew more, and if he wished he could impart still more shocking revelations. But for all that, he appeared unsettled. It made me recall to mind how I had wondered whether Stephen Anderson had enjoyed an affair, which his wife had later learned about. That might explain much.

In any case, I commended Stephen for his respect for the dead woman. There was no need for his wife's accusations. She was assuredly a poisonous witch. There are some gossips who cannot restrain themselves when they hear of another's misfortune, and are always keen to denigrate them and their behaviour. Although, it had to be said that Mistress Kate did have some right to wonder at the cause of Mistress Rachel's pregnancy. She had been a lonely woman here in the parish, I guessed. Dishonoured since her 'husband's' supposed divorce, and her own marriage annulment, it would have been difficult to see how to make her way in the world. It was quite possible that she had chosen to lie with a man and play hide the pudding, seeking only some comfort, and then to discover, as so many enthusiastic young lovers do, that such games can lead to misfortunes. Perhaps that was a reason for her eager sponsorship of the journey to Paris; she thought it would be good to escape her usual haunts for a while?

'She was no better than she should be,' Kate pronounced again, and with that I knocked back the last of my drink and took my leave of them.

It was a relief to be out in the open air once more and away from her poison.

Briefly.

Outside, I made my way homewards with some annoyance. The eagerness with which Kate Anderson made her accusation was enough to make me want to defend the dead woman. Rachel was no woman of loose morals, I was sure.

I continued on my way without paying attention to my surroundings, until I was accosted.

'Master Blackjack? I hope I see you well?'

I was about to give a short response, when I realized it was Richard Croke. On the basis that it's always a good idea to remain on friendly terms with the wealthier members of the parish, I gave him a good day, and looked at his companion.

It was one of those over-dressed and overly ornate types you see occasionally. He had a slim figure, and expensive clothing, set off with a smart cloak and a very fine sword which looked like a rapier. In short, he was a Spaniard. Croke reluctantly introduced me to him. He was called Diego de Toledo, he said.

Diego de Toledo looked at me without any great enthusiasm, rather as though I was a mere peasant in his path, and I was fully aware that my company was not required. It was embarrassing, and I soon left the two and continued on my way. I wanted nothing to do with Spaniards. So many of them had appeared in London since Queen Mary's marriage to Philip, and their arrogance while strolling about the city had not endeared them to anyone. Besides, just now, I didn't want John Blount to hear that I was consorting with the enemy.

That was a thought! A Spaniard would definitely have good reason to be keeping a watch on Rachel. She was known to be a companion or accomplice of Lady Elizabeth. What if they had heard she was planning to flee to France? Perhaps Croke or the Spanish had discovered the plan to journey to France, and they decided to prevent her?

I continued towards my home deep in thought.

The first intimation I had of encroaching danger was the loud slapping of cheap shoes from behind me. I was not concerned, for it was still daylight, and footpads were unlikely to attack at such an hour when there were plenty of people on all sides to bear witness to an assault. A woman hurried past me, and it struck me that the pursuit was for her, not me. I was confident enough, and mildly relaxed after a number of drinks. Besides, it was a pleasant evening.

I was suddenly wrenched from the roadside by a hand on my shoulder, and as I span about, burping with some confusion, a fist the size of a cannon ball came into view. It was clenched as tightly as a ship's cable about a belaying pin, and I felt my eyes widen in that brief moment before oblivion beckoned, and then tried to duck from its path.

My evasion was not entirely successful. The fist still struck me on the brow, but at least that meant I was merely stunned, rather than utterly destroyed. I had a brief moment to recognize the gorilla before I saw the fist renewing its assault on my features. With a sharp yelp, I tried to escape. It involved bending almost double, lifting my leg, and kicking out for all I was worth while closing my eyes from that horrible sight. There was a moment's crashing pain as he used his fist to club me over the shoulder after missing my face, and then there was a moment's peace. When I opened my eyes again, I saw that there was a look of wonder on his features. That lasted a mere moment, and then his eyebrows seemed to run together and crashed over his nose, before rising in an inverted 'V' of agony. He emulated my own foetal posture, but although he was not enjoying this new sensation, he did not release his grip on my shoulder. It took a second kick to make him give a slight 'oof' of intense emotion, and then his hand relented, having two or three cherished items to nurse.

I fled.

It took me little time to cover the distance from his anguish to my front door, and I hammered quickly on finding it was barred, desperately throwing a look over my shoulder, concerned that I might see the lumbering brute dragging his knuckles over the stones of the roadway towards me. He would not be in a happy frame of mind, were he to discover me. Before I met him again, I was determined to get a good grip on my hand gun.

I was still standing there and beating upon my door when I noticed a movement in a shadow farther up the street. With a yipping sound that strained my throat, I thundered still more determinedly, convinced that the gorilla, or John Blount, had sent a second assassin to pay me their close attention.

To my relief, the door opened and Raphe stared out at me in consternation. 'Master? What is the—'

I shoved the fool aside, and just as I was about to slam the door, I caught sight of the man's face. I didn't recognize him, but I could see him peering at me, and he was not impressed to see me disappear, I guessed, for his face wore that appearance of contemplation and regret that a determined assassin would carry after seeing a potential purse of gold snatched away from his grasp.

FOUR

Tuesday 30th March

It was a horrible morning to which I awoke the next day. My head felt like a very sorry pig's bladder after a brutal football match during which every player's boot and fist had attacked it. There was a lump the size and colour of a plum on my forehead that rather spoiled my looks.

Naturally, after the shocks of the day before, I had resorted to a jug of wine as soon as I had made my way to my chair in the parlour, and sat ignoring the non-verbal recriminations of my cook and steward. They had no understanding of the terrible danger which I had only by the finest scrape averted. They should have feared my situation since, were I to die, both would need to seek new employment. But no, even when I blurted my concerns, and let them know how close I had come to utter destruction at the hands of the gorilla, Cecily appeared unmoved. She merely sniffed meaningfully and stared at my jug of wine; meanwhile Raphe complained bitterly about my requiring him to keep fetching more wine.

After their lack of sympathy, it is hardly to be wondered that I ejected both while I sat and stared into my fire, mulling over the injustices of my life and the lack of compassion even of my staff.

I sipped wine. It made me think: at least I did not feel so cragged and worn as after the visit from Rachel that day. It must have been a better batch of wine. Which meant Raphe had emptied the last from the old barrel, the thieving turd. I would have words with him.

There was no doubt in my mind that the man in the shadows last night was the same fellow who had followed me to my home, only to be witnessed by Raphe watching my doorway. If so, he must have waited for a long time; the man was patient, if nothing else. Had Raphe followed him, as I had instructed? I would have to question the fool later.

The gorilla was a different matter. He was a brute, and had tried to capture or murder me. I could not be certain which, but I was convinced that he would not hesitate to make another attempt. He would seize any opportunity. I must be cautious. In future, when walking abroad, I would have to avoid any narrow ways, and must keep a careful watch over my shoulder. Perhaps I should retain a fighting man, my own henchman, to protect me. A sudden vision of young John Anderson crept slyly into my mind. The boy was a fool, but a man did not have to be a genius to outwit the gorilla. Only quick mentally and physically.

The gorilla: why had he tried to assault me? He would not hesitate to throttle me even before tens of witnesses; I had seen that in his eyes, even as they narrowed in pain. It was, I confess, a matter of pride that I had managed to cause him such agony, but the result was not going to be to my taste, I was sure. The man would not relent. Why, though? John Blount had indicated that I had some days to seek a solution to this murder, so why set his man on me so soon? Unless, of course, it was not an attack at John Blount's bidding, but another's?

It was enough to make my hair turn white.

But just now, the uppermost thought in my mind was security. And that meant I must prepare.

First, I retrieved my handgun from its holster in my chest, cleaned it carefully, and loaded the barrel with fresh powder and a ball, wadded well with some greased canvas. I checked the dog to see that the lump of stone was sharp enough to spark when it was set against the wheel, and installed it in the holster on the belt, hidden behind my back. To balance its weight, I hung my ballock knife from the front of the belt. Then I pulled my baldric over my head and settled the sword sheath on my left hip, and draped the shot flask and powder horn to dangle at my side as well. It made me feel twice my usual weight, but I didn't regret that. The gorilla had followed me, as had two others, and I was not of a mood to take risks. At least with weapons on view any assailant would be a little wary of trying to launch an assault on me.

Walking downstairs, I confronted my useless servant. 'What happened to you following the spy? You were to trail after him and learn where he came from!' I snapped. I was, after all, very angry to have been left in potential danger just because he was too lazy to obey my clear instruction.

'I did.'

'Oh, really? Where did he come from, then?'

And this was when he dropped his first bombshell.

'From Mistress Appleby's.'

He looked away, but not before I caught a glimpse of the smile on his face. He knew, of course, of my assignations with the lady of that house, and he would have been perfectly aware of her husband's suspicions. If Saul were to be assured that his wife was visiting me at intervals, he would be incandescent, and that could only create more difficulties for me. Suppose the fool decided to demand a test of courage in some kind of martial combat? In London there were regular demonstrations organized by the Masters of Defence, and I had often enjoyed witnessing the bouts with staffs, swords, daggers, and even fists, but it had never occurred to me that I might be expected to endure a similar combat. No, and if I had anything to do with it, I would not now.

'What of the second?'

'What second?'

'When I returned, I was followed again.'

'I don't know about that,' he said, and added unnecessarily, 'although you had drunk more than usual by the time you got home.'

'What does that mean?'

'I've heard of a man said he saw pink flies everywhere after he'd been drinking too much for too long,' he said in a throw-away manner.

'I do not see any pink flies,' I said heatedly. This servant was getting above himself. It really was about time I discarded the pestilential menial, and if only I did not need yet another reason to annoy Master John Blount, I would have turfed the lad from my door on the spot. But the fact that his uncle was my master, and the fact that I still needed an attendant for my protection against the footpads who were undoubtedly seeking me, saved his employment for the nonce.

'I want you to go back to the garden and keep an eye on the street. See if there is anyone who seems to be paying too much attention to my front door.'

'Yes, sir.'

He remained standing there.

'Now, Raphe!'

'Now? But it's raining like . . .'

'Now.'

He gave me the sort of look that Cinthio's Moorish captain gave his underling just after killing his wife, and wandered out. From the slump of his shoulders, I could only imagine that he was feeling distinctly unhappy in my service.

It made me feel so good that I called loudly for ham and eggs. Loudly less so that Cecily could hear, and more so that Raphe could, while out in the rain, which I now heard beating down heavily. That was enough to make me smile. All was well with the world so far, even if Cecily seemed still more disgusted with my Lenten lapses.

And next, I had to enlist the assistance of young John Anderson or someone. I needed a guard for when I was out and about. I certainly couldn't rely on Raphe.

There are times when a man gets lucky. In my experience, those times can be few and far between, but today I was fortunate enough to check some points.

Now, I know that you will have the same thought that had occurred to me: although John Anderson had told me that he could not have been involved in the murder of Rachel and the destruction of the church, because, as he said, he was busy with a friend up at the Green Dragon inn, I had not yet verified that. After all, I may well discover that the fellow giving him that alibi may well have been his closest companion from childhood. I had to fight to recall that he had told me the fellow was Elias Spink, which meant it was Gawtheren Spink's son. There could not be many Spinks within the parish.

The Anderson house was a large and imposing hall, in every way a reflection of the alderman's, but for the fact of the fresh limewashed walls and timbers. It gleamed even in the miserable, dull, rain-cloaked morning, and I was forced to stand at the door for an unconscionable length of time while waiting for someone to respond to my knock. It did at least give me the opportunity to keep a wary eye open on the street and ensure that I had not been followed all the way here.

It opened, and I stepped in before the bottler had an opportunity to refuse me entry. I was not going to wait outside any longer. Soon I was installed before a feeble fire that smoked and puffed without ever seeming to give flame or hallowed warmth. The logs must have been made from old elms, I think, or timbers cut for coffins, for all the heat they gave.

'Master Blackjack, what a pleasant surprise,' Mistress Anderson said as she entered, wiping her hands on a towel. Her expression and the set of her mouth indicated that any pleasure she felt was of a distinctly limited form. 'I trust I see you well?'

After the usual pleasantries, I managed to enquire about her son's whereabouts.

'John? I believe he has gone to visit the Bull. They are to hold a small play in the rear yard. Some play actors are giving a demonstration of their skills, such as they are.'

'You have little sympathy with such pursuits?'

'Acting? Of course not! It is an activity for heathens, sodomites and evil-doers who cannot be trusted to hold down a real job or take on a career! If I could have my way, I would have them all arrested, and burned at stakes set in their acting wagons. Such a fruitless occupation for any man! They should be set to work on the roads as paviours, or made to form cobbles, some form of serious work that would benefit all, rather than this foolishness!'

'Many enjoy the actors' efforts,' I tried.

'Many enjoy fornication and gluttony. Does that make them worthy activities?' she said sharply.

I could have disputed that case, but sought not to antagonize her, so did not respond. 'I understand your son is a friend to Elias Spink,' I said. You see here I was cleverly testing the boy's story. He had told me that he was the enemy of Spink, and I was asking whether he was the boy's friend. I know it seems devious, but I had limited time, and had to seek the truth before my life was put in real danger.

'In which case you understand a great deal more than *I* do, master!' she said, and if it was possible to be knocked back by a woman's blast, this was the time. It felt like a monstrous gale of wind striking me forcefully, as though I was trying to walk into a zephyr. I was all but blown over.

I heard steps hurriedly approaching in the screens passage, and she held up a hand to send the page or bottler away. Clearly the fellow was not brave enough to enter to try to protect me from his mistress.

'Who told you that?'

'I . . . I am not . . .'

'It is a lie! A foul, despicable untruth that was made up just to insult my family! I will not have the name of that woman mentioned in this house, nor that of her son! My son would have nothing to do with . . . with *him*! They have nothing in common, and do not move in the same circles!'

'I see,' I said in my most placatory manner.

'Don't squirm so! If someone tells you a similar lie, you should let them know that it is not true, and that if I learn who is spreading such mendacious gossip, I will see to it that the full force of justice lands on their heads!'

'Yes, I quite . . .'

'And if you ask me, the damage done to the church? The murder of that woman? I would not be at all surprised if they were found to be the responsibility of that boy of her's. He is a scoundrel, no doubt. He was born in sin, and he will die in sin!'

'I see. Um. I should leave you in peace, madam. I am very sorry to have been the . . . to have brought this . . . to have mentioned it.'

I left, and although it is hard to admit it, I must have looked like a terrier slinking away from the butcher's shop after being seen stealing a sausage.

I have often enjoyed a little play-acting. It is a pleasant diversion for fellows such as myself, who have a little spare time of our own, and who wish to spend it being entertained.

Sometimes the acting is of a high standard, and the audience can be transported back in time, to the days of Athens or Imperial Rome, or to the wonderful histories of the English kings, or to a bawdy tale of widows seeking a man to scratch their itches – those always get the audience guffawing. If the acting is not so good, there is a lot of entertainment to be had from watching the audience reactions, with perhaps a cabbage or two being hurled, or a rotten egg. Those moments can be hilarious.

Today's actors were quite impressive. They had brought a wagon of their own into the yard behind the inn, and having brought down the sides, the wagon bed became their stage. The play was something to do with the tale of a fellow from the wild countryside, who came to London and became Lord Mayor, if you can believe it. Hardly likely, was my view, but it was competently acted, and the crowd quite liked it. There were some good jokes in it, and the actors were glad that the rotten eggs were kept back. From the look of their clothing, they had experienced plenty of eggs in their time, but that is, after all, the risk of a life as a strolling player.

John was in the front of the audience, standing with the rest with his mouth agape as he swallowed up the scenes before him. I did not push through the crush to get to him, preferring to remain at the outer fringes of the mob, from where I could see the entrance to the inn, the gates to the yard, and watch for any sign of the gorilla or the young fellow who was sent from, if Raphe were to be believed, Saul Appleby's house. I saw no sign of either of them, and after a while, I could lean against a pillar and enjoy the remainder of the play, such as it was.

At the end, to nobody's surprise, the crowd quickly dispersed before they could be importuned into handing over a penny for their enjoyment, John remained rooted to the spot, obviously eager to speak with the players. He managed to engage two in conversation, even as they were packing up stage props and trying to evade him. It was plain that their interests lay much more in the contents of the hats being passed around and seeing whether they could afford a beer or two on the proceeds.

'You enjoy the play? Your mother didn't seem keen on your visiting the actors,' I said when I finally gave up and walked to meet him.

'She has little understanding of what I enjoy,' he said, a trifle moodily.

'You would like to be a play actor?'

'What a life! To travel all over the country, visiting new towns and cities, a new audience in every inn – it must be marvellous!'

'It must be *horrible*! Think of the days of rain, like earlier today, when the wagon leaks, and you have become soaked to the skin with no chance of a fire to dry yourself or a bed that isn't sodden! Have you tried travelling? And then there are the fleas and lice from cheap inns, and the risk that the landlord or one of his trollops will cut your purse strings and make off with all your money. And the food!' I pulled a grimace. It was reminding me all too strongly of my visit to Dartmoor, and the horrors I had been forced to endure along the way. I could not conceive of any man desiring to experience such misery.

'I doubt not that you are quite correct,' he said sadly. 'But I would dearly love to be able to make my way as an actor. To join a wandering band such as this and spend my life in their company perfectly content. Instead,' he added glumly, 'I am trained as a leather seller, and forced to spend all my days here in London.'

'Yes. In London, in a large hall, with servants to see to your every need, with women available at all the better watering holes, with wine and beer and food to tempt an epicurean,' I pointed out.

'When all I really want is excitement. The open road, the opportunity—'

'To be knocked on the head and left dead at the roadside,' I said sharply. I had been poor, and I knew full well that given the choice, rich in London was far better than poor anywhere. 'But that is not why I am here. Do you have a little time to answer some questions?'

'Gladly!'

'Good.'

I procured a table in the inn, and we drank a quart of weak beer each while we discussed the affair. It was my belief that the murderer was probably someone who knew of Rachel's mission to France, but of course I could not admit that to my new accomplice. That would involve news of my loyalties becoming common knowledge. For that reason I had to appear to defer to his own theories.

First, he suggested that the murder could have been the result of the vandalism, that the murderer was in reality only there to desecrate the church. 'There are many who would wish to bring harm down upon the church now that it has once more returned to the Catholic fold,' he said, nodding sagely.

I did not disagree.

'Then again, it might have been a man who was so desperate to possess her, that he took her inside and slew her when she refused him. Perhaps she had an assignation with that man?'

'I doubt that,' I said firmly. I did not want people to pursue that theory too far, in case someone overheard John Blount discussing the message Rachel had apparently received from me.

'But it is a possibility,' he persisted. I could not deny it was possible.

'However, I think it far more likely that this is a matter of someone who knew her well, someone who felt slighted, or who knew something she had done.' I was racking my brains trying to think of reasons why someone would have killed her that did not implicate me in any way.

'I know Elias accused the priest. But that is hardly likely,' John said.

'No,' I replied thoughtfully. I mean, there are always rumours about priests, their carnal desires, their urges and lusts concealed under an unconvincing cloak of celibacy, but in the main the priests I have known have all seemed moderately sane and unconcerned with such things. They tend to be more worried about the size of the tithes they collect than the quality of the women in the parish. Of course, there were always exceptions.

'Talking of Elias,' I said, 'I spoke to your mother about him, and she was furious. What has he done which has incurred her ire?'

He looked shifty. 'Why do you think she might be angry?'

'I listened to her.'

It took a little longer to wheedle the truth from him, and when I succeeded, I was astonished.

'Really? Him? Your father?'

'Yes. He has had affairs with several women, but with Gawtheren Spink, there was this . . . unfortunate outcome. Elias has no fault in this, obviously, and my father has paid for his upkeep and some money for food – he had little choice. Having made Gawtheren pregnant, she would find it difficult to persuade a husband to take her and her boy, and she is loyal to Elias. So my mother holds a certain dislike of Gawtheren and Elias.'

'I see.'

'There are many who we should question,' John added. 'Men like the alderman,' he said knowingly.

'Kirk? What of him?'

'I have seen him with Rachel several times, having quiet conversations.'

I blinked. 'I am having a quiet conversation with you now, but that doesn't make us . . . anything of that sort.'

'Well, no. We are men, naturally. But an alderman making an effort to speak with a woman like that, it seems curious to me, that is all,' he said, offended by my rejection of a favourite theory.

So it came down to this: we had no idea who might have been the murderer and desecrator.

Reluctantly, I decided that I should speak to the priest himself and assess whether he had formed any conclusions. And John would stay with me as my henchman.

When we reached the church, Father Peter was at the door, sweeping out the remains of broken splinters from the screen. He looked up at us as we approached, and his face set into a rictus, his jaw muscles working, as though he was chewing on a particularly gristly piece of meat.

'Father, I wondered whether I could have a short word with you?' I said with a smile.

He glared at me, looked at John, then glared at me with renewed vigour, saying nothing.

'Perhaps we could go inside,' John said, his face a picture of affability and courtesy. He held out a hand in a gesture proposing that the priest should lead the way.

Peter stood glowering a little longer, before setting his broom against the wall and reluctantly leading the way into the church.

With the broken trash swept away, the larger pieces removed and stacked outside, the damage was far less visible inside. We walked down between the pews, genuflecting deliberately in case the priest thought us lacking in reverence, and only when we were at the front of the church did he stop, turn and face us. 'Well? You are plainly not here for any form of absolution. What is it you want?'

All this was directed at John. The priest clearly thought I did not exist. Perhaps I was a ghost?

John glanced at me, and then said, 'Father, we are trying to learn all we can about the damage done to the church, and about the terrible death of the maid in there.' He nodded towards the vestry.

'She was not there when I left the church on Sunday.'

'When would that have been?'

'After dark. I always remain here in prayer until dark, and then lock up. There are thieves and vagabonds all over the city. No one is safe, not even in a church, so it seems,' he said, and his eyes were cast fearfully towards the vestry as he spoke.

'So you left after dark? And you are sure she was not in there when you did so?' I asked.

He was wool-gathering. When I spoke he turned to me as though surprised to see me there. 'Hmm? Oh, yes. Yes, I am quite sure. The poor maid! She must have been terrified, in the dark, to be caught – and then her throat cut! It is a horrible thing to conceive! That it should happen here, in my church! Oh, God, forgive this poor sinner!'

And I think he was about to collapse to the floor in a reverential fit, but before he could, I called his attention back to me. 'When you arrived here yesterday morning, you didn't see her at first?'

'No, not until you brought the vestry to my attention. I was so disturbed at the mess in here,' he said, a hand waving weakly over the damaged rood screen. 'What else could I do? When I entered and saw all this, I was appalled. To see such destruction in my church, *my* church! How could it have happened? And during Lent! Oh, God!' He turned from us and meandered to the altar, where he collapsed on the floor and spread his arms out in imitation of the cross, and set up a wailing that would surely have competed with any sinner in hell.

'Come, John. There is nothing more for us here,' I said, and we walked from the church.

On a usual day, this would be the time when most of the people would be arriving for Mass. Not today. Not until the bishop had come to reconsecrate the church after the murder. Blood had been spilled, and that had to be washed away by a senior priest.

You know, I have to admit it. I really felt rather sorry for the old man. He looked as devastated as his church's interior.

After our talk with the priest, I decided I should speak with Alderman Kirk to see if any more news had come to light.

My associate was reluctant to join me on that enterprise. 'You should question him alone. My father and Kirk have had a serious falling out,' he said.

When pressed, it soon became clear that the problem was based on good neighbourliness – or, rather, bad neighbourliness. The two households had been on good terms for many years, but recently the Kirks, according to John, had become difficult. There was a dispute about the edges of certain properties, to the extent that the Andersons had been in receipt of some warnings, because they were leaving garbage on the edge of the alderman's lands, as Kirk claimed, whereas the Andersons said it was on their land. The precise boundary was in dispute, and as a result there were sharp words spoken and a certain tension existed between both households. John did not feel he could join me on my enquiries to the Kirks.

I made my own way towards the alderman's hall, but on the way my steps slowed as I reconsidered. After all, what good would speaking to William do? If I were to see him and his wife was present, he would clam up in the face of her matronly jealousy; if she was not there, he would still be reluctant to discuss matters further, since although he and I may work for the same mistress, he could not be certain of that. He might consider me as a danger, a spy sent to persuade him to open up about his own loyalty to Lady Elizabeth, and thus a traitor to the queen.

Still, I had little choice. I must ask him.

I was in luck. After knocking tentatively on the door, I was admitted, only to discover to my relief that Agnes Kirk was not in the house. She had gone out with a mission to buy some fabric for a new dress. From personal experience I knew that must mean she would be away for some time.

So, I decided to take a more positive approach with him. The last occasion we had met, he had attempted to take a high-handed tone with me, until he wilted under the gaze of his terrifying wife. This time I intended to take the high tone with him.

'Master Blackjack,' he said as he joined me in his hall. 'I hope I see you well.'

The usual greetings are, I have often found, rather a distraction when a fellow is intending to interrogate a man. Common politeness means it's necessary to respond to the usual questions, and then soon all conversation is bogged down up to the axles in small talk. This time I chose the direct approach. We had reached that point at which we were both running out of small conversational items, and I thought I had best leap in.

'Master Kirk, I know you were outside the church talking to Rachel on the night she died. What were you discussing?'

He blinked and stared at me in astonishment. 'Me? With Rachel? I . . .'

'There is no need to deny it. I have witnesses who saw you there,' I said firmly, if dishonestly. I had, after all, only John Anderson's word for it so far. 'I am seeking her murderer, and to do so I needs must learn what you were doing there, and what you discussed, as well as anyone else you saw.'

'I . . .' His eyes went to the door to his private chamber.

'I did not want to embarrass you, so I waited until your wife had left the house,' I said.

He gave me a look that was mingled gratitude and . . . well, contempt, I think. 'Come with me,' he said.

As with Marbod, I soon found myself in a garden, although this time the bench was against the farther wall away from the house.

'I cannot discuss such matters in the house. Agnes' maid-servant hears everything said in there,' he said with a kind of desperate urgency.

'You were with Rachel outside the church, weren't you?' I said.

'I admit it, yes. It was impossible not to see her. She called me, you see. She had her little maidservant bring a message to me, asking me to see her one last time.'

'One last time?' And that was when the expression on his face when he found her body in the vestry was explained.

He threw me an agonized look. 'I loved her,' he said simply. 'Oh, I know it's hard to imagine, a dry old stick like me with a young, vibrant, *exciting* woman like Rachel, but it's true. I fell in love with her the first time I met her, and I flatter myself . . . I think she was very fond of me. We . . . well, it was our child she was carrying.'

I think at that point I could easily have dissolved or melted and fallen through the slats of the bench. To think that the woman could have turned my advances down, and all the while she had been swiving this tedious fellow, was enough to disorder my brains. I gaped at him.

'We had reason to meet and discuss matters of some importance,' he continued, 'but soon it became obvious to me that there was more to our meetings than that. We chatted, and learned that we had much in common, from spouses who were bullying and unkind, to missing affection, and . . . well, everything. And then she fell pregnant.'

'And that was *you!*'

'It was.'

'Why did you arrange to meet her there?'

He gave a harsh bark of a laugh at that. 'I? Arrange? God's

pain, I couldn't arrange anything with her. Damn it, she was in command at all times. Even when she . . . it was always she who made the choices, who decided. I had nothing to do with it.'

'What did she want to see you for, then?'

Kirk then surprised me. He covered his face in his hands and began to sob, silently, his shoulders jerking. It was so unexpected, I barely knew what to do. After some moments, I patted him on the shoulder in an attempt at comforting him, but it achieved little.

'I adored her,' he said, and his voice was very small and far-away.

'Rachel?' That was easy enough to understand. She was entrancing.

'Yes. We had been seeing each other since she first arrived here. It was so difficult to imagine that I . . . and my wife would have been furious, had she learned. But Agnes was going to learn, I had decided. I could not hold the secret any longer. And it need not have inconvenienced her. I could provide a home for Rachel and our child, I am wealthy enough to afford anything she might need. And then Rachel asked me to meet her there, outside the church.' He took a deep breath and sighed.

'I had to wait, oh, so long. But at last I saw her making her way towards me. She was alone, a dangerous thing for a woman like her as dusk fell, but she was never conventional. She didn't fear anyone. And she told me, right there and then, that she was leaving. She would go with my son, and I would never see her again. She couldn't remain here with me, and see the hurt it must give Agnes, seeing another woman bear my son. Instead, she would go far away and save her that shame and grief.'

'So you struck out at her?' I guessed.

'Are you mad? I loved her! I could no more harm her or my child than fly to the church roof! No, I begged and pleaded, but she left me and went into the church, and I waited, and then made my way homewards.'

'Did you see anyone else enter the church after her?'

'No. The priest had already fled. I saw him hurtling away

when I was almost there. Then, when Rachel left me, I was
. . . I was broken, I suppose. I walked to the Green Dragon
and drank more than I should have. It was late when I returned
home. But I didn't hurt her. I couldn't hurt her.'

'You are sure? There was no one else there?'

He scowled with the effort of recollection. 'I think I saw
Croke and a companion of his just before I saw Rachel. They
were chatting, and I kept to the shadows until Croke had
walked on. I didn't want to be seen with her.'

'And when she said she was going away, did she give you
to understand where she was going?' I asked carefully.

'No. Not at all,' he said, and then dissolved into tears
again.

Walking from his house, pensively mulling over his words, I
bumped into Gawtheren Spink, and it occurred to me that
she was an excellent source of information about people. She
appeared to have a fair amount of knowledge of the locals.

'Mistress Spink!' I called, and hurried my steps to her.

She stopped, and gave me that knowing smile which I
recalled from the first time I had met her. 'Ah, Master
Blackjack!'

We exchanged the usual polite salutations, and when I asked
where she was going, she told me she was to visit the butchers
row at Newgate Street Shambles. I offered to walk with her,
and she shrugged and said she would be glad of the company,
so I fell into step at her side and we ambled along quite
pleasantly.

'It was a shock to see Mistress Nailor slain,' I said.

'So, you want to discover who killed her?' she said, and
then laughed aloud at my expression. 'You men are so
unsubtle!'

'It is that obvious?'

She smiled again. Her mouth was perhaps her most desirable aspect. It drew a man's attention to her face. When she
spoke or laughed, it was hard not to watch her lips moving,
and with her attractive round features and general amiability,
it was hard to conceive of a more delightful companion under
the blankets on a chill winter's evening. She would be an

enthusiastic bed-walloper, I felt. Certainly, she was some ten or more years my senior, but I could happily appreciate her charms.

'You are as transparent as a window pane,' she said. 'Come, ask away! What do you want to know?'

'Who do you think could have desired to see her dead?' I asked. 'It was no robbery, but almost certainly an act of . . . what? Jealousy? Bitterness?'

'I do not know, but she was with child. You heard that?'

'Yes. I had heard,' I said.

'So, who was the father? That would be my first question,' she said.

'Yes?' I said, doubtfully. I had no intention of sharing what Kirk had just told me. Besides, as far as I was concerned, the likelihood was that this death was due to the politics in which she was engaged, not the parentage of her child.

'If the father was a local man, he might well have decided to try to conceal his responsibility,' she said, and now there was a grim look to her mouth. It was a sudden, and rather startling, alteration in her appearance.

'Why would he do that?' I wondered, thinking about Kirk.

She gave a short laugh like a bark. Where her usual laughter could shatter a steel bar, this was more painful: quieter, but more concentrated, like a chalk slowly scraped over a slate. It made every nerve in my body shudder.

'Who wouldn't? Any man around here would be reluctant to admit to fathering a child with her. You have seen Agnes Kirk, wife to the alderman. What would she not do to him, were he to confess to playing hide the porker with another woman? He could hardly conceal the matter, if Rachel had gone to him with the wain and demanded support. He might deny it, oh, men always do, don't they? But she would bring shame on him and his household. Agnes may be a weak and somewhat shrewish woman, but she would find her husband's dalliance shameful, and she would make his life thoroughly unpleasant as a result.'

'I see,' and I did, of course. From what I had seen of Agnes Kirk, the idea that she would make her husband's life a living hell was easy to believe.

'And so there you have one man who could have killed to conceal his affair,' she continued. 'But there are others who would kill, too, if it meant hiding news of such a matter.'

'Who do you mean?'

'Agnes herself, for example. For her, news of her husband's infidelity would be so shameful, she would prefer to prevent news of it ever getting out. But not only her. What of the *good* – her voice seemed to bathe in acid at that word – 'Master Anderson? He is such an upstanding member of the parish, after all. Were he to be discovered as a fornicator with Rachel, it would affect his wife's position.'

'Him?' I chuckled at the thought. 'I think Mistress Rachel had better taste than him.'

She gave me an odd look. 'You think so?' she said sharply.

I suddenly recalled that she had borne Elias when Anderson made her pregnant. Perhaps, I judged, my comment was a little unsubtle, bearing in mind Gawtheren had fallen for his blandishments. 'I didn't mean—'

'Yes you did, and perhaps you're right. She wouldn't have fallen for his lies, I suppose. It takes a special fool to listen to him. You know of Elias, then. I see it in your face. But if Stephen had succeeded in shaking the sheets with Rachel Nailor, and his wife heard of it, she might well take a knife to the poor woman.'

'Madam Anderson? But she is a meek, mild woman,' I said, and it wouldn't be too much to say I scoffed.

'Don't be confused by the meek appearance. She's as hard as coffin oak. You think her husband is sharp enough to reach his position without a hard-headed woman behind him? And then there's their son, John. What would she do, if she learned that he had been seduced by that woman – and don't huff at me, master! It is what Madam Anderson would say and think. What, her little boy could have seduced a worldly-wise woman like Rachel? Nay, he is too young, too immature, too wayward to be able to conceive of seducing a woman like her, but she, with her wiles and deviousness, she could inveigle the poor young fool into her bed with ease. That is what Madam Katherine would believe, and she would protect her son from the expense of supporting a foundling or of having his name pulled through the shit by any means available. Then there are others, too.'

'There are more?' I said, frankly appalled at the number of suspects being presented to me.

'Well, you know what they say, Master Blackjack. When a maid is discovered with child, first look to her household. Her master, Gerald Marbod, seems a strong, masculine fellow. Perhaps he found Rachel's presence in his house to be just too tempting. He wouldn't be the first master who had taken advantage of an attractive younger woman under his protection.'

I left her at the shambles and turned to make my way back homewards, my mind in turmoil.

The idea that almost everyone in the parish whom I had met could have individual reasons for wanting Rachel dead had not occurred to me. Now it was brought home with sparkling clarity that almost everybody could have had a reason to see Rachel dead. And that was without the other aspects, those of her position in Lady Elizabeth's household, her mission to Paris, and the trust which had been placed in her.

It was a most perplexing situation, and I was now realizing just how confusing was my situation. The fact that my own personal safety depended upon my discovering someone who could realistically be blamed for her death was no aid to me. What, was I supposed to discover who was the father of Rachel's child? Kirk fondly believed that he was, but a man might often mistakenly believe his wife's child was his as well. There was little by way of proof of paternity. Still, Kirk had the proof of his own bedding – unless I discovered a witness who could tell me that he or she saw a different fellow with Rachel, in bed and making the rafters creak, I would have to take his word for it. The likelihood of such a witness appearing was remote.

I had reached the conclusion that my best option would be to go to John Blount and lay the whole sorry tale before him and hope for some sign of compassion, when I suddenly saw an appealing little figure in the street ahead of me. We were only a short distance from the parish now, and the figure was that of the young maid, Moll, from the Marbod home. It struck me, that were anyone to know about Rachel's possible relations with men, a maid who perhaps shared the same bedchamber was about as good a possible witness as I could hope for, and accordingly I trotted to catch up with her.

'Moll! Moll, I am glad to see you here,' I called when I was some six feet from her.

She turned with a face so filled with fear and alarm that I did not approach closer. Instead I gave her my best Honest Jack smile and slowed to a walk, keeping a decorous yard between us at all times.

'Master Blackjack,' she said after a few moments. Her face did not ease. I could have thought her terrified of me – but that would be ridiculous, of course.

My first impressions had been quite correct, I decided. She was a sweet-faced, slim but full-figured young woman of perhaps seventeen years or so. Her eyes were almond-shaped, and greenish grey in colour – quite entrancing. She would definitely be worth pursuing, once I had completed my investigations and secured my future. For now, I had other interests, and I tried to approach my questions with my customary tact and diplomacy.

'You will allow me to escort you back to your home, I trust? These streets are none too safe for a young woman such as you,' I said.

She made no comment. In her arm she held a great wicker basket, and her head was lowered as if staring at it. I wasn't surprised, because after all, how often would a young maid like her have the attention of a man of culture and position? She was unused to such acknowledgement, and it would have been more shocking had she accepted my company without any sign of nervousness.

'Tell me, Moll, are you well enough? It must have been a terrible shock to learn that Rachel was murdered.'

She cast a glance at me, fixed her gaze on me, and then her bottom lip began to tremble. 'Oh, sir, sir, it's horrible! She was like a mother to me, or an older sister. She was my only friend!' Her words began on a level tone, but her speech ended as a wail as the poor chit began to sniffle and sob.

Several passers-by noticed, and some gave me very hard stares, as though suspecting it was all something to do with me, and I got the impression that some fellows were close to stepping between us and accosting me.

'Moll, please,' I said, and she calmed herself, wiping at her eyes with her sleeve, sniffing and blinking hard.

'I'm sorry, master,' she said at last, passing me a watery smile. 'It's just she were my only friend, and without her, well, I don't know what I'll do.'

I had to be careful, I could see. 'Your master must understand, I hope. It must be obvious that you have lost a close companion, and you need some time to recover from the shock.'

'Oh, sir!' and another wail and eruption of tears.

It was some little while before this spasm was controlled again. 'Is it such a terrible household? Surely you have other friends in the hall?'

She was wiping her eyes, and gave me a watery smile. 'Oh, the other servants try to help. They keep my spirits up.'

'But you mourn so strongly because Rachel was an ally who has gone? Come, now. I know that Rachel herself was not happy there. She told me as much only the day before she died. Is Master Marbod so harsh a master?'

'No, sir. He is very kind and understanding. But Madam Marbod, she can be . . . prickly.'

'Ah. She is a demanding lady?'

'She has a . . . a clear view of how things should be done,' the maid said hesitantly. It was plain to me that Moll was trying to avoid stating that her mistress was a harridan who demanded too much. And now no doubt Moll would have even more work, since Rachel's disappearance. I gained the distinct impression that Rachel had been a moderating influence in the house.

Meanwhile I was aware of several men eyeing me with less than friendly expressions, as though I was some kind of fiend. I explained calmly, 'Friends, this maid's companion has been murdered,' but that didn't seem to help.

'Why're you remindin' her, then?' was one response. Another was rather more pointed, referring to my own features and parentage. I see little point in repeating such infantile comments from an ugly, goblin-featured son of a whore.

'Moll, come, let us hurry back to your home.'

'Yes, master, thank you.'

But her face showed no pleasure in the thought of returning to her hall.

We had covered more than half the distance, when I essayed once more. 'Moll, I want to discover who it was who did *that* to Mistress Rachel. Will you try to help me?'

Her eyes were large and luminous as she looked at me and nodded seriously. 'Anything!'

'Thank you. Did you know that Rachel was with child? Did you know that before her death?'

She nodded, slowly and solemnly, and although her eyes brimmed once more, I was relieved not to have a fresh inundation.

'Do you know who the father was? Was she seeing a man regularly? Was there a special friend she used to see often? Did she talk about him?'

'Oh, master, no!'

'It wouldn't have been . . . could it have been your master in the house? Was it Master Marbod?'

She looked quite shocked at that. 'Oh, no, Master Marbod wouldn't think of it, I'm sure!'

There was no doubting her certainty on that score, which was a double relief to me. First, it meant I didn't have to worry about him being the potential murderer, and second it meant that I could happily trust him for advice and assistance to do with my investigation.

'I am glad to hear it. So you feel safe enough in the house? That is good. But are you quite sure that Rachel never mentioned a special man to you? Not one?'

'She did tell me once that she was hoping to marry, but a particular man. She just said that if she did, a man who would look after her, I mean, she would have me brought to her house with her.'

'Would you have liked that?'

She showed uncommon wisdom then. 'I don't know, sir. I liked her, lots, but that was when we both worked together. It would be different with her the lady of the house and me her servant, wouldn't it? And Master Marbod is very kind to me. I would be deserting him to go with her. I wouldn't want to do that, no.'

And that was all I could discover from her. When we reached the hall, I left her at the door, and set off homewards, my head down as I mused over all I had learned – or, rather, had not learned. Who was this strange fellow who managed to get Rachel pregnant? And who was it who had sent her a message purporting to be from me, asking her to meet me in the church?

It was a sign of how deeply I was engaged in thinking about these questions that I did not notice the men gathering about me until one stopped me with a hand on my breast.

'Hallo, Jack,' he said.

I think I have mentioned already that there were certain people I wished to avoid, and it was in part these fellows who had tempted me away from my old haunt and persuaded me to find new lodgings in St Helen's.

This will, I am sure, seem a trivial incident, but there had been a small tavern with a cockpit not far from my old house, in which I had occasionally played a few rounds of skittles and enjoyed the entertainments. They regularly had musicians come and play for the players and drinkers, and it was always a convivial gathering. However, one evening while I was there, I was accosted by a fellow who, and my memory of the precise conversation is a little hazy, asked whether I would be content to continue the party at another location and, being somewhat befuddled with ale at the time, I invited all back to my own lodging.

Now, this would be fine, but of course when the reckoning came two days later, I discovered that I owed for drinks and some food for some thirty guests. I had never offered to pay for all their food and drink, but it seemed that my friend in the tavern had assured the landlord that all the comestibles were to be paid for by me personally. The man must have seen the landlord for the fool that he was, clearly.

Equally clearly, the fellow confronting me was that very landlord: Albert Pudge. Who, now I was arrested in my walk, removed his hand from my breast and experimentally tapped his hand with a large and thoroughly brutal-looking blackthorn cudgel.

'Ho! Master Blackjack, I believe. I've been wantin' to see you for some weeks. Now, master, about this little matter of the money you owe me.'

There are times when it is best to take to flight and think about explanations later. Accordingly I turned to left and right, only to find that three men behind me were effectively hemming me in.

In the absence of flight, there is always the option of threatening violence. However, on certain occasions such as this, it is all too likely that an offer of physical combat is likely to be accepted, and with odds of four to one, that did not appeal.

Which is why, with the other possible escapes accounted for and rejected, I fitted a welcoming smile to my face and greeted my companions with every sign of joy. 'Why, if it isn't Pudge! How are you, Pudge? I haven't seen you since, oh, since . . .'

'Since you ran away from the debt you owe me.'

That was difficult to evade, admittedly. He was still slapping his palm with the cudgel with the appearance of a man determined to test his blackthorn on something else nearby.

'Hahaha! You thought I was running away from you? No, no. I was just . . .'

'So you'll have the money for me here, will you?'

'I will have it for you tomorrow morning. Shall I bring it to you?'

'No need, master. We're here now. I know! Let's go back to your house now, shall we? And then we can fetch it right away.'

'Oh, well, that would be fine, but I don't have it all in my house,' I said.

'No matter. We can go to the banking house where you keep it, master. Can't we?' His tone was altering slightly. It sounded, I suppose, rather menacing. It was not a pleasant sound. 'Because otherwise, Master Blackjack, we might have to assume you are trying to avoid paying your debts, if you see what I mean. And we wouldn't want that, would we? If we got that sort of thought, we might get a little angry, if you understand me? And you wouldn't like me to get angry with you, now would you? You owe me for drinks for thirty of your companions, plus the food they took, and damages.'

'What "damages"? I entertained them at my own house!'

'The damages were the effect you had on my reputation,' he snarled, leaning down until our noses were almost touching. It was not a pleasant experience.

I don't think I quite explained the sort of fellow Pudge was. He was built rather like the wall of my house, by which I mean absolutely solid, square, and hard as ancient oak and brick. He was a good six feet tall, so a little taller than me, and had a grizzled beard that almost concealed his mouth, a broken nose, eyes as black as the pit, and a forehead with a scar that jagged about from one side to the other. I once heard that he was knocked down when a reluctant customer attempted to escape without paying by picking up a beer barrel and hurling it at Pudge. The metal barrel hoop at one end caught him on the brow, and knocked him down. But as the customer turned to walk away, so it is said, Pudge stood up again, picked up the barrel, ran and broke it over the man's pate. I understand the man's head suffered more than the barrel. Pudge was that sort of a man.

He smiled now, and that was a truly fearsome sight. 'Lead the way, Blackjack,' he said.

I had little option but to obey. Starting out by walking up Bishopsgate, I suddenly struck an idea. After all, they may not know where my home was. It could well be that they wanted me to lead them there so that they would know in future. In short order I had a plan of escape outlined, and immediately put it into action. I led them up to the Bull, and before any could stop me, I turned into the yard.

They must have bumped into me by an evil chance. Fate does that sometimes. In any event, now we were in the Bull's yard, with the noise and bustle of a busy inn's stableyard, it would be more difficult and troublesome for Pudge and his merry fellows to murder me.

I took the door on the left which led into the bar areas,

and went to a table where I waited expectantly. Pudge and his men entered and stood about my table. There were, by my reckoning, at least forty other drinkers and eaters in there at the time, and I could see Pudge's eyes roving over them all, assessing which might or might not intervene in a discussion with me. When the smile returned to his face, I could see that he saw no great defenders of my character in the room with us. He sat opposite me and laid his cudgel on the tabletop.

Sitting there, he knew I was trapped. There was no escape behind me, I was sitting with my back to the wall, and in the narrow way between the screens that sheltered this table from the next, there was little space to make a run for it. Besides, his three friends were standing and glowering like a wall of halberdiers facing cavalry. I wouldn't be able to pass them, even if I escaped Pudge's clutches.

'So you thought to lead us a merry dance about London, then,' he said. 'That was pleasant. It's good to have some exercise before business. How about you give me your house key, and we'll go and fetch our money. You can remain here and drink while we go, if you like.'

I was searching among the faces at the inn. There was one man I was sure must be there. He had my measure generally, and would be unlikely to be satisfied hanging about my house. He must be here.

'Well? Perhaps you keep your key in your purse, eh?'

His cudgel was back in his hand, and he prodded my purse with it. It was a sharp prod, and made me catch my breath. 'Stop that!'

'Or what, little mouse? Will you squeak all the way home to Mother?' he drawled.

'I have no key,' I said.

'We know that.'

I smiled cynically. 'Of course you do.'

'Pleasant little place you have there, isn't it? And easy to find, once you know the face of your bottler and cook. All a man has to do is keep an eye on the local shops, and soon the servants can be spied. It's taken me some weeks, but you see, I do believe in returning a favour. And when someone steals from me, I like to get full recompense, if you know what I mean.'

He nodded, a nasty smile tugging his lips wide, and suddenly my world began to topple. My eyesight went blurry, and I felt a quickening discomfort with a loud roaring in my ears. It was one of those moments when I thought I might faint at any moment, and it was deeply unsettling and unpleasant. I rocked back on my seat, while his men all sniggered, and their humour only ceased when I pulled out the gun.

I pointed it straight at him. He was only a matter of a yard or so away. I could not possibly miss at such a close range. 'You must move away, now.'

'No.'

'Oh.'

It was one of those moments when what had seemed a brilliant plan sort of fizzled out, like a fuse which had been lying in a puddle. I stared at him, and all four stared back at me. It was not a moment I care to recall.

And then I heard the voice. 'You *bastard*!'

Rarely have I been so happy to see a man. The gorilla had, as I had anticipated, waited long enough to become thirsty while watching my front door. Thinking to himself, if such a term is not over-optimistic, that a quart of ale at the nearest hostelry would be refreshing, he bent his steps to the Bull, and on entering, he was immediately confronted by the sight of me and four others. It was a sight to confuse a man with so little brain capacity. I could see his brow wrinkling with the effort of thought. I should have been at my house. Here was someone who looked like me, but this was an inn, not a house. Could there be someone else who dressed and looked like me? No, so this must be me.

The gorilla moved to me. Pudge's three men barred his way. Each seemed to realize by some inexplicable communication that the real danger lay not before them, but was approaching from behind. Perhaps it was the curious sound of his knuckles dragging on the sawdust and rushes. One by one, they turned to face him.

I would like to say that it was a glorious fight. In most

tavern brawls I have witnessed, there have been moments of thrilling excitement as one man is cornered and fights back, or brief periods of pity when a bold warrior disappears under an ocean of flailing fists, or despair, as in the face of the landlord as he sees his newest table collapse under the weight of struggling, kicking, bludgeoning bodies.

There was none of that today. The gorilla was not interested in histrionic battles. He wanted me, and as the first man essayed a punch at him, he barely seemed to notice. The fist caught the side of his chin, and I could see it was a blow with real weight. Behind it was a man of Pudge's height and build, and his face registered shock to see that the gorilla's head was moved three inches to the left. Shock turned to horror when the gorilla's face slowly clenched and contorted as it turned to face the fellow who had hit him. A hand the size of a moderate water pail suddenly sprang forward and that man disappeared amid a cloud of soggy sawdust.

A second Pudge pugilist attempted a similar blow, but this fist never reached the gorilla. He caught the fist in his own and peered at the man with fury in his face. Then he squeezed. The other whimpered and his legs began to crumple, but before agony could force him to the floor, the gorilla punched him. It sounded like a sledgehammer striking an oaken log. That fellow was out.

Pudge stood. His last companion was already retreating before the gorilla making oddly pathetic keening sounds, rather like a newborn puppy desperately seeking a teat, and as his legs met with a bench, he suddenly collapsed.

Looking at me, Pudge pointed a finger at my head and nodded as though reminding himself of my face and looks. Then he cast a brief look around at the two incapacitated warriors and his one remaining, still mewling, companion, sneered at the gorilla, and stalked from the room.

The gorilla glared at the whimpering figure on the bench and then took his own seat beside me. He glanced at me with a frown of confusion, but apparently the rapid violence had dissipated his feelings towards me.

'What's all this about?'

* * *

I never would have thought that I might say this, but that was one occasion when I truly warmed to the gorilla. He had approached me with the intention of perhaps pulling my head off, or disembowelling me, but the fact of the other men there planning on doing that before him had distracted him. He had the sort of mind that was capable of only one thought at a time. They lined up in his head, I daresay, and followed in military order. First in the line was: catch Jack; second was: pull his arms off; third: probably, kick him in the fork like he did to me; and finally: pull his head off and see how easy it is.

The trouble was, of course, that he only got to the first thought, and then became diverted by someone punching him on the jaw. That worked like a bar lying in the road before a coach. As with a coach, it made his mind halt, and seek a detour. His detour of choice, naturally, was to defend himself. And having done so twice, his queue of thoughts were so discombobulated that he was forced to sit and attempt to reorder them.

Here lay my danger. If he were to have too long to consider, he may just recall that first instruction. Rather than give him an opportunity, I hailed the inn's serving girl, a pleasant, sharp-witted young wench, who glanced down at the two men on the floor, one moaning, one snoring, at the white-faced man sitting opposite the gorilla, and then at me. 'Yes?'

'What will you have?' I asked.

The gorilla gave that deep thought. It was clearly difficult. I smiled at the girl. 'Three quarts of strong ale.' I glanced at the gorilla, and he considered, and then nodded. He glanced at the man opposite, who tried to squeeze himself between the planks of the screen behind him, but had to submit to the laws of physics.

I'm not sure why the fool didn't merely sidle out from the table and take the streets at a canter. I've seen the gorilla try to run, and it's not a pretty sight. If you have seen a foal born, and trying to work out which leg is which, it is rather similar. The gorilla is good at a fast walk, but faster than that and his coordination begins to fall apart. I suppose the uninjured warrior wasn't aware of that, not having seen the gorilla trying to run.

'Who're these?' he said at last, looking over the table again.

'These gentlemen came to talk to me about some debts,' I said. 'We have a dispute about the sum involved.'

'Oh.'

His mind apparently cleared, for the wrinkles on his brow were ironed away as his mind relaxed into no thinking whatsoever. Then a perplexed little frown returned. 'I was going to kill you.'

'That's not very friendly.'

'You wasn't friendly when you kicked me.'

'Ah, but you were trying to kill me.'

'Oh. Yes.'

'Why?'

He peered at me as if trying to remember. 'Oh, Master Blount told me it would be hard to replace you, so . . . I thought I'd show as I could do it.'

'I see,' I said. He was taking part, so he thought, in a form of interview requiring a practical demonstration. I supposed it made sense. To a degenerate mind like the gorilla's, anyway. 'Why do you want the job?' He frowned again, and I quickly spoke to divert his attention once more before he returned to the four-stage process he had been considering. 'Because, I think I may have a job for you.'

'I 'ave a job. Following you.'

'Ah, this will be perfect for you, then. I will pay you to be with me.'

His frown moved from suspicion to perplexity. 'Eh?'

'I will pay you to remain with me for the next day or two. You will be doing the job John Blount wants you to do, because you will be keeping your eyes on me at all times. But I will be paying you as well. That way you will be paid twice. And at the same time, I can show you all about my work.'

His face showed his inner torment, but then the act of consideration grew too much. Luckily our ales appeared and I raised mine in a toast. The gorilla lifted his, as did the remaining Pudge warrior, and we all three clashed our pots. I drank, and as I did, the gorilla absent-mindedly punched the fellow over the table. His eyes glazed over, and he slid slowly

from view to the floor. His quart pot was rescued from his
hand before a drop was spilled by the gorilla.

He smiled. After knocking down three men, his world was
set once more on solid footings. And he had two quarts of
ale.

'Yus,' he said.

With the gorilla in tow, I left the inn with its three dozing men
before they could fully recover and blame me for their misfortune, and made my way homewards. En route we met with
young John Anderson once more, and I managed to persuade
the gorilla that the young fellow was no threat to him or me,
before John discovered how far one of the gorilla's arms could
fling him. It was a close-run thing, and I have to confess that,
now I had the gorilla in my train, it was an appealing vision.
Anderson was, after all, hardly necessary now.

We repaired to my house and, while there, I went to my
locked iron box and retrieved a small purse of coin. Installing
that inside my shirt for safekeeping, having withdrawn two
silver coins, I relocked my box, locked the door to my strong-
room, and rejoined the two downstairs, where they were
discovering the quality of my wine while a truculent Raphe
watched them. I gave them a coin each in thanks for their
assistance, giving the gorilla to understand that there would
be more to follow, so long as he guarded me well. He bit the
coin, looked pleasantly surprised (in so far as his appearance
could ever be said to be pleasant), and pushed it into his
purse.

I left the two in the kitchen, with John making enthusiastic
sallies at a stern-faced, uncommunicative Cecily, much to
Raphe's concern, and the gorilla sitting with his back to the
wall and staring at nothing. I felt sure that he could occupy
himself happily for hours like that, waiting for a random
thought to spring into life. And if it didn't, he would remain
happy.

At last I could settle in my chair before the fire in my
parlour and consider what action I could or should take. It
was clear that my home was now known to other people. The
lad from Saul Appleby had followed me home; Pudge and his

men had followed Raphe – I would have to have sharp words with him shortly over his lack of caution while shopping, the fool – and obviously John Blount and the gorilla knew where I lived. Any one of the first two could appear at any time to assault me, and while the gorilla appeared glad enough to take my coin for now, there was no telling how brief such loyalty would prove once John Blount gave him the order to remove me. And that was likely not to be far in the future.

What had I learned? Remarkably little, in truth.

Moll had told me that Gerald, her master, seemed a good master, although his wife was more tetchy. But that was normal for any number of ladies who spent their days dealing with the servants. To them went the responsibility to make sure that the maids were cleaning and working as they should to keep the household in good order. Her moods did not mean Marbod himself had made Rachel pregnant.

Gawtheren was interesting. It was obvious to me that she had cause to be jealous of Stephen Anderson's latest affairs, if he was responsible for Rachel's baby – not that I considered that likely. She was a beautiful, intelligent woman. What would she see in the bloated merchant? And as for Kirk, he was too insipid for her, surely.

The murder was no nearer resolution. I felt the best course for me now was to visit Gerald Marbod again and ask for advice. He was one of those men who appeared to have extreme clarity of thinking, and the idea that he may be able to offer sensible advice based on his knowledge of Lady Elizabeth and the mission to Paris which Rachel had been instructed to undertake, was reassuring. After all, unlike my own master, Gerald Marbod gave every sign of trusting me. He believed that I had been unfairly cast in the light of a villain by the actual murderer, and that was reassuring to me.

I made my decision, I would go to see Marbod again, and let him know all I had learned, which was little enough, but he may be able to advise me – even if his advice was to flee the city.

It took only a few minutes to walk to Gerald Marbod's hall, and soon I was standing with him in his garden again, having deposited the gorilla to stand guard at the front door, looking curiously like a statue carved from rock.

The two men who had escorted Rachel to church and back were with us. One, I took to be the bottler, while the second I think was a groom, but both carried staffs and long knives and appeared proficient in their use. Marbod had one stationed at a gate at the farther end of the garden, while the bottler remained near the threshold of the house.

'How may I help you?' Marbod said.

I gave him to understand the trouble I was facing with my investigations, and indicated that Pudge was also a threat to me.

He puffed out his cheeks. 'You appear to have a facility for making enemies, Master Blackjack.'

'It's not my fault!'

'So you are pursued by a man who claims you owe him money, a jealous rival in love –' I had not explained that Saul was married to Susan. I felt it was a little easier to ask for assistance from Gerald if he thought I could have a valid claim to her affections – 'and now because you are suspected in poor Rachel's death, you have Master John Blount's men seeking you. And over all, somebody tried to snare you with the murder of Rachel. That should be your start point.'

'But how can I learn anything? Everybody seems to have a plausible motive, whether it's a jealous wife, or a lecherous husband.'

'Everyone apart from me, of course,' he said with a keen glance at me.

'Well, naturally, you and I are innocent,' I said.

'What does intrigue me is the two incidents,' he said after a moment. He sat on the bench, glancing about as he did so to ensure no gardeners or others could be within earshot. His voice dropped. 'The murder of poor Rachel occurring with the desecration of the church. I suppose a man who would murder a woman in church would feel few qualms about causing such damage, but it is hard to imagine the mind of someone engaged on such an evil path.'

'I wonder, whether the desecration was done before the murder or after?' I said.

'After,' he said with conviction.

'Why?'

'I am assuming that she walked into the church of her own free will. If she entered the church and saw such damage, she would surely have fled the scene to fetch help – the priest, the watch, the coroner – and report her discovery. Were she to discover it, she would be unlikely to go to the vestry.'

'But she might have walked in upon the murderer in the act of his destruction,' I said.

'Perhaps. Yet I doubt it. The noise of breaking the screen would have been loud, and surely it would have been heard from the churchyard as she went to enter. Those noises would have demonstrated to her that there was something amiss inside. If she went, it would be to look, and seeing the damage done, she would surely immediately run from the place.'

'The destruction could have been done long before,' I mused.

'If so, the fellows would have fled with their booty.' He smiled.

'Perhaps they did?'

'And left a silver communion cup? And the cross? Surely they were the two most valuable items in the church. Nay, my friend. They were either still there, in which case Rachel was far too bright to enter, or they had not begun their campaign of destruction. They were there, or they followed her inside, and after killing her, they engaged upon the ruination of the church, and fled without stealing the most obvious precious items. Which also leads me to suspect that perhaps they did not intend to kill her, but because she saw them there, they had to silence her, and then went about their breaking and smashing in a hurry. Yes,' he added thoughtfully, 'the more I think about it, the more convinced I am that the truth here is that the men guilty of Rachel's slaughter and the deliberate rampage in the church must have been men who were determined to bring about the return to King Henry's Church of England. They were the sort to despise the Catholic church, and sought to strike a blow for the true church.'

I maintained a dignified silence here. After all, I had no strong feelings for either church. To me it seemed far-fetched to believe that any Englishman would be so sacrilegious – but there, such men do exist, the fools. 'If she were to enter and walk through the church, perhaps she heard the other men arrive, and went to hide in the vestry?' I guessed.

'Why do that, if she was there to see you? She was expecting to hear someone appear.'

I was straining my brain to work this out. 'But if there were several men, she would be suspicious. And if there were only one or two, she might have thought it was the priest, and hid so as not to have to explain herself to him. Or, she was . . .'

I was suddenly still. 'So perhaps the man who went in to desecrate the church entered after Rachel? He attacked the altar and screen, and then noticed her body, and fled?' That was a thought to conjure with.

'You may have a point there,' he said when I explained my thinking to him. 'Perhaps you should speak with him.'

'He will tell me nothing,' I said.

'Then let me join you. He will be reluctant to ignore my questions,' Marbod said. 'And if he lied about one thing, perhaps he lied about killing poor Rachel too.'

The weather had turned again, and a fine rain was spitting at us in the grey light as we made our way from his hall to the church, avoiding the excrement and mess of the streets. Hawkers still wandered, their cries more dejected than hopeful of persuading someone to buy their wares, and I was glad to see that the usual street urchins and beggars had taken refuge rather than remain in the cold and wet. One tried to make me feel guilty, holding out his hand, but I ignored the little brute. He didn't bother to ask for anything from the gorilla, who lurched along behind us.

Reaching the church, we entered, genuflecting hurriedly as we passed into the nave. There were a couple of men at the back of the church, and one sitting in the pews on the left, mumbling his way through his rosary, while two women knelt in the pews in the middle of the chamber. Of the priest there was no sign.

We walked through to the vestry, and out to the small chamber beyond, but Father Peter seemed to have disappeared.

*　　*　　*

We spoke to the other people there in the church, but no one had seen him for a while. Not all that day, apparently, which surprised me. After all, he only had light duties, didn't he? The church was waiting to be reconsecrated, after all, after the violation of the vestry. He was supposed to be on duty at his church, I assumed, just not taking Mass. Then again, he also had to go and give extreme unction when called, so perhaps he had hurried off to help usher someone into the next world – whether into the land of angels, the land of demons, or waiting in-between.

I was all for leaving, but there was something about the place that struck me. I walked over to the vestry and glanced inside. There was a darker patch on the flags where, I imagine, Rachel's blood had been spilled, and where regular washing had left this stain. It made me curl my lip. I didn't like to think of her sprawled out down there, but I could not eradicate that memory. She had been so vibrant, it was hard to believe that she was actually dead, and that her body was even now mouldering and decaying. Perhaps Father Peter was at her graveside? But if so, she would have to have had her funeral service in another church. I would have hoped to have heard if there had been a funeral arranged. The parish was not so vast that important ceremonies of that nature could be missed.

There was nothing in the vestry to help me. No little knick-nacks or evidence of a priest's presence.

'I saw him here this morning,' I said, 'but now he seems to have gone out for some reason.'

Marbod stepped past me and peered into the vestry. When he returned, his face was set. 'This is a fresh mystery,' he said with a frown. 'All Father Peter's belongings are gone.'

I suddenly gaped. After all, I know most people would not have been able to come to any conclusion about his disappearance, but for me it spoke volumes. 'He must have been the murderer!' I gasped.

Marbod looked at me as though I was suddenly struck lunatic. He spoke slowly and gently. 'I don't think so, Master Blackjack. Why should he have murdered Rachel?'

'I do not know, but it is the only explanation,' I said.

'Perhaps it was shame – he got her with child, and killed her to conceal his guilt, and now realizes I will track him down, so he's fled!'

Marbod said nothing, but I could see he was more than a little doubtful. It was plain enough to me, though. The priest had called Rachel here, driven by some fiendish motivation, and when she appeared, he slew her, and now he'd run away. He didn't run immediately, of course, because he was still there in the church yesterday, cleaning up the mess, but he was definitely guilty, for why else would he bolt from his church?

Outside the gorilla was still standing where we had left him. Marbod cast an eye over him without giving the impression that he had formed a favourable opinion of the man. I cannot say that I blamed him for that. We walked off, Marbod to his hall, where he said he was going to sit and think about the whole affair, and the gorilla and I towards the Bull. It was a matter of good fortune that we happened upon Gawtheren and Elias Spink not far from the church, and I invited them to join us.

To my certain relief, the three comatose figures of Pudge's companions had all woken and departed. The gorilla looked disappointed, as if he realized he had unfinished business with them. There was a wet mark on the floor where a hostler had emptied a bucket over the head of one to stir him, and the gorilla stared at it morosely. I took a seat at the same table, and invested in drinks for all. The gorilla sat and gazed into the middle distance as we spoke.

Gawtheren was all ears when I told her that Father Peter had left.

'I knew it,' Elias said. He had a nasty curl to his lip as he spoke, as though it pained him even to think of the priest. 'I said to you, I said to everyone, the man was the murderer.'

'How can you speak of him like that,' his mother said. 'Hold your tongue. He's a priest, you fool!'

'I don't care! I'd speak if he was the bishop! I don't care! Everyone knew how he stared at the women in the congregation. He undressed them all in his filthy mind, even you,' he added, I thought rather ungraciously, to his mother.

She didn't seem to notice. 'Just because he was a randy old stoat doesn't make him a murderer.'

'It makes perfect sense,' Elias stated with all the boundless confidence of youth.

I don't know why it is, but in my experience, the most unforgiving and judgemental of people tend to be those in early adulthood, from fifteen to twenty years or so. Perhaps it is their lack of exposure to all the temptations that life can fling at them: they assume that surviving temptation is as easy as refusing one more cup of ale, or deciding not to go to the stews to enjoy the whores.

'Why?' I asked.

'Think how he spoke about you, when you were first in the congregation,' he said. 'Do you think he treated you differently to others? No, if any man there were to look at a woman, he would instantly rant at them for their presumption. But whenever he could, we would all see him staring at the women. Sometimes at their faces, but usually at their breasts and buttocks. It was all he could do to keep his tarse in his cods, the filthy old goat.'

'Was he known for promiscuity?' I enquired. I was keen to know who was so degenerate that they would bed a priest – only from casual interest, you understand. The sort of woman who would seek to lie with an old man like Peter was not the sort to be blessed with *my* favours.

'No,' Gawtheren said firmly, and threw a stern look at her boy. 'He was just lonely, I think. Oh, he would often stare at my bubbies, but then, they are a good size, aren't they?'

She hitched them up with a hand under each. It was enough to bring tears to a fellow's eyes. I crossed my legs, feeling that my codpiece really was not quite adequate.

'So, anyway,' she continued, letting them drop once more, 'I think he was a man to be pitied more than censured. He had tasted the pleasures of the flesh, and then had them whipped away while he was yet a young man. And he had no choice.'

'His wife was forced away?' I said.

'Yes. She did come back a few months ago, begged him to help her, demanded money, food, anything, but he could do nothing, and sent her away. He had no choice. That is the law.'

'Where did she go?'

'Out the other side of the city wall near the moorgate. There are some shanties there, where the beggars live. Poor woman. She had a little boy, too. It must have been hard for him,' she said with a certain wistful understanding, 'to have to reject his family or take the consequences. There are times when I wonder whether he realized just what he was giving up, and whether he would have chosen the same, if he had the choice to make now.'

'So he was desperate,' said her son the judge, jury and executioner. 'He wanted a woman, any woman, and told Mistress Nailor to meet him in church, and he raped her and killed her. That's the sort of man your priest is, Mother! A murdering, raping, child-killer.'

Gawtheren boxed his ear for that. 'You foolish rakehell, you keep talking like that and you'll end up in Newgate! The bishop doesn't approve of roarers accusing his priests of misbehaviour.'

'Aye, well, he has. He even tried to with you!' he said sulkily. He took a long pull at his beer and then leaned forward. 'You think he's a good man, a *godly* man? Ask any of the women about here.'

'Elias!' Gawtheren snapped.

'But he hasn't killed one before, has he?' I said, reasonably, I think you'll agree.

'There's always a first time,' he said, nodding with all the knowledgeable conviction of youth. 'He must have done it.'

'Why?'

'Because he's too excited by the women in his congregation. You watch him, his eyes are all over them even when he's supposed to be saying the Mass. He tried to get my mother to *pray* with him,' he added with acid sarcasm.

'That is his job,' I said.

'Not the way he wanted to do it,' the boy said and nodded again.

Gawtheren rolled her eyes. Elias ignored her. It was plain that he expected me to understand what he was driving at. Which was fine, except I had no idea. 'How did he want to do it?'

He rolled his eyes. 'He wanted her to kneel before him, and he'd give her absolution from behind.'

'Oh!'

Gawtheren tutted. 'You're letting your imagination run away now, Elias!'

'You speak to the other women here, you ask the maids and youngsters. They'll tell you. You can imagine what sort of absolution he was thinking of. Dirty old hardhead! If he'd suggested that when I was there . . .'

'Yes, I understand,' I said hurriedly as his mother gave a sigh of exasperation. 'But why should he think she would agree to such a . . . um . . . benediction?'

'He knows all the sins of all the women, doesn't he? Easy enough for a man like him to try to turn their past behaviour against them. Aye,' he added, 'and he was desperate, I daresay.'

I looked at him.

He had the grace to redden. 'Well, he had been married, hadn't he?'

'You need a wench, Elias. You've been letting your imagination run riot,' Gawtheren said.

I couldn't disagree. After all, the boy could have little knowledge of women and the natural desires a man must feel. He was still in the embarrassed fondling stages, when a youth tries to negotiate the cheapest rate from the local whores.

Which was a thought. 'Who has said this? After all, the fellow could easily go and preach to the street-drabs if he wanted to ease his tarse. I doubt Rachel Nailor would agree to sleep with him.'

'He'd have to pay money for a dribble-tail, wouldn't he? Why'd he do that if he could take his pleasure by fooling them?'

He did have a point there. I sipped beer while considering his words.

'Besides,' he added. 'I saw him. He ran out of the church like the devil himself had appeared on his altar. I saw him.'

'Yes, well, that might have been something else making him run out,' I said.

'Like what?' he sneered. 'He tells us all the time that it's a sin to look and dream, but that's what he does all the time!'

'It's not proof of murder,' I said.

'Then mayhap the fact I saw him run from the church as darkness fell, full speed like all the hounds of hell were after him, is proof!' the boy said.

'You mean that? You saw him running from his church?'

'Aye,' the boy said, nodding slowly. 'And why else would he run like that? He'd just murdered Rachel Nailor, and ran away in horror.'

Later that evening, I was able to spend time with the gorilla and John, Raphe fetching and carrying wine for us all in celebration. John had entered the inn just as I was preparing to leave, and I was glad to be able to explain the story to him. I doubt the gorilla had absorbed more than a couple of words from earlier at the inn, and I was not convinced that spending time re-explaining it all to him would work now, either. He had an astonishing ability to sit and divorce himself from his surroundings.

'You see, it became clear to me all at once,' I said to John and Raphe. There seemed little need to mention Gawtheren or her gormless son. 'This priest was always uncomfortable here in London. I expect he came here from a country town, or perhaps a village, and was glad at first to have the living here. But then, of course, he could marry and enjoy life with his wife and child. He was a father, a husband, and he had a happy congregation. All was good. But Queen Mary's arrival on the throne, things became altered. She brought about the quite correct return to the Catholic faith, naturally . . .' You will see that I was not foolish enough to denigrate the faith. 'The old religion was a relief to so many people, but some were distressed, as was Father Peter, I suppose.'

I took a refreshing gulp of wine. It was a long story, and I needed to wet my throat.

'The first change for men such as Father Peter was the return to celibacy. Any marriages supposedly entered into were declared null and void. They did not exist for priests, because under the Catholic rule a priest must remain celibate. All those priests who had taken wives were forced to give them up, or lose their positions in the church. It must have been a sore trial for them, and I know many did give up their holy orders, but most could not give up the cure of souls and they, like Peter, decided that their calling was more important than their families. A terrible choice to have to make.'

'So he threw over his wife to keep his job?' John summarized.

'Exactly,' I agreed, although a little coolly. It was a flippant way to describe the matter. Meanwhile the gorilla remained staring into the middle distance, as he tended when there was no fresh spark of excitement to attract his attention. I ignored him.

'I have heard that he was lonely in his parish. He longed for the companionship of a woman, and doubtless he sought solace with a number of women. Perhaps it made him lunatic? Perhaps it was the effect of his desperation? He found Rachel in the vestry, and driven by lust, he slew her. Then, I suppose, driven mad by his appalling act, committed inside the very church where he should have maintained peace and the protection of all the souls in his parish, he ran away, just as Elias told me.'

I sighed. It was perfect. Father Peter was the obvious felon. He fitted the story I had woven. He was there on the evening, he had been there the next morning looking like a madman, and today he had disappeared. If that wasn't the act of the guilty man, I do not know what is.

'I see,' John said, and he had Raphe top up his cup. Raising it in a toast, he drank to my health, and Raphe did the same. The gorilla didn't seem to notice.

'But . . .'

John was frowning. I smiled graciously. 'What?'

'Didn't someone say that Rachel went to the church because of a message from you?'

'Maybe, but it doesn't change the facts. He murdered her. Perhaps he sent a message, believing she and I were having an affair, and thought to entice her so he could kill her.'

'Why would he do that?'

Rather grumpily, I pointed out that the inner thoughts of a madman were not my expertise.

'So what do we do now?' Raphe said.

'Oh, the priest will have to be hunted down and discovered, and then he can be presented to the bishop for punishment. I daresay he can recite the *pater noster*, so he will be safe from a hanging, but he'll spend some time at the bishop's leisure to repent and beg forgiveness,' I said airily. I had no idea what punishment would be meted out to a felonious ecclesiastic, but the main thing for me was, it saved my skin.

I mean to say, if I had failed to uncover the murderer, the suspicion would remain in John Blount's head – and probably in the mind of Lady Elizabeth too – that I was somehow involved, and perhaps responsible for the death of her ambassador, Rachel.

After a few more celebratory cups of wine, I went to my bedchamber resolved to visit John Blount the following morning and explain all to him. And then, perhaps, my life could return to something similar to normal.

FIVE

The next day was as different from the day before as it possibly could be.

When I opened my eyes, it was to the gleam of sunshine spearing through the window, lancing down at my face. I luxuriated to feel her warm kiss. When I paid attention, I was aware of the merry chirping of the birds outside. A pigeon cooed loudly, closely followed by a loud rattle as some scallywag loosed a pebble at it from a sling, the stone bouncing off my tiled roof. I wondered whether the little miscreant had hit his target, or whether the pigeon had survived to coo another day, but that was of little interest, in truth.

Nay, I stretched in my bed, feeling the comfortable glow of satisfaction. I had bested fate. Although my life had been in danger, and John Blount and Lady Elizabeth might well have sought to remove me from their service, and from life itself, my ingenuity and diligence had produced this wonderful result. The flight of the priest was proof of his guilt, and left me secure.

Even after the pints of wine last evening, my mind was clear and untroubled with headaches or nausea. Instead I felt as refreshed as a man who had slept the sleep of pure innocence. I felt, in short, like a fellow who has achieved a great quest and returned to general acclaim and reward. It put me in mind of the tales of King Arthur and his round table. Then, knights who left the court to undertake missions for the king for truth and honour, were often rewarded on their return by the affectionate ministrations of their lovers. It made me think, lying there in my bed, that it could only be improved, were Susan Appleby there to join me in a little early morning wrestling. I decided I would have to visit her house again and see whether we could arrange a bout or two.

But first, of course, I must go and visit my master. It was

essential to let him know the good news before any unpleasant instructions could arrive giving him the command to remove one assassin and replace him with another.

I dressed slowly, and when I had my jack on, I looked at my weapons. It would be good to say that I felt no need to walk the streets armed, but in truth, I was still more than a little wary after my experience with Pudge. I tied my pistol belt about my midriff, thrust the gun home into its holster in the small of my back, hung my ballock knife from its sheath, pulled my baldric over my head and settled the sword in the scabbard, and then over all I donned the powder horn and shot wallet. The purse with silver coins lay on my shelf, and I took this up and thrust it into my shirt once more.

Thus encumbered, I made my way downstairs.

My airy and cheerful demeanour seemed only to confuse Cecily, who had not seen me in so good a temper for some days, and when I refused her offer of breakfast, she looked almost distraught. There was, of course, no sign of Raphe. I would hardly have expected to see him about at such an early hour, for he was a miserable soul in the mornings. It has been said by a wise sage that some people, like me, are good in the early morning, while others, like him, are not. Usually it would annoy me to have my own servant lying abed when I was up and about, but today nothing could spoil my cheery temper. I was convinced that the day was mine, and all I need do was grasp it firmly for all good things to come to me.

I walked to the front door and opened it, stepping out into the bright sunshine and closed my eyes, inhaling deeply.

And then there was a most unpleasant sensation. It was that of a particularly sharp weapon lying across my throat. I looked down with extreme caution to see the heavy blade of a bill. The staff to which it was connected ran over to my left, and my eyes ran down and along the shaft to the coldly smiling face of Pudge the innkeeper. I swallowed, very carefully.

'Lovely morning, ain't it?' he said.

I was not of a mood to agree just then.

'That was a nasty trick you played on us,' Pudge said.

We were in my parlour. Pudge and two of his men with him

(I believe the third was still feeling the after-effects of the gorilla's clubbing over his pate) had taken hold of my arms and pulled me unprotesting inside. In the process, as if by some magic, my sword, dagger, gun, shot and powder were all removed from me before I was set on a stool, my hands bound. One of Pudge's men was testing the blade of my sword, and swishing it about his head with cheerful abandon. The other had taken charge of my gun, and was studying it with all the attention of a choirboy seeing his first picture of a naked woman.

Cecily, I am glad to say, had remained in the kitchen. I didn't want to think what these misbegotten sons of poxed stales would do to her, and if Raphe were to walk in and find her being accosted by an unwelcome visitor, he might do something very foolish indeed.

Not that it was the thought uppermost in my mind, I confess. More serious to my mind was my own wellbeing, especially as the second fool pointed my gun at various targets muttering 'bang' at each.

'Be careful with that,' I admonished him.

In reply he deliberately pointed it at me, making a fresh 'bang', which entertained him hugely. I imagine such fellows do not have recourse to more instructive amusements. My only hope was, that he might loose the dog and let it send a ball into Pudge's thick head. Not that my luck would permit such a merry event.

I looked up at Pudge. 'If he sets it off, you and I will be equally at risk.'

Pudge glanced over at his friend and glowered, pulling the gun from him by the barrel. There was a whizzing sound, and a little flash from the pan, and Pudge opened his mouth to bellow at the fool for pulling the trigger, I imagine, but I was too busy by then, throwing myself backwards to the floor, as the cannon's roar filled the room with harsh, brimstone fumes. The yellowish smoke made breathing difficult, as though inhaling raw, hot woodsmoke, and I was soon choking with the intensity.

Meanwhile, the incident set off a number of events.

First, the fellow with my sword dropped it, gaped at the scene, and suddenly seemed to shimmer and disappear as though he had been converted into a cloud himself. The other, who had been holding the gun, was gazing wide-eyed at his employer with more than a little horror. He turned to me as if in a plea for understanding, gave a sort of embarrassed grin, and then quickly decided that his friend had in fact shown great discretion; for he was now in a chamber in a man's house, whom he had bound with a cord, whose pistol he had stolen, and with which he had now murdered his own master. This was, in short, a situation that could only be improved by disappearing. No sooner had he reached this conclusion, than he had it away on his heels as fast as the quickest racehorse. A faint image was left in the reeking fumes for a moment of his body, before the clouds realized he was no longer there, and they could fill the gap once more.

I could not see Pudge. Lying recumbent, I tried to peer to my left and right, but it was only when I took a glance between my legs that I saw him. He was sitting, apparently utterly baffled, as he stared down at the hole just below his heart. Blood was slowly pulsing from it, and he looked up and saw me with an expression of mournful loss.

'Oh, *bugger*!' he said.

'*Raphe!*'

I have been known to hold a grudge against some people, but I have to admit that I didn't feel the need to add to Pudge's woes any more than I already had. His own accomplice and assistant had managed to punch a hole through his lower chest that may well do him irreparable damage. It was more than likely that he would die from this wound, and were he to do so, a petty act of spite would help no one; whereas, were he to survive this blow, he would be forever in my debt, if my actions now could save him.

To my relief, Raphe appeared, waving a hand before his face at the foul atmosphere in there, I bellowed at the fool to run to the apothecary who lived a little further along Church Lane, and bring him back. To tell him that there was a wounded man in my room with me, and if he had skill as a physician, to bring his tools with him, and to be quick. I deliberately ensured that he should leave me on the floor and to fetch the man at speed. It may be thought that this was proof of the natural kindness of my heart, leaving myself in considerable pain in order to attempt the rescue of Pudge's life, but it has to be mentioned that I had another thought: in my experience, men of Pudge's build have been known to survive a bullet shot, and were he to survive, I would prefer him to know I had done all I could for him.

There was the other point which occurred to me speedily: when the physician arrived, he would be able to swear that I was bound. I could not have fired the shot that threatened Pudge's life. Yes, in my own house I would have been free to ensure that a robber who threatened my life would be at risk of injury, and perfectly correct. However, if it were to be heard that I owed him, according to his tale, a large sum of money, and then it was assumed that I had caused a gun to injure him, I was less sure of my position. A man defending his life and limb in his own property from a house-breaker was one thing; a man evading a debt by inviting his debtor indoors and then loosing a pistol at him could expect somewhat less sympathy. I had little desire to test a court on their view of the matter. I have had enough experience of lawyers and judges to know that their perspective of events can be startlingly opposed to those of people actually involved, mainly depending upon the importance of the protagonists – or the size of their wallets.

Raphe, for once, was as good as I had commanded. He must have run all the way there and back, and in his wake came a puffing and panting gentleman with a leather apron like a smith's, and a leather satchel that rattled and clattered somewhat. He stood in the room, coughing slightly from the residual smoke, and I sharply suggested to Raphe that he might open the window at the far side of the room before we all expired from the choking vapours and then, if he was not too busy, he could perhaps untie my hands?

It took me a good while to get the blood back into my hands. When Pudge's men had bound me, they had not thought to concern themselves about my wellbeing, and instead they had ensured that I would be exceedingly unlikely to release myself from their bonds. In that they had been entirely successful.

As far as Pudge was concerned, I could do nothing to aid the physician, who himself kept muttering dolefully that he was no barber surgeon, but he would do his best to save life when he could, and who would have thought a fellow would bleed so much from so small a hole? I left him to it, with Raphe to assist as he may, and soon I heard Raphe in the street calling for assistance to save the man's life. There was a need for some hefty fellows, apparently, to hold the man down while the physician had a dig around to find the ball and any cloth that might have penetrated with it.

All I was sure of was that it was not the sort of task to which I was fitted. When my hands had stopped tingling and stabbing with the return of blood to them, I retrieved my weapons from the floor, while the physician and Pudge engaged in a foul struggle against each other, while two men and Raphe attempted to hold the struggling innkeeper still, and beat a hasty retreat. There is something deeply unpleasant about the operations of surgeons and their ilk.

I made my way to the Bull, where I took a table and spent a little while cleaning the pistol, checking the dog, and reloading it, while consuming a large pot of wine to settle my nerves.

While I was there, I was surprised to be discovered by John Anderson. 'Master? Is all well?' he asked, eyeing the pistol on the table before me with some suspicion and concern.

'Nothing to concern you,' I said loftily. I had no wish to explain Pudge's interest in me, and just then my skills of invention were not at their strongest.

'Everyone is talking about the priest,' he said.

'Yes, the suspicion is, that he felt so guilty at his crimes that he took to his heels,' I said.

'So you will go and capture him?'

'Me?'

This was a new idea to me. I have been involved in the capture of dangerous criminals in the past, and it is not a pastime which I cared to repeat. Generally, hunting down a man involved days and nights spent out of doors, in the cold, often the rain, and all too often the individual concerned was less than enthusiastic about being captured, and would fight tooth and nail to escape. Men could get hurt acting as volunteers in a posse. I mean to say, I have endured many hardships in my time, and saw no need for putting myself into harm's way yet again. Apart from anything else, I still needed to get over the bullet that could so easily have been fired at me.

It was a thought that brought a sudden prickling of sweat to my brow. After all, it was Pudge grabbing the pistol which had made it go off. He had grasped it by the barrel and pulled, and since his companion's finger was on the trigger, he had set it off while it was pointing at his lower chest. It was easy to see how the accident had happened now, but the thought uppermost in my mind was, if Pudge had yanked it with his other hand, the barrel may well have been pointing less at him, and more at me, you see. And the memory of the size of the hole in him produced a kind of sympathetic horror in me. The physician might think it was small – I had no such conviction. I could almost feel that heavy ball striking my belly or breast, and I was less sure of my ability to survive such a massive missile.

'Do you think so?' he said.

'Eh?'

'Should we go and see whether he is there?'

'Where?'

'At the beggars' town outside the wall, where his wife lives now.'

I looked at him blankly, my mind still filled with the idea of the agony of that bullet, but gradually I was brought back to the present, and recalled that we had been discussing the priest. 'You think he'll be there? In that case, we should tell the alderman so he can send a force to arrest the man.'

'You think a man like Father Peter would require a show of strength? I would expect him to submit immediately.'

'Perhaps.'

'And think how we should look, the two of us, capturing the man who destroyed the church and murdered the poor woman in the vestry,' he added.

In my mind's eye I saw our broken, bloody corpses stripped bare, purses long gone, lying on a dung heap.

'Walking back here with the guilty man held between us,' he added helpfully, perhaps after seeing my expression.

'I don't know.'

'I thought you would like to. After all, it was he who accused you of killing her,' he said, almost as an aside, toying with some spilled wine on the tabletop. It made him look as though he really had little interest in the matter. And it worked.

'I had forgotten that!' I said, and thrust the pistol home in the holster once more. I called for more wine and some for John as well. I did feel the need for a little liquid sustenance after the shock of the morning, and it has to be said that I was reluctant to head towards my home yet. The thought of Pudge straining under the grip of the three men holding him was . . . unpleasant. I had no desire to return and discover him lying on one of my beds, whether alive or dead.

When the wine materialized, I finished mine in three gulps and stood. 'Let us go!'

Obviously, as a man of courage and spirit, I was not anxious about the thought of footpads and cutpurses, but it did strike me that a young fellow like John could be at risk, and I thought it sensible to ensure his protection for the journey, so I sought out the gorilla and William Kirk, who in a cowardly manner refused to join our party, but did send two of his own servants with strong staves to help protect us. Personally, seeing the gorilla join us was infinitely more reassuring than an army of young men with staves.

As we walked, I said to John, 'What do you know of Adam Bonner and his dealings before he died and Kirk took his place as alderman?'

'From all I have heard, Bonner was a thorn in the side of William Kirk. The two were both close to daggers drawn, mostly over buildings and investments they had made together when they were friends, but then their amicable arrangements were broken, and what had been a companionable and profitable friendship became hatred.'

'How so?'

'Kirk invested in a group of buildings. He advised Bonner to do the same, and both anticipated a good return. But the buildings burned down, while holding a certain quantity of merchandise inside. Bonner was very angry, and accused Kirk of having spirited away the goods before setting fire to the buildings himself. Kirk angrily denied arson and fraud, but it was enough to destroy any friendly feelings between the two.'

'What happened?'

'Apparently Kirk tried to get on to the council, but there were no seats. There is only one alderman per ward in the city, and Bonner had it. And then Bonner was killed.'

'How?' We were passing under the gate house itself, and I shivered at the thought of murder.

'A knife in the dark. The fool wandered along an alley late at night, and was found the next morning with his throat cut. No one saw the murder, nobody was there to see a man flee from the alley.

'But one man stood to gain by Bonner's death: Kirk. As soon as Bonner was confirmed dead, the council chose Kirk to replace him without election, just seconding him to the seat. I imagine he has benefitted hugely from the position. If he was wealthy before, he will have increased his riches massively since. An alderman can make money in so many ways: accepting bribes, fiddling with the weights and measures, it's a racket for a man who knows what he's doing.'

I puffed out my cheeks thoughtfully. It was interesting that the murderer of Bonner the alderman had used the same method of killing his victim. But that was obviously mere coincidence.

We left the city by Bishopsgate, and made our way along the northern wall of the city, following the line of the ancient fortifications. In places they were still strong enough, but in most it was a depressing sight. For me, having been pressed into service during the last rebellion when Wyatt's mob attacked from the south, all I could think of was the risk of a mob from the north deciding to come and rob every Londoner blind. With a wall in this state of disrepair, it would not pose too much in the way of an obstacle.

We left the smoking kilns of the charcoal burners who plied their trade near to the wall, and then the pits in which chalk was burned to make lime, before we entered the miserable shanty hovels where the poorest folk lived.

These were the people who were shunned, or who had not enough money to conceive of renting a property in London, let alone buy one. Their crude homes were planks leaning against the city wall, or some few built of lathes set into posts with thin mud plaster filling the gaps and thatch of grass or a thick bed of reed. The denizens of these dwellings were suited to them: thin scarecrows, few with shoes of any sort, some with so few clothes they might as well have not bothered.

For the most part they were no threat to anyone. The majority had the sunken eyes and cheeks of the always-hungry. Those who had eaten recently were the men and women serving the great clay-built charcoal kilns and lime works. Their trades made them unpopular, but at least they had food.

John tried to avoid the most beggarly of them, averting his gaze from their appeals, almost as if he felt he was responsible for their poverty in some way. I mean to say, it is hard to see people in such straits, obviously, but it's no one's fault. It is just the way the world is.

With all the people gathered here, I began to wonder whether we would ever find Father Peter. It was almost a large town in size, and although there were not so many people as lived within London's walls, there were enough to make the process of searching all but pointless. In the end I started questioning the burners. Although many ignored me, or cast wary glances at the men with me, one woman, who kept her eyes fixed on the thin smoke emanating from the top of a kiln as she spoke, engaged with me.

'Yes, Peter is with his family. They're up there. Ask for Jane.'

I followed her pointing finger. She had indicated a path leading away from the city, which had tents and other flimsy structures at either side of the street. We set off up this muddy track, hopefully asking everyone we met where Jane and her family lived, but in the end it was unnecessary. As we climbed a slight incline, I saw him.

The priest was sitting on his rump, holding a child in his

lap, rocking backwards and forwards. We approached, and I carefully slowed my pace just a little, so that John overhauled me and was nearer than I when we accosted the man.

Not that there was any need for me to worry. That was soon plain enough.

Father Peter did not look up as we came close to him, and although we formed a loose circle about him and the door to his tent, he paid us no heed.

'Father Peter?' John said, his voice a little strained. I put my hand on his arm to still his tongue.

The priest was clutching a small figure to his breast. It was plain enough that this was his child, and it was equally obvious that the child was dead.

'Father?' I said. 'I am sorry, but you must return with us. You are required to explain yourself to the alderman.'

He rocked back and forth, but did not speak. Some mumbling came from his mouth, but nothing else. I glanced about me, and shooed the gorilla and Kirk's two men away. Having all five of us was too intimidating for the priest. I was about to speak again, when the tent's flap opened and a woman stood before me. She was shabby, but stood as erect as a lady. Her clothes were clean, which must have been little short of a miracle in this filthy parish, and although her face wore every travail of misery carved into it, there was a strength in the set of her jaw and the directness of her gaze.

'Who are you?' she said wearily.

'I am Master Blackjack,' I said. 'And you are?'

'I was his wife,' she said. 'Now, I don't know.'

I understood, of course. This was the only course open to so many women who had been married to priests after the queen's decision to return to the Catholic faith. The 'wives' were cast out and left to fend for themselves, as newly declared whores. What else could they do? With children in tow, very few men would look at them as possible wives. The only choice they had was to take to prostitution full time or beg and die by degrees. This woman, I guessed, fell into the second category. There was a set to her face that showed confidence, poise and fortitude. This was a woman who, it was easy to imagine, had once been a pillar of the community of St Helen's. She had been a woman of substance. Now she was reduced to living here amidst the mud and manure on the edge of the moors.

'His church was damaged and a woman murdered, and there is suspicion that your . . . this priest was responsible. I am sorry, but he must return to answer to the justice.'

'Look at him! You seriously think he could kill a woman? Can't you leave him alone? At least for a day? We need to think what to do for our son.'

'What happened?' John asked.

In answer, she sighed, 'What do you think? A fever, a chill, and a slow wasting. I did all I could, but it wasn't enough. I cannot afford an apothecary, and the medicines friends here recommended did no good. My poor little boy Peterkin died.'

'You should have asked Peter to help,' I said.

'What do you think I did?' she snapped, and I saw the stark despair in her face. 'I went to him two weeks ago when Peterkin was first ill, and then again last week. Then,' she said, looking down at her once-husband, 'Sunday I went again at noontime, when Peterkin had a fit, and Peter swore he would come.'

I suddenly recalled that day, when I had been drinking myself to oblivion after the shock of Rachel's and Blount's visits. This woman had walked to see her husband in her despair and loss. It made me feel a sudden sympathy for her.

'It was too late. I went to tell him that little Peterkin was on his last legs, and would he come to give our son the last rites, and he promised he would. But he was forced to delay to hold Mass for the parish, and then . . . then it was too late.'

The misery in her eyes was enough to make me want to throw my arms around her and give her a little compassion. But I knew she would not appreciate it. She was a very strong lady and a stranger's condolences would not help her.

'He has to come back with us,' I said. 'I am sorry.'

'*You're* sorry? What of Peterkin, my little angel?' she said, and her eyes were brimming with tears. Just recently I seemed to have developed the ability to make young women and mothers burst into tears. 'If you take Peter away, who will bury my boy? Peter at least knows what he must do. Other priests would refuse, they'll say Peterkin was born out of wedlock, so his soul is lost! But we *were* married, and Peterkin was born without sin in the eyes of God! I need to have him buried in a Christian fashion, not deserted in a trough by a crossroads!'

'He has to come back to explain himself,' John said callously, as I thought, without feeling. I could have slapped the lad. I moved to stand between him and Peter's wife.

Peter slowly rose to his feet, still cradling his son's corpse. 'Master John? Will you bury my boy for me? Will you say the last rites so that he can go straight to God as he deserves? He has done nothing to offend you. Why would you seek to see him damned?'

John had the grace to look embarrassed and closed his mouth.

'Mistress Jane, will you swear that your husband' – I was not going to insult her more by suggesting he was less than her husband – 'will indeed return to his church tomorrow and submit to the alderman and Keeper of the Queen's Peace? There have been accusations laid against him, and these must be answered.'

'I will. I swear it,' she said.

'There!' I said. 'I trust you.' And I turned away, but before I could take a step, the woman grabbed my hand and held it to her lips.

'Thank you,' she whispered.

I spoke hardly at all on the walk back. There seemed little to say. Kirk's men left us at the entrance to my lane, and the gorilla left with them, I guessed to report to John Blount. It is a mark of my despondency that I invited John to join me in a cup of wine when I reached my house. There was a shock awaiting me there.

The invitation for him to accept a cup or two of wine was not only for company, but also because, since the discharge of my gun into Pudge's podgy body, I wanted to be assured that there was no one else in my house who might decide to assault me. Accordingly, I opened the door and motioned my guest inside first, and almost fled when I heard his gasp. I turned to flee, but before I could put my initial intention to flee into action, I discovered a keen interest in what was happening inside as I heard John guffaw with laughter.

Pushing the door wide, I found my servants engaged in rapidly attempting to disentangle themselves. They had been enjoying the benefits of a warm fire, a thick rug laid before it, and my absence, to get to know each other rather more intimately than I would have expected. Indeed, it would not be dishonest to say that I was bereft of speech.

Raphe, with a face as purple as a ripe plum, was desperately trying to pull his breeches up while tucking in his shirt and concealing the proof of his recent excitement by turning his back to the door. Cecily, meanwhile, stood and sedately tucked her hair back into her coif. Of course, for her it was the work of a moment to stand and allow her skirts to fall and preserve her modesty, such as it was.

I stood and I suppose I must have gaped and stared for some while. Raphe managed to get himself fully dressed and waited with his head hanging, while Cecily met my gaze with a solemn dignity. She was not the sort of young woman to feel shame. In fact, I felt that if I were to attempt to rebuke the two of them, she would be more than likely to reprove me for interrupting them.

'Um, John, I think I prefer to go to the Bull,' I said. 'Raphe, I will speak to you later about this.'

I said nothing to upset Cecily. After all, she was a very good cook.

Walking to the Bull with John, I was unsure what to say. John, for his part, found the whole situation hilarious. He laughed all the way to the inn. 'His face, when I walked in! She looked daggers, but he was just appalled, I could see that in his eyes, the poor dummerer! He couldn't speak, and just stared at me in horror as she climbed off him and let her dress down. But he . . .!'

I was not of a mood to engage with his hilarity. We reached the inn and I entered and went to my usual table, but it was occupied. Instead we took a stool each near the fire and waited for our drinks, he with continued amusement, me with rather more solemnity. The main thing, for me, was that the pair should uncouple and show a little decorum. Where would the world be if servants felt that they could behave so freely?

We sat, and perhaps I was not particularly convivial company, because after only one drink John decided he should return home. I, on the other hand, was just starting to enjoy myself. Pudge was out of the way, the gorilla was more or less amiably disposed towards me, and I had a wonderful feeling that all the blame for Rachel's death and the damage done to the church would rest on the priest's shoulders. He was clearly guilty. Everything, in short, was looking most agreeable.

Once John had departed, I settled back and closed my eyes. It was tiring, going out and investigating murders, I decided, and decidedly more so when there was a risk that I myself might be put in peril of my life.

I was just settling down to enjoy a fresh cup of wine, when I heard my name called.

It was Richard Croke who had hailed me, and now he joined me, taking John's seat, a pint pot of ale in his hands.

He was a curious fellow, this Croke. Tall, slim, ascetic, he had a narrow chin and gaunt figure. His eyes were dark, but inside the inn's chambers, that was true of almost every man. 'Master Blackjack, I hope I see you well?'

We went through the usual pleasantries before he asked whether there was any news of Rachel Nailor's murderer.

'I don't think so,' I said. Memories of seeing him with the Spaniard came to mind. I was not keen to share too much about my investigations, and reluctant to mention the priest. After all, these Catholics tend to stick together like birds to lime, and Croke might invent another guilty person just to help Father Peter escape justice. Instead, I said, 'But I am new to the parish, so I daresay I will be last to hear any news.'

'A terrible event,' he said, shaking his head slowly. 'To think that she could be slain here, in St Helen's.'

'People get slain all the time,' I said.

'Not here in our parish,' he said with some asperity. 'The last man to be killed on our streets was poor Adam Bonner, and that was, oh, a year ago.'

'Really?' On the streets of London it was rare that a body would not be found most days.

'We are unused to such sordid matters in our parish,' he said, looking down his nose at me.

It was enough to spark a response from me. After all, London might be dangerous, but at least the men here had courage and the determination to take no nonsense, and I said as much, leaning rather on the aspect that those who disagreed may just not be bold enough to protect themselves or the city. 'I have served in the ranks when it mattered,' I added. 'During the rebellion, I was engaged in defending London Bridge.'

'Oh. I recall that,' he said without enthusiasm. 'I lost a warehouse to fire during that horrible affair, as did Adam Bonner. A terrible time. But business picked up again soon afterwards. There was good trade with the Spanish after the wedding, too. There were Spanish all over the city for a while, and they were very keen to spend their money.'

'You sold much to them, I suppose?'

He didn't notice my sarcasm.

'Yes. They were happy times. Although, of course, many disliked them – and still do. There was a Spaniard in the parish only a few days ago, and several folk drove him off. It was shameful. Oh, but you met Diego, of course.'

'Yes – but when was this? When was he driven away?'

'I don't know – a few days, as I said. Before last weekend, I think. He returned the other day. You met him with me.'

'Ah, yes. I remember.' If it were not for Peter's admission, I would have been worried. Rachel had been trying to travel to France to negotiate a path for her mistress in direct contravention of the plans that Philip, the queen's Spanish husband, had planned. He would be infuriated to learn that Elizabeth was attempting to escape to Paris, to their enemies. If I was not certain of Peter's culpability, I might have thought that Rachel had been murdered by a Spaniard – and he might have tried to put the blame for her murder on the one man who was known to be her associate: me!

Of course, it was all nonsense. But I pushed my ale away. Suddenly my belly felt uncomfortable.

SIX

Thursday 1st April

I mused over the previous day's discoveries when I sat down to a plate of eggs, cold beef, some pork, cheese and bread the next morning, much to Cecily's obvious disapproval. I gave her a cold stare. After all, after her behaviour with Raphe yesterday, she was in no position to lecture me about Lenten abstinence.

Croke was merely croaking, I decided – and the alliteration made me smile to myself. There was no need to worry about Spaniards, when it was obvious that Peter was guilty. Why he should have taken it into his mind to murder Rachel – jealousy, guilt, misdirected passion – I did not know, but he was surely responsible.

John had muttered, on the way back, that we should have brought the priest back with us. Yet, what would that have achieved? We would have him back one day earlier. And in reality, for what? It would devastate a woman who was unable to bury her son in hallowed ground, and would cause enmity between her and the parish – all for no reason. Of course, if Peter did not come back to the church today, I would look foolish in the eyes of many – but I could explain that I trusted the word of a priest. Besides, when he arrived today, then all would be well and good.

I finished my breakfast with a pint of weak ale, belched, and stood. Raphe was in one of his surly moods, but that did not bother me. With my weapons all in their places about my baldric and belt, I felt dressed for the day. I left the house and walked out to take the road to the church.

When I had returned home the night before, it was to find Raphe grumpy. Apparently it was not only the effect of being discovered tasting the cook's delicacies, it was the fact that he had not enjoyed serving as a leg-holder during the operation to remove the bullet from Pudge's body. It was not, he gave me to understand, a pleasant experience. Well, what of it? A fellow had to learn to deal with such matters, and he was a man, when all was said and done, as he had demonstrated with Cecily, I pointed out. He was not so keen to discuss that. Yet, when a lad passes twelve years, he is adult, and must behave in a grown-manly fashion, as I reminded him.

I did learn from him that the physician had stated that his patient required peace and rest for his recovery to be ensured, and had instructed Raphe to bring porters to carry Pudge from my house to his own. I reckoned the physician knew the best way to guarantee his fee was to hold Pudge in his lodgings and nurse him there. To my mind, it was optimistic to think that Pudge would willingly part with whatever fee the physician chose to inflict on him, and to me it seemed likely that the physician would soon have an opportunity to treat his own black eye, but that was his choice.

The day was one of those grey, cold ones. It was not wet, which was a relief, but the sun remained concealed behind a thick layer of clouds which cloaked her presence as effectively as a barrel would hide a candle. Walking along, I was aware that it felt grim, as though dark matters were underway, and the attitude of the people I saw was hardly any better.

At the churchyard, I was surprised to see the sexton hard at work on a small grave. He looked over at me, a sallow-faced man with deep chasms cut into his leathery face at either side of his mouth, giving him a dour appearance. When he recognized me, he ducked his head and touched his cap with respect. 'I thank 'ee for this, Master Blackjack.'

'Me? What for?'

'Givin' us time to prepare for the burial. Mistress Jane's grateful to you for lettin' her keep her husban' with 'er last night. They 'eld vigil with their boy all night. Won't be long now. Then we can put the lad in 'ere.'

I nodded, acknowledging his respect and walked on to the church. And at the door a clutching sensation grabbed at my heart.

Oh, God's hounds! The man thought I had given express

permission for a renegade priest to spend a night in the company of a woman! Worse, that I might have given permission for a burial to take place on consecrated ground for a dead but illegitimate boy! If this was to become common knowledge, my own life would be in danger. A vision of the bleak tower where Queen Mary held those whom she wished to question sprang to mind, and I suddenly felt as sickly and feeble as Raphe had looked the previous evening.

Before I could do anything I heard the sound of a mob. However, this was not drunken rioting apprentices, rather it was a mass of steady, solemn people. When I stepped out to observe, I saw Peter and his woman at the front of a column of assorted beggars, charcoal burners, lime workers and others. Peter still held the frail little body to his breast, and although my impression of the priest was not greatly improved since the first day he had railed at me, I confess that there was a dignity to him now. He caught my eye and looked away, but then returned to meet my gaze, and this time he bowed his head briefly. For some reason that made me feel honoured and honourable.

Yes, it is strange, but to be recognized and approved by the priest made me feel just a little better in some way. I suppose his appreciation of my allowing him the previous night was enough to show him that I was not such a wastrel as he had imagined.

In any case, I was not going to hang around there while they conducted a ceremony in defiance of the law. I hastily made my way from the church and up to the Bull. I could rest in there a while, I thought, and when the ceremony was over, I could return.

It was almost midday when I returned, and I found that Alderman Kirk had already arrived, as had Sir Gerald Marbod and Richard Croke. Father Peter stood in his church and answered their questions with a slightly tremulous tone, as though he knew he was pleading for his life, like a child discovered with a stolen loaf of bread. It was a pitiable sight.

'You admit to meeting women here in the church?' Marbod said.

'I admit meeting one woman, my wife Jane. And that was only to be told of—'

'You are not married. Your marriage was declared void,' Croke stated firmly, his grim features all the more forbidding upon hearing the priest's words. 'She is a woman confirmed in her miserable, sinful life.'

'That is a lie. I swore my oath to her before God, and He didn't object! What right do you have to question Him?' Peter said. There was more firmness to his response, but his anxiety was still visible.

'You "saw" her here, you say,' Croke pressed, 'when you know it is illegal for a priest to have relations with women?'

'She is my wife,' Peter said stoutly. 'Our son was dying. To my shame I didn't go to see her and him.'

I glanced at the alderman. Kirk looked deeply uncomfortable, but clearly saw little opportunity to interrupt Croke's interrogation. Croke had authority here; I assumed he was known to be a dedicated Catholic and had little truck with those who adhered to the Church of England.

'How many other women did you entertain here in the church?' Croke snapped.

'None, I—'

'What was it about Rachel Nailor that attracted you to her?'

'Nothing!'

'You deny asking her to meet you here?'

'Yes, certainly!'

'But she came, and you killed her in the vestry there,' Croke said, pointing. 'What had she done to you?'

'I did not!'

'She was pregnant – was that your child? Did you murder your own child as well as your concubine?'

'I never . . . I didn't . . . it wasn't me!' Peter stammered, his face now white.

Marbod was studying him closely, I could see, and now his glance flitted to me. I was sure he was thinking of the fact that Rachel had come to the church in response to a summons she thought came from me. And it struck me: why would Peter have sent that summons? I was still convinced that Peter was the murderer, and yet the message was incongruous. Someone must have delivered the note to her. Perhaps I could learn who, and thereby learn who had actually sent the message. Perhaps Moll would know.

Kirk interrupted Croke's accusations. 'The woman's body was found in your vestry. How do you explain that?'

'I don't, master,' came the response, all firmness and conviction fled. 'I can't.'

Alderman Kirk nodded, and gave Croke a sour glance before continuing, 'Father Peter, this is not a matter for the secular world to pursue, this is an ecclesiastical affair, and we must wait to hear from the bishop as to how to take matters further. For my part, I intend to seek the murderer of this poor woman, and ensure that he suffers the full penalty of the law for his evil crimes, both those against the church and against her body, murdering not only her, but the infant in her womb. Will you swear to remain here in the church until we hear from the bishop and how he wishes to proceed?'

'With all my heart,' the priest said.

'Then I consider this matter is closed for now,' the alderman said.

I watched them leave, debating whether to join them or not, and in the end decided to leave them to their affairs. Kirk walked with his head hanging. He looked truly miserable. I could only imagine that he was sorely distressed to think that Rachel's mission had foundered so early. Later I must speak to Marbod about that message. Why would the priest have sent to Rachel in my name to ask her to come to the church? It made no sense. Meanwhile, Jane had walked to her husband and the two were holding hands in a rather touching display of affection.

'I think you acquitted yourself well,' I said to Peter.

He glanced at me, but returned his gaze to his wife. 'I think I showed myself to be weak, vacillatory, incompetent and a coward. I showed that I dared not go to my son when he needed me, I did not go to my wife and support her when she needed me, and only took the honourable course when I had exhausted all others. And by sheer misfortune, that was the night that some murderer chose to break into the church and murder that poor woman.'

'Did you really have nothing to do with her?'

I agree – asking him that while his wife was there holding his hand was hardly subtle, but these were troublesome times.

He sighed. 'It is hard for any to accept, but no, I did not. Even if I had desired it, her attitude towards me was always respectful, but cold. She was not the sort of woman to give herself to just any man. She was a strong woman with convictions of her own.'

'I don't understand.'

'She refused many offers from various men in the parish. Even . . .' His brow clouded. 'But I cannot say. I did see many men attempt to engage her in conversation. You were one of a very few with whom she would talk. It was one reason why I attempted to stop you from pestering her when I saw you ogling her. I knew she would be likely to deprecate your overtures.'

I bridled, but then his words sank in. 'You mean you had confessions from men who had tried to inveigle her into their beds?'

'I cannot say.'

The sanctity of the confessional had never been more annoying to me. No one is more stubborn than a priest determined to keep secret the confessions told to him. Even now Peter's lips had closed as firmly as an oyster's shell.

'When you left here to go to your wife, did you see anyone here?'

'Perhaps. I cannot tell. I was so distraught by the news of Peterkin that anything is possible. I took flight to find Jane and . . . and . . .'

His eyes filled. It was embarrassing. Jane put her hand to his face and wiped away the tears, then took his hand, and we all stood in quiet reflection.

I had to break the silence, and cleared my throat. Most of the audience of the little trial had left, and there were only a few people huddled at the porch, and some three or four in pews praying. I saw one of them was Gawtheren Spink, and it brought back to mind that fateful day when we found Rachel's body.

'Why did you accuse me when we found her body, Father?'

He blinked several times, then wiped his nose with a hand kerchief. 'You were new to the parish. I know all the other parishioners in my congregation. I couldn't believe one of them could do such a thing, so thought it must be you, the foreigner.'

'Yet when the young Elias Spink saw us here, he immediately accused you.'

'He is a troublesome fellow.'

'How so?'

The priest frowned, and for a moment I thought that yet another snippet was to be declared a secret of the confessional, but then he shook his head. 'Gawtheren was never married. Elias has suffered all through his life from being a bastard. And, of course, when I was forced to reject my own family, it made him feel that Peterkin and Jane were no better than he and his mother. Which was wrong, of course, for we were married in church, and a change in the kingdom's law does not change God's acceptance, as I told Croke just now, but that is not how Elias viewed the matter. For him, it was clear and simple: I was a hypocrite. I suppose when he saw Jane coming here to see me, it reinforced his opinion of me, and then, when Rachel was found dead, he gave voice to his own inner turmoil and his disgust at what he saw as my unfairness to him. But I could do nothing for him.'

'I see,' I said. 'Tell me, when you were here, before you left, she could not have entered the church without you knowing?'

'No. I was here praying until I left,' he said, and there was a sudden shiftiness in his face.

'Just kneeling at the altar and praying?'

'Yes, of course.'

'I know you were seen fleeing the church in great haste, Father.'

'Yes. Elias saw me, of course.'

'Yes. Was there anyone else you saw as you ran?'

'No. But I was not paying attention,' he said.

'It seems strange to me,' I said. 'Would she have entered the church if she saw all the destruction?' It did make little sense to me. But then, perhaps she saw the damage to the church and assumed that the message calling her to meet me had been because I had become aware of some danger, that I had become involved in a fight, and was waiting to see her. She would have courageously walked to the vestry, where . . . no, I didn't want to think of the murderer grabbing her and cutting her throat. The memory of her body was all too firmly planted in my mind already.

Peter and Jane were still holding hands. It was obvious to me that the death of their son had brought home to these two that their love was far more important than the queen's instructions on chastity.

I left the church soon after, taking the street to Marbod's house, but I had only managed a short distance when I encountered the gorilla. He was loitering at the gate to the churchyard with a sullen expression on his face.

'You paid me for two days,' he reminded me.

I was ready for that. I retrieved another silver coin from my purse and was about to pass it to him, when I reconsidered. I dived into my purse again and brought out a second. 'Take both of these, master . . .?' It suddenly struck me that I still did not know his name. 'What is your name?'

Taking the coins with an air of disbelief and near-religious awe, he stuttered slightly as he said, 'They calls me Ned, Ned Clement.'

'A good name,' I said, mentally wondering how a man whose surname could mean 'gentle' could have ended as he had. 'I will need you for at least two more days, Ned. Can you do that? You will still be watching me for John Blount, after all.'

'Aye. I think so,' he said, carefully installing the coins in his purse.

We continued on our way to Marbod's house, and I left him at the gate to the street as I entered.

Marbod came to me in the hall, and I asked him about the message for Rachel.

'Who brought it? I do not know. But I think Moll took the message. Let us ask her,' he said.

Moll was brought in by the bottler, who was sent away while we spoke with her.

'You recall the evening that Rachel went to the church, when she was slain? You said that she received a message inviting her to the church. Who brought that message?'

She was a terrified little thing. It was hardly surprising, the poor maid being confronted by two such important men. She was more than a little tongue-tied, staring at Marbod, glancing at me, and then back to him.

Of course, I quickly realized her difficulty. Knowing of the message, she knew that it was purportedly sent by me, and thus the logical conclusion was, that I had myself murdered Rachel, and equally logically, the chit would be very anxious about accusing me before her master. Yet her master had demanded a response. She was no doubt feeling that she was caught in a cleft stick.

I sought to reassure her. 'Moll, I know what you are thinking, but have no fear. Tell the truth, maid, and help us to find the murderer. I sent no message to Rachel, so whoever did so must have sent it by a boy or some other device. Was it a verbal message? Was it written down? Who brought it? Anything you can tell us would be most helpful.'

'I . . . I don't know, master,' she said, giving Marbod the sort of look a hare would give the hounds. Utterly petrified and preparing to bolt.

'Come, now, Moll!' he instructed her. 'It cannot be too difficult. Was it a boy?'

'I . . . I suppose so.'

'Who?'

'I don't know.'

'Master Blackjack,' Marbod said, 'perhaps you should take her about the parish, and see if she can recognize the boy?'

'Oh, master, no, I have so much work to do, and Mistress would be angry if I fall behind!' There was genuine fear in her voice at this thought.

'Then you must hope to find the boy quickly, eh? And catch up on your work when you get back. Or rise early tomorrow to clear it up. This good gentleman wishes to find the boy so we can find the murderer. We do not want a murderer loose, do we? All you need do is find the boy. We can question him later.'

It was not to her taste, and she looked thoroughly distressed, as well she might. If she still considered me the murderer of her friend, how could she not be concerned at being sent away with me? But to be fair, it did strike me that the likelihood of finding the boy was remote. After all, boys were ten a penny in London. They might have come from any lodging, any tavern, any street, or even from outside the city in one of the makeshift settlements like Jane's. The chances of coming across the boy in an hour's walk about the streets were remote in the extreme.

'No,' I said. 'I feel sure that Moll would find it difficult to spy the lad. How many fellows are there in the city? And this one boy could be anywhere: on the streets, in an alehouse, or asleep in an attic. But I thank you for the suggestion, and for offering Moll to help. Moll, my thanks, but you have work to do here,' I said grandly, and she scurried away like the little mouse she truly was.

'You should be cautious,' Marbod said. 'If you refuse assistance like that, others might impugn the reasons for rejecting her aid.'

'What do you mean?'

'I should have considered myself clear,' he said. 'Since you were supposedly the man who sent a message to Rachel asking her to meet you, now that Moll has been offered to go and find the boy concerned, who brought that message to the house, well, most people would expect you to be keen to find the fellow. If you refuse Moll's help, it could be thought that it is because you don't want the boy found; because that messenger was sent by *you*.'

When I left his house I was deep in thought, and they were not pleasant thoughts.

It had not occurred to me that my attempt at kindness could be construed as a means of avoiding my own guilt being discovered. I was only trying to save myself, and Moll, the ridiculous effort of hunting high and low in every street nearby for a boy. The city was full of them, and it would be nothing short of a miracle for us to actually discover the right fellow. With no name, all we could do was seek the lad by peering at every young apprentice thief until one or another decided we were suspicious and should be knocked on the head. I had no desire to submit to having my head used once more as a stress-tester for some villain's cudgel. Over the years I have endured a number of assaults and my pate always appears to be the favourite target for those who wish me harm. Well, I had been attacked too often and would not put myself in harm's way again.

Finding Ned the Gorilla at the gate, I beckoned him and continued on my way, frowning as I considered the danger I was in.

Everything I did seemed to turn to dust on inspection, and yet my own alleged participation was still hanging over my head, like the sword of that fellow that dangled over his victim . . . Damn of Cleves was it? Whoever it was, I could appreciate his dilemma just now.

Marbod was right to warn me about failing to hunt for Moll's messenger boy. I was also perfectly well aware that a man of such importance and wealth would not be a reliable ally. I have had some experience of men of his type, and I knew that if at any time he felt I was becoming a threat or risk to himself, or to Lady Elizabeth, he would instruct a man like Ned the Gorilla to come and pull my head off. Ideally after pulling off both legs and arms as well. It was not an appealing thought.

Ned was currently testing his height by allowing his knuckles to drag on the cobbles, or so I thought. He was showing every sign of reluctance. 'What is it?'

'Never had my breakfast.'

'Why not?'

He considered this a moment. 'Didn't want it.'

'But you do now.'

'I want a meat pie,' he told me, and turned off up Bishopsgate to a little pie shop.

I sighed, but continued on my way. It was only a short distance further along the road that I saw Master Croke and his Spanish friend. They were both watching me, and it was unsettling. I don't like to get involved in politics, and to feel the attention of a Spaniard in these difficult times was worrying.

I turned into the church close, forgetting that I was alone. My mind was wandering, as were my steps.

It was only when someone tapped my shoulder that I realized how far I had misjudged my safety. I turned to find the grinning face of the man who had appeared outside my house on my return from the Appleby's house on Monday. I registered his face, and felt that quickening of excitement and panic that so often in the past has been my saving. Turning, I made the best of my opportunity to flee, but as I turned I found myself confronted by a thickset, bearded fellow, who grinned wickedly, blocking my way. I only managed the one step before someone dropped an anvil on my pate. Or so it felt. All I knew was, one moment I was up and about to run as fleet of foot as any greyhound, and then I was falling, falling, into a blackness that opened in the lane at my feet, as if I was swallowed up by the deepest privy in London, a vast, black hole that went on and on, and just before I lost consciousness, all I could think was that landing in the bottom of that pit was going to be vastly unpleasant.

The sad fact is, my predictions so often prove to be accurate.

There have been other times when I have woken from an unexpected nap in the middle of the day.

The sort I appreciate tend to be those little snoozes which come after a good lunch, when I have enjoyed messing with friends, and have discovered a new brothel, or when I have learned of a new wine, and have partaken to the fullest possible extent. Those rests are delightful, and I always yawn and stretch afterwards with a feeling that I have had a successful day. They are refreshing and leave me full of energy – especially if I wake up in the bed of a young wench who is keen to entertain me once more.

And then again, there are the other occasions; those when I have been forced to slumber unwillingly. This was one such. The first instinct, upon waking, is always to perform a swift check. Are my legs still there? My hands? Am I bleeding? These are the initial mundane considerations before I can even think of the next level of question, which usually involve:

Where am I? Who knocked me out? Why did they knock me out? How do I get out of this?

Today was one of the latter experiences. I woke to a splitting headache, but at least all limbs appeared to be available for instant use, once my head had stopped its imitation of a log under the splitting axe. There was a steady pounding, which to my mind spoke of a heavy blow to the back of the head with a cosh or cudgel.

Why had I allowed Ned to go to the pasty shop? The gorilla would have been most convenient in that alleyway, and whoever my attackers were, he would have soon put paid to their presumption in waylaying me. Not that the reflection was comforting. All I knew just now was a terrible, all-encompassing fear. Yes, it was of course based on the knowledge that I had been struck down, but the more important concern just now was the fact that I had no idea *who* had decided to hit me, where they had brought me, and *why*? These seemed to me to be the more pressing matters for me to consider just now. And the fact that some form of sack was draped over my head was not aiding my clarity of thought.

I was in a building; likely a basement. There was a faint dripping from somewhere nearby, and the air felt damp. When I turned my head to listen for the sound of traffic and hawkers in the street, I could hear nothing, other than an occasional low rumble. That could have been the noise of carts, but then again it might have been distant thunder, for all I knew. What I did know was that I was not going to get up any time soon. My hands were bound behind my back, and my ankles were also tied, and my captors had contrived to bind my ankles with a rope connected to my wrists, simultaneously making flight impossible and life deeply painful. It was not a happy wakening.

That I was not among friends was soon made clear. A boot thudded into my breast, hard enough to make me jerk, which had the nasty effect of making me try to curl up to protect my front. With the rope bonds, that had the result that my hands were wrenched down and back.

'Stop whimpering, you pathetic horner!'

'Me? I don't . . .'

'You know very little, don't you, *Master* Blackjack. You go about town whoring and turning decent women into scurvy hobbies, don't you? And all the time the husband is left to wear the cuckold's horns and be laughed at, eh?'

Another boot, in the belly this time. It made me gasp for breath and then squeal at the pain in my wrists.

'You're not laughing now, though, are you? Mayhap your past is catching up with you, you pricklouse knave!'

'I don't know what you're talking about!' I said. After all, if at all possible I needed to negotiate an escape.

'Don't whimper, you pathetic tarse! What any woman could see in you, I don't understand!'

'Who . . .?' A sudden horrible conviction was coming to me. There were clues in what he said, after all. I hadn't touched another man's wife in ages, apart from Susan. And this voice, strained as it was with real anger, was rather familiar. I pictured him in my mind, the unfriendly, scowling face, the suspicious glances, the weakly glower . . . yes, I was sure it was him. And while he was a rather feeble imitation of a man, his kick was powerful, and I was bound and entirely at his mercy. It was not a good situation.

'Um, perhaps if you remove this sack, we can talk?' I suggested.

'So you can try to persuade us to release you? Don't waste your breath!'

'If you aren't, what are you going to do with me?' I said boldly.

'Don't squeak, little mouse! I'm going to castrate you, and then hang you!'

'But . . . What have I done to you?'

'You took to fornicating with my wife, you totter-legged trash!'

This was not the calm, even-toned neighbour I remembered. This was a raving madman, driven mad by jealousy, of course. Well, it was hardly surprising, since I had the benefits of youth, style, energy and looks. All he had was money.

Oh, and his wife, I suppose.

I tried to give the reasonable approach. I often find it helps when someone is screaming. 'Perhaps we ought to go to the tavern and talk this over? I am sure that—'

'You'd like that, wouldn't you? No, black-hearted, black-souled Blackjack, you are never walking to a tavern again. You with your whoring about! What, you think I'd let you loose to go and chase another man's wife? You may not have much respect for other people and their wives, but I have enough respect for them to want to protect them from shame and humiliation at your pursuit of their womenfolk!'

'It's not my fault if . . .' I suddenly realized that saying it wasn't my fault if his wife desired me, perhaps wasn't the safest topic of conversation. I closed my mouth.

'Yes? Yes?'

'Nothing.'

'Go on, say it! Not your fault if my wife wanted to lie with you, that's what you were going to say, isn't it? Eh? Well?'

'No, no. Nothing of the sort. I'm sure your good wife is far too enamoured of you to want to seek out alternatives.'

'Really? Then you will be surprised to hear that she succumbed to my persuasion, then? I had to beat it out of her, but she admitted to lying with you after I thrashed her! Eh? What, no more amusing little tales? No more jokes? No entertainments to share with us?'

I didn't like that 'us'. It struck me that Saul Appleby was by no means the sort of man to kill a fellow in cold blood – nor, I hoped in hot. However, if he had brought accomplices with him, they may well have been paid to murder me. That was not an appealing consideration.

'Oh, damn you!' he screeched, and suddenly my hood was ripped from my head and I could see my captors.

It was not reassuring.

'Oh, hallo, Master Appleby,' I said. And although I was alarmed, no one would have been able to tell.

He sneered at me. It wasn't a good look, especially when he resorted to kicking me and swearing. For such a small man, he had a powerful kick, I have to say. I was forced to try to roll away, and avoid the torrent of abuse as well as his boots.

Behind me, I discovered, were the two men. The first who

had followed me to my house, as it now seemed, and his companion, the man who had been in front of me when I was struck down. His beard was thick and dark with spatters of grey, so he wasn't as young as the other. I mutely begged them, but they watched with every sign of indifference as Saul continued to batter me.

'Just stop!' I cried at last, when the pain was growing.

'Why should I?'

'You're wrong. I never did lie with your wife! She was lying to make you jealous!'

'Why should she want to make . . . me . . . jealous!' he screamed, kicking to emphasize his words.

'Maybe you don't pay her enough attention! How should I know? I hardly know your wife!'

'You know her so little that you see her regularly! Yes, I know all, Blackjack!'

I looked up at the two again, but saw little sympathy there. It did not look as though I was going to be able to count on their aid. Tears began to spring in my eyes and I had to blink them away.

'Take off his hosen. I want to cut off his tarse,' Appleby said.

I tried to fold to protect my cods, but with the rope at ankles and wrists, it was impossible. I could have wept as Appleby stood before me, a wolfish grin on his face, slowly drawing a knife from his belt.

But this seemed to be the final straw for the two with him. The bearded one glanced at his companion and then shook his head. 'No. You wanted to scare him, and we were happy to help with that. He's been scared, but we aren't going to kill him or cut off his cods. You'll have to do that on your own.'

I could have kissed his feet, had I been able to roll to him, but my poor, bruised body was incapable of travelling that far.

'I paid you!'

'You paid us to catch him and bring him here. We've done that.'

'Give me my money back!'

Now the bearded man's expression became as black as his hair. 'Try to take it back.'

'But I wanted you to help with him and let me have my revenge!'

'I think we've helped you enough.'

'God's bones! He's been swiving my wife, man!'

'Well, as he said, if you let your wife loose to do that, it's your fault, not his,' said the other fellow. I began to look on him more positively. I could almost forgive his following me to my home.

'Then go, both of you! I'll do it myself!' Appleby said.

I peered up at the two, pleading with them to save me, but there was no answering kindness in their eyes. Their sympathy extended so far, but no further. They turned on their heels and left. I tried to call them back, but my throat seemed to have dried up, and I could not make a sound beyond a slight bleating.

'Let's see what she found so enticing, then,' Appleby said.

I tried to fix my knees together, but bound as I was, I could not protect my member and ballocks. All I could do was roll away, which I did as fast as I could. With legs bent and ankles at my arse, it was not possible to hurry, and he was after me like a ferret seeing a rabbit, with the nastiest fixed grin on his face I have ever seen on a man. It was an expression I would see in my nightmares for years to come, with luck. But then he caught my codpiece and sliced the bindings. I could feel the sudden coolness, and I confess I screamed.

'Shut up. Shut up, shut up, shut up!' he shouted, the blade resting seriously uncomfortably underneath my proudest piece. And then I screamed again as I felt the blade drag at my skin, and I closed my eyes in horror.

And there was a clatter of a blade striking stone, and then a sort of sob. I opened my eyes cautiously, to see him standing with his forearm on the wall, his face resting on it, while he choked with emotion. I cast a glance downwards, and was glad to see that I was still entire. The relief was such that I almost fainted, but managed to swallow back the bile that had risen, and began to breathe more easily.

Without his companions to back him up, I had been fearful that he might stab me in an ecstasy of rage, jealousy and sheer nastiness. However it was perfectly clear that there was no such possibility. He was not the sort of fellow to murder his victim while tied up and on the ground before him. And there was no chance that he would willingly threaten a man like me if I were unbound and able to grab my own dagger. He was not made from that mould. If he had other men in his pay with him, then perhaps he would try to kick or stab a man, but not alone.

'Could you please release me?' I said after some moments.

He turned to me, his face a picture of misery for a moment, and then he appeared to recognize me, and he snarled something particularly rude about my mother before returning to his solitary conversation with the wall. While he did so, I sat gazing longingly at the knife on the ground beside my codpiece. It looked so appealing there, rather than in the hands of a lunatic determined to castrate me. It represented freedom with a hilt. If only I could grasp it and use it to cut my bonds – but if you have ever been tied as I was, you will know that it's impossible. The mere act of rolling over to place myself near the blade was utterly impractical; the idea of rubbing my wrists near that hideously sharp blade when it might leap and jerk, unfixed as it was, was enough to make my toes tingle. It made me feel quite faint. I had heard of people who had cut their wrists, and tales told of their long, languishing agonies as their life's blood seeped from their wounds. It was not something I was prepared to attempt for myself.

'Saul, come. This is all a horrible mistake. Release me, I pray. We can talk about this somewhere in comfort, rather than here.'

It took all my powers of persuasion, but at long last the fool wandered to me and slashed at the rope at my ankles. In little time my legs were free, and I could sit wincing as pins and needles stabbed at both feet with a horrible regularity. It was quite impossible to think of standing, and meanwhile, my hands had lost all feeling, and I had to plead with the foggy carrion before he finally ambled over and I felt his knife's blade slicing through the last of my bonds. I did have a moment's concern, when the man remained behind me, and it occurred to me that a man who was too cowardly to strike a man in the breast, might yet be courageous enough to stab him in the back. It was all down to the eyes, I think. A fellow might flinch and quail at killing a man who was looking him in the eye, but to inflict the same damage from behind was easier.

In any event, I was safe. As soon as I felt the ropes fall from my wrists, I brought my hands before me. My mitts were pasty and useless for quite some while, and felt as much a part of me as two crabs. Then, as the colour returned, so did the pins and needles in them, too, and I could have howled with the pain.

'I'm glad that hurts,' he said with a sneer.

I punched him then, right on the nose, and discovered that pins and needles are not as painful as a beak on the fist. While I capered, clutching my hand to my breast, he fell back to the wall, both hands on his battered snout.

'Why'd you do that?' he demanded peevishly. 'Look! You've broken it! I could have you in court for that!'

'By the Mass! Look at my cods, you fool!' I snarled, shaking my bruised paw. It hurt like hell. 'You dare to accuse me of assaulting you? You tried to castrate me, all because of some nonsense about me chasing your wife! Look at me, you've ruined my codpiece, you nearly ruined *me*! I could . . .'

I loomed over him menacingly. He had dropped his knife when I punched him, and now he quailed as I clenched my fists again. If he had spoke one more word, I swear I would have battered him to a pulp, but as it was, the fellow looked so pathetic and miserable that I couldn't. I have said many times before, that I am constitutionally incapable of killing people, and much though my bold, warrior-like soul was demanding compensation for the sheer horror of that knife's blade at the root of my prickle and ballocks, it was pointless. I could no more kill him or beat him than jump to the moon. Besides, I knew how much it hurt to belabour a face. My hand felt as though it would never be the same again, and I had no desire to injure that hand again, nor to give my other hand similar treatment.

I saw that my weaponry was all stacked on a stool at the far side of the chamber, and I went to it, slowly gathering up my property as the feeling returned to my hands and muttering under my breath about foolish merchants and their ridiculous ideas, while visions of his wife naked in my bed teased me wickedly.

Picking up my codpiece, it took some effort to tie the laces and make it function once more, but I did eventually manage it, even with my fingers feeling as dextrous as clumps of pudding.

Finally, with a last, contemptuous glance at Saul, I was about to leave, when his abject misery struck a chord with me. My hand on the door, I was torn. He was sitting, his rump on the dirt of the floor, a hand at his broken nose, whimpering and whiffling. I couldn't leave him there like that. It would be like deserting a waif in mid-winter.

'Master Appleby, let us forget our altercation. Let me buy you a warm brandy.'

It was not as if we were hard-pressed to find a good inn. The area was filled with drinking dens of all types. The lower alehouses, I knew, Master Appleby would not wish to enter, since they were too far below his perception of his own status, but there were plenty of good taverns and wine shops in the vicinity, and we repaired to one not too far from Bishopsgate. There, he insisted that he should buy drinks. After a short reflection, we both chose wine in preference to brandy, and then he realized he was hungry, too, as was I, so we purchased a couple of beef pies, and sat near a fire eating and supping as contentedly as two companions of long-standing.

'My nose hurts,' he said, once we had finished our meal. His voice had a curiously nasal quality now.

'Not as much as my . . .'

'I apologize for that, master. I was so enraged, convinced that you must be the rake who was putting the cuckold's horns on me.'

'And your wife actually told you . . .'

'No, she refused. I was merely certain it must be you when you visited her the other day. I had instructed a man to follow you home. I had to act, you understand? That man discovered your home, and I hired him and a friend to help me today.'

'If they had been hardier, they might have killed me on your command,' I said with some heat.

'Believe me, I am glad that they were right folk,' he said earnestly. 'I beg of you, forgive my foolishness!'

I drew away slightly, anxious that the fool might fall into my lap and begin weeping again. That is no way to behave in a London wine shop, after all. Then I gave a disdainful sniff and gazed away.

'Master, will you not forgive me? No harm was done . . . to you,' he added, his fingers pawing gently at his swollen snout.

'I could even now be dead, my throat cut, and cast into the Thames, if your commands to those two had been heeded,' I said. 'The honesty of those two men was all that saved my life! You would have had me murdered here!'

'Oh, master!'

I gave every sign of relenting in the face of his appeals. 'Very well, but assure me of this: you will give up such foolishness as trying to hunt your wife's lover. Fie! I believe you are wronging the woman! I have ever seen her to be a most chaste and sensible woman. When I lived in your street, I never saw a man with her who could have been thought to behave disrespectfully or lewdly in her presence.' This was true. I did keep a close eye on her, for after all, if a man were to be entertained by her, I wished to be assured that it was not some poxed cod's head who could pass to me his infection.

'I swear it!'

'You will treat her with respect and honour?'

'I will!'

'Then I shall forgive you, Master Appleby,' I said loftily, and we drank a toast to friendship and forgiveness.

I swore to myself that I would entertain his wife as soon as possible, just to take revenge for the terrifying experience to which he had subjected me. But for now, it was pleasant to be drinking. I had no idea beforehand of his position in the city, but now, as we chatted, I learned that he aspired to become an alderman himself.

'It is a wonderful position, after all,' he said, his chest puffed up like a pigeon's. 'A man with such status can truly be said to be amongst the aristocracy of the city. Aldermen run the city for the benefit of all.'

'Do you know many aldermen?' I asked.

'Oh, yes. I am acquainted with all those who serve at present,' he said with a kind of wine-inspired smugness. He had reached that stage of inebriation where the world could be viewed with paternalistic affability. Any thoughts of my possible involvement with his wife had dissipated as the tide in the jug of wine gradually went out.

'Do you know our alderman, William Kirk?'

'Oh, yes. I have had dealings with him,' Appleby said. He laid a finger aside his nose and winced. 'Aye, yes, one of those fellows a man would be cautious with.'

'Really? He did not strike me as a dangerous man. His wife, now, she was terrifying.'

'Oh, ah! Kirk would take the nails from your fingers if it would serve him. I heard tell that he paid for an assassin to remove a past alderman, just so that he could take the post. He had made sure that he would be invited, if there were a seat available, and then, lo! A seat was made ready for him.'

That gave me pause. He had not appeared that determined, but a man might easily be driven by money or, perhaps, even a particularly over-demanding wife, to acts that he would not usually have considered. I have some experience of women, of course, and I know that many can be vixens if they do not have their way. A woman with ambition can be a terrible thing. It doesn't matter what her motivation, whether it be competition with her neighbours, a desire for a larger house, a wish to have her wardrobe replaced with furs, all too often a fellow seeking a quiet life would accede to his wife's demands, no matter what. In Kirk's case, could he have resorted to murder to satisfy his wife's desire for status and position? Quite possibly.

'Do you mean the alderman called Bonner?'

'Yes, Adam Bonner. He was a mercer, a good man, so I have heard, who was very enthusiastic about supporting charitable ventures and gave himself up to patronage of those in a worse position. But that didn't help him. He was found one

morning in the lanes near Mercer's hall, where he had been
enticed, so it was said, by a young draggle-tail. When he
reached the corner of an alley, he was set upon and slain most
cruelly, his throat cut. Nobody ever learned who had committed
the crime, but Kirk became an alderman in his place, a post
he retains to this day.' His face took on a wistful expression.
'I should like to be an alderman. My wife would regard me
with more interest, were I an alderman. It is hard,' he said
dolefully, leaning towards me as if sharing a secret unknown
to most, 'to have a wife who does not respect a fellow. She
did when I first engaged her to become my wife. Her father
was pleased to have snared such a successful man as me, but
she has been so uncaring in recent years . . . it is hard when
a wife doesn't show proper respect.'

I said nothing. It was on the tip of my tongue to advise
him on how to deal with Susan, but a moment's reflection
persuaded me that such a course may not be the most judi-
cious. In preference I made a few sympathetic noises chosen
to indicate support.

At least now I had something which I could follow up. I
left him still sitting mournfully staring at his cup, while
I hobbled outside on stiff legs.

There were plenty of men who would take a fee to murder
a man, but it struck me that it was curious that two murders
occurred in the parish only a year apart, and both committed
in the same manner. Could the same person have killed both?

When I turned into my lane, I was intrigued to see that lights
were moving in the church. On a whim, I turned my steps
towards the west door and peeped inside.

The damage done had been all but mended. The broken
struts and lathes replaced, the screen returned to its former
state, and I could see that the communion cup had been to
visit a metalsmith who had teased out the lumps and dents. It
reflected the candlelight smoothly once more.

'Father?'

I called out hesitantly, for the priest was kneeling before
the altar, his hands clasped in earnest prayer, head bowed,
eyes screwed tight shut. He looked like a man pleading for

absolution. In the light from three guttering candles, his face looked horribly unhealthy. A man's face in such light will usually glow with a ruddy hue, but tonight the priest looked waxy and almost greenish.

On hearing my call, his head snapped about and he stared at me with apparent terror, his mouth dropping open, eyes filled with something like panic.

'Father, what is the matter?'

'I . . . my wife . . .'

'She is unwell?'

'A man came and accused her of seducing me. They forced me back here, away from her. At the moment when she needed me most, to try to come to terms with our loss, the bastards dragged me away!'

'Who?'

'The catchpoles. Sergeants. I don't know! Men with staffs of office who have more power than they should, and who can wield it with impunity! Men who would come between a man and his wife and force them apart even when the wedded couple have just suffered the loss of their son!'

'Why would they have hunted you down?' I wondered aloud. After all, while many sought to persecute the occasional priest for misbehaviour, and Heaven knew that the queen was keen to do so, and had stated so often, yet it was unusual for such a pursuit to be conducted so swiftly.

'Because . . . because of the night Rachel Nailor was murdered,' he said. And then he gave a sob. 'Because of what I did!'

I gaped. Yes, I gaped. I had heard much which had shocked me in recent months, but to hear this obvious admission of guilt was not what I had expected. It is not common to hear a man of any sort confess to the slaughter of a woman, let alone a priest. And never in the confines of his own church. '*You* did it?'

'*Yes*! I regret it, of course, I have been wrestling with my conscience ever since, but I was overwhelmed!'

'*You* did it,' I said. I moved away slightly.

'You have to understand: I was forced to leave Jane and my boy. I should *never* have agreed to leave them destitute.

If they were to suffer, so should I, in God's name! I should have stayed with them.'

'And that was why you did it?' I said. He stood and moved towards me, rather like a man who was asleep and yet walking, I edged back further. I had a sudden premonition of the priest covered in gore, laughing, his face smothered in my life's blood as he bayed at the moon. It was all too easy to imagine him cutting my throat. After all, a priest who could murder a woman like Rachel out of some twisted form of revenge for an unfair law, was more than capable of slaughtering me too. A madman was said to have the strength of a score of men, or something, I had heard once. This priest deserved to be installed in Bedlam, it was plain.

'Yes. I was driven mad when I heard of my poor boy's death.'

I took another two paces back. My heart was in my throat, and it felt as though the constriction must choke me. 'But I've done you no harm!' I said. It may have sounded a little squeaky, but that was the blockage causing that.

'I didn't say you have,' he said, puzzlement washing over his face.

'Rachel Nailor didn't either, did she?' I said.

'No. She was a perfect gentlewoman,' he said, his increasing confusion evident. 'Are you well, Master Blackjack?'

'I am fine,' I squeaked, stepping back again.

He was holding out his hands like a supplicant now, and I was convinced that soon I would be dead. I grabbed for my pistol, but in my terror, the slippery metal slipped from my hand and it fell to the ground. He was clearly mad, he could pull my head off. That thought was enough to set me gibbering.

I had managed to reverse all the way to the back of the church. Here a few timbers, no doubt from the renovation of the screen, had been left haphazardly across the aisle. I realized that afterwards. For the present, all I knew was that something prevented my rearward travel, and I gave a loud shriek of terror, and tumbled to the ground.

'Master Blackjack!' he cried, and ran to me.

I was having none of that, and tried to disentangle myself from the baulks of wood hurriedly, in the process managing to get my cloak entangled in some trash, and as he approached, I was mewling to myself.

'Master, please,' he said, offering his hand. I tried to pull mine away, but he grabbed it insistently, and with his aid I was drawn to my feet again. Being a competent man with a sword, I would have unsheathed it in an instant, were it not for the fact that he turned from me and stared once more at the altar.

'I have already made my peace with the Lord. I have begged Him to understand that when I did all that damage, it was not a reflection of my feelings towards Him, but the overwhelming confusion and despair at the death of my son. If only I had remained with him and Jane, perhaps Peterkin would still be living now. It was unjust of me to desert them, it was cowardly and despicable. It was my disgust with my own behaviour that led to my outburst of rage and unseemly desecration.'

'And the murder,' I could not refrain from mentioning. I wanted to clap a hand over my mouth as soon as I spoke, suddenly fearing that he might be provoked by my thoughtless words.

'Murder? I had nothing to do with that,' he said, a small frown of confusion on his face. 'Good God, no! I was brought to such rage on hearing of my boy's death that I swept the items off the altar and broke the screen, but that was all. It was the enormity of my crime that caused my destructive rampage, and as soon as I had seen what I had done, I fled. I had nothing to do with Rachel's death.'

I breathed a sigh of relief so complete, I felt quite faint. For a moment or two there, I had been convinced that mine would be the next body discovered in the vestry.

When Peter turned to me once more, there was a sadness in his eyes that told of his inner turmoil. He essayed a brief smile, but it never touched his eyes. It was obvious that his soul was tormented by the loss of his son, and by his feelings of guilt at deserting his family. 'What will you do?' I asked.

'I will go to my wife, and damn the consequences,' he said. 'What is there for me here? I cannot perform my priestly duties even if I want to, since the church must be reconsecrated.

Blood has been spilled here, and that evil must be washed
away and purified by the bishop. To me it makes more sense
that I should return to my duties to my family, rather than a
flock which I cannot service. I should be glad to return to my
calling, were I permitted to enjoy the comfort of my spouse,
but if the law refuses me that, then I am less than competent
to serve the parish as priest. I cannot do it while constantly
thinking of my woman and how she fares.'

'Is that why you were always railing at me? Jealousy?'

He gave me a quick glare at that, and I was instantly
reminded both of his first sermon, directed at me as it had
seemed, and by the suspicion that he was a madman. I took
an involuntary pace away from him.

'*Jealousy*?' he repeated, and then his eyes drifted away from
me and took in the nave and all the pews. 'Is that what you
thought? Perhaps, yes. After all, you and the other men here
could leave at any point and go and talk with the women of
the parish. On the first day you came here, I could tell you
were eyeing the women in the pews, and after the service I
saw you with Rachel Nailor, and you seemed to be enjoying
her company. She was a strong, intelligent woman, after all.
And very desirable, of course. I could tell you were attracted
to her.'

'Only a fool would not be.'

'So, yes. Perhaps it was jealousy on my part. I knew that
outside this church, out in the real world, men like you were
meeting with women like her and enjoying the natural desires
of the flesh, while I was cast out of my own marriage, forced
to desert my wife and child, rejected from society. An outcast
fully absorbed in the parish, yet not a part of it. Others could
marry and enjoy the companionship of a good woman whereas
I must toil in loneliness. Yes, I suppose I was jealous. Who
would not be?'

That was a question I could not answer. However, I could
ask my own. 'When you left here after spoiling the altar and
nave, was it possible that Rachel Nailor could have been
dead in the vestry already?'

'Had she been murdered before I left? Surely not. No, I am
sure she could not. I was here from the late afternoon, and

did not leave until after dark had started to fall. I doubt she was here before I went to the vestry after my lunch, so I assume she must have come here after I left for Jane.'

'You did not leave the church at all? Not even to fetch a drink or food?'

'I was called away briefly,' he admitted. 'Yes, Master Croke came and asked me to meet with a friend of his, a most surly and ungracious Spaniard.'

'What did he want?'

Father Peter grimaced. 'I think Master Croke wanted to show how even recalcitrant priests were being forced to adhere to the Catholic faith. He was showing off, but he concealed that in a talk about hearing confession.'

'Were you out for long?'

'Not terribly, no. And then, as I reached the door to return inside, I learned of Peterkin's death, and the rest of that evening is blurred in my memory. I know I went inside, and the effect of Croke and his friend's arrogance, the thought of the Catholic church and all it had done to my family . . . well, I became enraged and committed the acts of destruction you saw.'

'When Croke spoke to you, where was that? In sight of the church?'

'Yes, although I did have my back to it. But I was only out of sight of the church for a very short while.'

No doubt it was a short while, I thought. But it was long enough, perhaps, for Rachel to slip into the church and for someone else to meet her there and cut her throat and escape. Unless Rachel and her killer arrived later, when Peter had already fled.

But there was one other thing that occurred to me. 'Father, I had heard that William Kirk was here that evening. Did you not see him?'

'The alderman? No, I did not. He was not here. But then, he and Croke do not get on well. Perhaps he left when he saw Croke arrive?'

When I returned home, I found Raphe in the kitchen with Cecily. They were laughing together at my table, and it was some moments before I could attract their attention and point out that I was in need of a glass of wine.

With a bad grace Raphe rose, drew off a jug of wine, and passed it to me. I was astonished to be treated in such an indifferent manner, and was so surprised by it that I confess I had walked into my parlour with the wine and a pot in my hand before a suitable response occurred to me. Of course, I should have chastised him immediately, but the moment was already passed, and I could hear the two of them giggling like apprentices after their first taste of ale.

Hector, Raphe's dog, was sitting before the fire, and threw me a lacklustre glance when I sat behind him. 'I know. Raphe has lost interest in you too, hasn't he?' I said.

SEVEN

Friday 2nd April

E arly the next morning, when I left my house, I saw John at the door to the church, but for once he did not appear to want to engage me in conversation, and I was keen to avoid him, so hurried past to Bishopsgate and on to Marbod's house. As I reached the front gate, I saw Moll farther up the road. She bore a basket in the crook of her arm, and I hurried my pace to catch up with her.

Her route took me down the main road towards the centre of the city, and soon I was walking along a baker's row of shops, each with a variety of good loaves of bread and the scent of sweetened cakes set to tempt any jaded palates. They mingled with the odour of fresh meat pies, and I could have easily spent my fortune on a mixture of different pastries. It was always a mistake to leave home before breaking your fast. Just now my belly was rumbling like a slow wagon over cobbles, and I could not help but cast an envious eye at some of the foodstuffs on offer. In the end I succumbed to temptation and bought two meat pies and a custard tart sweetened with honey.

I waited outside the shop. Moll was three doors away from me, making her selection from a range of loaves of bread laid out on the display trestle outside the baker's. Soon she had two loaves, one made from finest white bread, the other cheaper maslin for the servants, no doubt. She had wrapped both in linen and installed them in her basket, and was making her way towards me when she saw me and her face fell. I suppose, were I to be told that a fellow had lured my master to his death, I would also be reluctant to meet the man in the street – or anywhere else for that matter.

'Moll, may I speak to you again, just a little,' I said. I sprayed pastry crumbs at her as I spoke, and she winced and took to patting her clothing to sweep the worst offending fragments away.

'I've told you all I know, master,' she said firmly. 'I di'n't know the boy with the message, and there's an end to it.'

'Rachel always went to church with you. I would gamble that you were her constant companion when she left the house, were you not? She had her two bravos to protect her in the street, but she also had you to keep her company. And with good reason, I am sure, for you are a bright little thing, aren't you?' I said coaxingly.

'What do you mean?' she demanded, as if I had offered her a penny for a back-against-the-wall knee-trembler.

'Nothing!' I protested. 'Only that you are intelligent and quick-witted. Rachel would have wanted your company because you would be more entertaining than others. She needed a companion with a brain rather than the two bullies who guarded her. You were her constant companion, weren't you? Even when she visited me, you joined her.'

'I suppose, but I didn't see who was father to her child,' she said.

There was a clear inference any man could make. I proceeded to make it. 'So you did not see her go out and about with a particular gentleman? You were not with her that last evening?'

'No,' she said, and there were tears in her eyes. 'She walked out without telling me. The bottler and groom were not with her either. It was the message from you that persuaded her to go, I assume.'

'So the message was not necessarily that she should meet me?'

'Yes, it was, but when I delivered it to her, she said that it was ridiculous and she would not leave the house so late. I left her in her room, and it was only later that I realized she had left and gone. When I was asked, all I could say was that you had asked her to meet you in church.'

'She was not in the habit of leaving the building without you?'

'No, master. She would always have me and two men with her. Master Marbod insisted on that.'

Now, I may be considered by some, and especially John Blount, to be less than a match for the brains of the average stone pillar, but that is only because I conceal my intellect carefully. And just now my mind made one of those leaps which shows the level at which a seriously clever man like me can operate.

You see, I was thinking about the way that a woman like Rachel might get herself pregnant. She had not shown any sign of carrying a child in her womb. Only the coroner, and perhaps a wise midwife, had noticed on seeing her corpse. The woman must have been in the early stages of pregnancy, surely, and yet Moll was certain that she had not been available to men outside her house. Clearly that meant only one man could have had access to her. It was a man in her house. And unlikely to be a servant, because if a bottler or groom had tried to put his hand up her skirts, from the little I had seen of her, Rachel Nailor would have not only screamed for her guards, she would have inflicted dire injuries on the unfortunate opportunist. In short, she would have marked him for life with her knife.

Which meant only one man could have been safe: Sir Gerald Marbod himself. It was enough to make me chuckle. After all, Marbod was an honourable enough man, but he was ancient compared with Rachel. Yet, she had left her husband, and now lived at the expense of Marbod. I had a thought: were she to denounce him, declare that he had raped her, what then? Eleanor Marbod would be unlikely to be willing to keep in her house a woman who was such a dread temptation to her husband. If Rachel were to make trouble, Marbod may make her life difficult, perhaps even throw her from his door.

The more I thought of it, the more it struck me as probably. Moll would not be with Rachel every moment of the day and night. She would have other duties to attend to. At any of those times, Gerald could have forced himself upon Rachel. What could she do, where could she go? She had been married, but her marriage was declared illegal by the queen, so she had few choices. She must accept hospitality where it was offered, and if there was a price to be paid, no doubt that was less than the price of losing hearth and home.

But Marbod was a powerful man in the city, and supposedly one of Lady Elizabeth's leading supporters. I could not simply denounce or accuse him.

'Ah! Master Blackjack, and how do I find you today?'

It was Gawtheren Spink, who bustled up to me with that smiling, bubbly demeanour of hers. For a woman of ten more years than me, she was a most appealing wench, I thought again. Enthusiastic and entertaining, with a degree of energy that would be sure to exhaust a bedfellow.

'Mistress Spink, I hope I see you well,' I said, smiling back at her.

'Well, I would be well, but for the thieves in the shambles. The prices they demand for a scrag end of mutton is enough to make a body weep! And as for the cost of an oxtail, well, I cannot describe the men who would seek to rob a poor woman like me, so old and frail.'

'You are still in the full bloom of youth!'

She punched my shoulder like a maiden at her first tease. 'I am old enough to be your mother, master. *Nearly*,' she added quickly. 'But since you are of a mood to pass compliments, how about passing another by treating me to a cup of ale?'

I was happy to agree, and soon we were in the Bull once more, a quart jug on the table, and a pair of cups filled to the brim.

'So, master,' she said, wriggling slightly beside me so that I could feel the warmth of her thigh against mine – a not uncomfortable heat, it must be said. 'How have you been filling your days?'

'I have been seeking to learn who might have killed poor Rachel,' I said.

'And learning much?'

'I think so.'

'Very secretive!' she said playfully.

I was distracted by the sight of Richard Croke at the entrance. He stood and gazed about, looking for someone. I wondered whether it was his Spanish companion. 'What does he want?' I wondered aloud.

'Croke? Most of the time he wants his ears boxed,' Gawtheren said with feeling. 'He's a miserable, dry soul. He has business with the Spanish and thinks himself above ordinary folk like us. He's suddenly the most religious man in the city, he would have you think.'

His eyes lit on Anderson sitting in a farther corner, and Croke strode over to join him.

'He is not sincere?' I asked, my eyes following him.

'He wasn't worried about religion before the queen changed the laws. But he's always looking to the next opportunity, and just now that means being devoted to the Catholic faith. He watches everyone for any lapses.'

'You mean he could be an intelligencer for the Spanish?' I said. Suddenly I recalled my musings just before Ned tried to use my head as a punch-ball. Could Croke have learned of Rachel's journey to France, and his Spaniard friend, or he, had killed her?

'Perhaps,' she said. 'But with the queen marrying a Spaniard, many seek to feather their beds.'

'Few as obviously as Croke.'

'Ah, well, he's not that clever,' she said.

'Who is?'

'Stephen Anderson is a clever fellow,' she said. 'But I don't see much of him. Mistress Anderson does not like me.'

'I had heard that, because of Elias,' I said. 'But at least Kate Anderson is not someone I should miss, were I not allowed to become her friend,' I said.

She chuckled. It was a good, dirty chuckle, and she leaned into me so her upper arm and shoulder met mine. They were warm too. I took a deep gulp of ale. I was feeling a little warm myself.

'Katherine Anderson has always had a dislike of me, but yes, you're right. It's not something I am concerned about. She is a poisonous biddy. She never had any fun when she was young, and seeks to burn away any passions that others might hold. I'm not like that, you see. I like passion, I do,' she said, and drank off the rest of her cup, before refilling both our cups. 'Katherine was always the sort to suck dry any pleasure from company. She's jealous of people like me, I think.'

'Why?' I asked. I could tell that my voice had risen slightly, and repeated it in a more masculine tone, 'I mean, *why?*'

'Oh, she knows I get more out of life and men than she does,' Gawtheren said quietly. Her mouth was very close to my ear, and I could feel the hot breath on my flesh. I was at that moment grateful for the size of my codpiece. With her full-scale assault on my male defences, I felt myself rising to the onslaught. She continued breathily, 'And she's right!'

'She is married, so surely she is content,' I said.

'Yes, she's married; but I'm not, and that offends her. I have a child, and that seems to her to be reason to despise me.'

'She would feel the same about Rachel, then, since she was with child?' I said.

'Yes, I dare say,' she agreed, but her tone was markedly cooler at the mention of Rachel.

'How about Madam Marbod? Would she not feel the same?'

'Her?' Gawtheren forgot to seduce me in her surprise. 'You think she . . .? Oh, you mean perhaps Gerald Marbod had been riding Rachel?' She draped herself over my side. I felt a hot little hand rest on my thigh, where it began to stroke. 'Possibly,' she said.

'Do you think he was?' I said.

'He's very rich, and what woman can refuse a successful, wealthy man?' she said, still kneading my thigh.

'He has always struck me as a decent fellow,' I admitted. 'He sent men to guard Rachel when she was out of his house, he looked after her when she was destitute, and—'

'He is a kind man,' she said. 'It makes a body wonder, doesn't it?'

'Wonder what? *Ooh!*'

Her tongue had flicked into my ear, and I yelped. It was startling. Her seduction technique was brazen in the extreme, and I found it off-putting. I mean to say, I have no objection to women trying to ensnare me. I enjoy it, and with my good looks and easy charm, I have found it a commonplace. But Gawtheren was that bit older, and more experienced, and I found her alarming.

'What?' she asked, all innocent and wide-eyed like a virgin in a brothel.

'You startled me.'

She chuckled again. 'Anyway, it makes me think. A man like him, looking after a woman so carefully. Did you not think he might have been pricking his lance in the wrong scabbard?'

'I . . . what?'

'Think about it. There he is, an upright, honourable man. He takes in a woman like her, with long legs, bounteous figure and big, "Come protect me" eyes, and you don't think he wouldn't take advantage? How many men haven't had their uses for maids in their homes? A servant girl is available, more often than not. A woman who's seen her marriage annulled against her choice, and who has no means of support, can hardly refuse to comfort her patron, can she?'

'But Marbod? He's too old for that sort of thing.'

She gave me a very straight look then that gave me to understand she might know considerably more about a man of his age and his passion than I could.

I emptied my cup. 'I think I need to return to my house,' I said.

'Oh, good. I haven't seen inside it yet,' she said.

'Eh? No, I meant, I have to go back and do some work,' I said.

'That's fine, although I haven't heard it called work before,' she said, and her hand was back on my thigh.

You will guess at my feelings when I say that at that moment it was a relief to see Moll at the inn's back door. She was, at least, a distraction. I was surprised to see her peer inside, and then she suddenly withdrew. I wondered whether she had seen Croke or Anderson, or someone else who had alarmed her.

Who was Moll seeking? It was curious at the very least. Although I had no inkling that there could be something to do with Rachel's murder, I was suspicious enough to get up and follow her. If nothing else, it was an excuse to leave

Gawtheren. Just at that moment, I was finding her single-minded pursuit of me to be terrifying.

What could she be doing here? After all, a young maid was not safe at the best of times, walking about the city on her own, and as for entering an inn – well, she could be mistaken for a draggle-tail looking for custom.

The door where I saw her gave on to a short alleyway, filled with the rank odour of urine where revellers and others had hitched their codpieces and relieved themselves against the walls. I hurried past that, trying not to think about the splashing of the puddles, and found myself in a courtyard with houses on each side.

I leaned against a wall before I could be seen, and was immediately glad of my concealment, for even as I gazed at her, she was joined by the Spaniard, whose eyes wandered all about the court as if expecting me, or someone, to be following him.

He went to Moll and immediately began to talk very quickly, but in a low tone. Moll stood close, but she looked scared, and I was sure that she was an unwilling participant in this little scene, not that she made any attempt to leave.

Shortly afterwards, the Spaniard left, slipping away by another alley at the farther side of the court. I watched as Moll stood there, growing rather tearful, and then she returned the way she had come. I had to sidle into a dark doorway as she hurried past, her head down, hood covering her features.

As soon as I felt safe, I leaned out, and saw her walking past the inn once more.

All of which made me wonder what in the name of God she had been doing with the Spaniard. Was she spying on Marbod for the Spanish? Was she a messenger for Marbod? Did that mean Marbod was an agent for the Spanish? If that was so, he could have betrayed everything about the plan for Rachel to travel to Paris. He would have to be a supporter of Queen Mary, rather than the Lady Elizabeth.

And either he had killed Rachel, or his ally the Spaniard had.

* * *

I was glad to find Croke and Anderson still together. The two remained at their table with a large bowl of meaty pottage between them, a white loaf of bread broken open on a board. They invited me to join their mess, and I was nothing loath. I soon had a stool at their table, and a fresh bowl before me, a mouthful of bread filling my mouth, while the two discussed the sale of a number of hides of leather. It was a boring conversation.

'You were here just now with Gawtheren Spink, I thought,' Croke said, once they had finished their deal-making. He was sitting back, licking his spoon of excess juice, but his eye glittered. I sensed a little frisson of tension. 'Has she left you?'

'Yes. She . . . she sat and had a little ale with me,' I said.

'She can be very friendly,' Croke said.

'Yes.'

'She likes to associate with younger men. Well, any men, really.'

'Enough, Richard,' Anderson said.

'I only wanted to talk about Gawtheren a little.'

'He has heard enough about her already,' Anderson said, rather more forcefully. 'Now, are you content with the price I quoted?'

'Yes, our business is concluded.'

'Good.'

'So, Master Blackjack, what were you discussing with Gawtheren?' Croke asked.

'Me?' My mind at the time was fixed on Moll. 'Oh, um . . .'

'I hope she was not overly flirtatious?'

'Leave it, Richard,' Anderson said.

'There is no need for you to worry about her.'

'I know what you're trying to do, Richard. Leave it.'

'What am I trying to do?'

'I have business to attend to. I thank you for your company, Master Blackjack. I will speak with you later, Richard.'

Anderson stood, and although his face was smiling, his eyes were not. They were cold and hard as flint. Science tells us that eyes emit a beam that brings images to the mind. If there was any power in his glance, Croke would have been burned to a cinder on the spot, and probably most of the inn about him. Anderson spat on the floor, turned and stalked from the room.

For my part, I merely stared at Croke with confusion. 'Why did you want to make him so angry?'

'It pleased me.'

I looked at him more closely. He had the same expression as always. His eyes were slightly hooded, and he had a twist to his lips that made him appear cynical. 'Why would his annoyance please you? You want to take pleasure in other men's misfortune or difficulty?'

'Occasionally, perhaps.' His eyes drifted away from me. 'We are in difficult times, we English. We have the threat of war hanging over us, we have the unsettling change in our alliances now that our queen has taken a Spaniard to her husband, and not least of our troubles is the resentment caused by our glorious return to the Holy Catholic Church. Anderson invested mightily in King Henry's religion, and he regrets its loss; he is also a man who has loved many times, and has two sons from different women.'

'You have no children,' I stated.

He did not meet my eye. 'We have not been fortunate. We had three, and all died young. But,' he added, 'I have at least succeeded in business.'

'What is your business with the Spaniards?'

'I bring in their wines and send back our own goods.'

'There is more to your work than that, surely?'

'What do you mean?'

'I have seen you many times with your Spaniard friend. Not many people trust the Spaniards now.'

'But many people are peculiarly stupid,' Croke said. He picked up his cup and drank quickly.

'You were outside the church the evening Rachel Nailor died, weren't you?' I said.

He turned now, and I was astonished to see that his eyes ran with tears. 'Yes, I was there. And I was angry, bitter and desperate. But if you are asking me, did I murder Rachel, the answer is no. I did not.'

'But you did see her there.'

'Only very briefly. I was with my companion, Diego of Toledo. We gave her a good day and continued on our way.'

'You did not follow her into the church?'

'You think I might confess to murdering her? No, Master Blackjack. That was not us. It was not him nor me. We were with each other from that moment on.'

I returned to my house and to my not inconsiderable relief, I opened the door to discover that my cook and servant were not writhing on the floor before the fire. When I called out to Cecily, she was meek enough and brought me some oatcakes she had prepared earlier. They were delicious, and I was reminded that this young woman might be rather a long-faced and humourless wench, but she could definitely cook, and if the cost of having edible food presented daily was that my manservant occasionally had an opportunity to shake the sheets with her, was that such a bad arrangement?

I had plenty to occupy me as I sat sipping wine.

Kirk, from all he had said, was clearly enamoured of Rachel. For all I knew, maybe he had fathered a child on her. Who could tell who the father was of any child? It was easy to see who a mother was at birth, but even at that time a man must take on trust the fidelity of the woman. Also, no matter what Kirk wanted to think, Sir Gerald Marbod was still a likely candidate for the father. Few patriarchs would refuse the opportunity of a young maid if she was available, and many young maids saw it as a significant step on the ladder to give their master a child – although all too soon, many of those same maids found their expectations dashed. Kirk had seen Rachel outside the church; could she have told him that the baby wasn't his? Perhaps he was so enraged at her infidelity that he lashed out. He followed her into the church and drew his knife . . . He could not cope with the idea that she was taking his child away, because he was so committed to the idea that he had himself fathered the child, even if that was wishful thinking on his part.

What was Moll doing, going to see that Spaniard today? Why would she? And what could be the subject of their discussions? Moll, the quiet, shy, anxious young maid who was constant companion to Rachel, and who seemed loyal to her master, although she was plainly scared of Eleanor Marbod. I could easily imagine that she was a hard taskmistress, with her cold and austere manner. Sir Gerald was a more approachable, kindly looking person. Moll had more devotion to him than his wife.

I finished my drink and set the cup down on the table. I would have to speak to John Blount in the morning and make it clear what I had learned. It seemed to me that the most likely man with a motive to kill off Rachel, Lady Elizabeth's ambassador, was the weakly merchant, Master Croke.

At last I was safe. If he were to accept that, my innocence was confirmed!

EIGHT

Saturday 3rd April

The sun was peering through my window when I stirred the next morning. I was relieved to find that even though I had consumed the better part of three jugs of wine, the quality was not in doubt. Although I did experience a sensation of being slightly jaded, there was nothing worse than that. I recalled the evening when Rachel had arrived to tell me of the proposed journey, and the horrible head I suffered from the following morning. It was truly horrible, and my belly had felt like I'd swallowed poison. I was much happier today.

I suppose I was slow. I have no doubt that many other, more suspicious fellows would have wondered at the sudden impact of my poorer quality wine. After all, I was used to large quantities. It is not in my nature to boast, but it cannot be denied that my capacity for strong wine has always been a matter of jealousy to others. I have a strong head and stomach.

However, it did strike me this morning that I had been significantly under the weather that day, and even when I drank more than I had that night, I usually woke up feeling considerably fresher. And that was when I began to have a niggling doubt: was it possible that my wine had been tampered with?

As I recalled, I had gone into the buttery to see where the wine was, and had found a full jug, which I had consumed. It was ready poured, and a cup was beside it. I had made the natural assumption that my useless servant had decanted it for me. It had seemed obvious at the time. Now, however, I began to wonder.

Down in the kitchen, I discovered Raphe and Cecily suspiciously red-faced and close together, as though they had been engaged in a clinch moments before my appearance. I ignored

Cecily while she moved about, heating a pot on the fire and preparing a breakfast for me.

No, my attention was fixed on Raphe. 'When Mistress Rachel was here, last Sunday,' I began. 'I said to you that I wanted wine, but you didn't bring it. Instead you went out with Cecily. When I looked, I found a barrel had been broached, and a jug filled. Was that you who drew off the wine for me and forgot?'

Cecily, the clumsy bint, missed with an egg, and the fire sputtered and sparked as the egg fell into it. There was a lot of smoke, and I can assure you that burned yolk doesn't smell pleasant.

Raphe was scowling like a cat seeing a mouse steal his food. 'I didn't pour you wine, no. I told you, I was out with Cecily at church.'

'In that case who . . .' I suddenly knew.

There was a good reason why Moll never seemed comfortable with me. It was rare enough for any woman not to be at ease in my presence for her behaviour to appear curious. And now I knew exactly why.

'I am going out,' I said.

'What about your breakfast?' Cecily said with a kind of panic. She hated the idea of waste.

'You can give it to Raphe,' I said.

All I knew just then was, I wanted to be away from the fumes of burning yolk. And besides, I needed to see John Blount urgently.

I opened the door, and squeaked in alarm.

There, outside, was a huge, hulking figure blocking my way. In my mind, it looked like an enormous demon about to grab me. I tried to slam the door, but before I could, Ned the Gorilla had already entered.

I eyed him with some disgust. 'What do you want?'

'I thought you wanted a guard.'

'You want me to pay you again?'

He shrugged. 'If you want me with you.'

I had a sudden memory of Pudge and his companions, then a knife held against my throat. They were pictures which melded with the thought of Saul leering at me, holding his dagger ready to castrate me. And then I remembered a horrible morning when my head felt dreadful and my belly roiled and bubbled like a pottage left on the fire too long.

Reaching into my purse, I handed him two coins and we set off for John Blount's house.

This parish was so full of passions and anger, it was easy to believe any one of the men could have murdered Rachel Nailor. The Spaniard still ranked highly as a political enemy. He had reason to want to prevent Lady Elizabeth's mission from succeeding, and it would be easy to prevent it: simply murder Rachel.

And now I realized what I had been missing all along. The reasons for Moll's visit to the Spaniard were obvious! She was a *spy*! What better for the Spaniard than to have an informer inserted inside the household of Marbod, one of Lady Elizabeth's leading supporters in the area? Moll was listening at the keyhole, or something – eavesdropping on the plans Rachel and Marbod discussed. She gathered up all the information she could, and then took it straight to the Spaniard. It explained everything. Perhaps even the murder of Rachel!

Croke had been outside the church. If he had learned from Moll or the Spaniard that she was going to leave England and negotiate with the French, Croke would want to prevent her. He was a committed Catholic, dedicated to Queen Mary. He seemed to me to be jealous of Anderson, perhaps because of Anderson's sons. Croke had told me he had lost three children. Jealousy and rage are unhappy bedfellows, but when added to a religious conviction, they could be explosive. He had presumably learned from Moll that Rachel was not devoted to his church and the pope, and those would be merely additional incentives to remove her. So he followed her into the church, cut her throat, and was from that moment deeply miserable. After all, not every man is cut out to be a murderer – especially of a beautiful woman.

And there was one key to all of this: Moll. The maid who was a spy.

*　　*　　*

I walked quickly to John Blount's with Ned the Gorilla, and soon I was standing before his desk again, Ned behind me, and two henchmen at my flanks. It was not a comfortable environment.

'You seem to have been very quiet since last we spoke,' Blount said. 'I am surprised. I thought I made it clear enough that you were the main suspect in this matter and for your own security you should uncover the murderer.'

I was painfully aware that the guards on either side stood within easy striking distance of me. Either could whip out a dagger and plunge it into my back in an instant. Why had I not disappeared as I had originally intended? Even going to Paris seemed more appealing just now. It would have been more congenial than this interview.

'I have been trying to learn all I can about Rachel to see who could have killed her. And I have learned who it was,' I said with a degree of hauteur. After all, it was good to have learned all I had. I had discovered much before him, and now I could lay out the facts. Not that they would appeal to him – discovering that Marbod had been loose enough with Rachel's plans was certain to upset him.

'Really?' he said, and there was a hint of sarcasm in his tone that I didn't like.

'Yes, really,' I said. 'If you had not been spending your days in here, and got out and about to investigate, you might have learned much. Instead you chose to accuse me of killing the poor woman with no evidence whatsoever. It was a ridiculous accusation.'

'Why, because you never killed anyone?' he said, baring his teeth in what I imagine he fondly assumed was a smile.

That was a hard one, because of course, I had not, really. Not intentionally, anyway. But so far as he was concerned, I was a hired assassin, and that was the reason I was valuable to him. Still, I decided to brazen it out. 'Who hasn't killed someone? But only for good reason, such as money. I didn't kill her, because I had no need to. I did not wish to go to France with her, but that was a different matter. There was no need to murder her to evade the journey. You think me foolish enough to risk my reputation by killing a woman

without profit? However, there were other men who wanted
her dead.'

'Enlighten me.'

His tone was curt in the extreme, and insulting. He was
talking to me in the same way he might speak to a particularly
dim servant. Someone like Ned the Gorilla, for example. I didn't
enjoy being patronized, and I decided to spin out the tale a little.
'There is a merchant called Richard Croke who appears to
be very close to the Spanish. They have been watching me.
Croke was seen near the church on the evening Rachel was
killed. He denies it, of course, but he was there, he was seen,
and he had good reason to murder her.'

'You are sure of this?' Blount was quick to appreciate the
risks of this news.

'Yes. I believe he gained an understanding of Rachel's
mission to France. That being so, he might have chosen to
murder her – or his accomplice did.'

Blount looked at me with suspicion. 'Are you making
this up?'

'Croke is deeply religious and supports the Catholic faith.
He is devoted to Queen Mary. He would obviously want to
prevent Rachel's mission succeeding.'

'And he has an ally who is Spanish,' Blount said. He had
his dagger in his hand, and was now balancing the tip on his
forefinger. His eyes narrowed as he looked up at me.

'Yes, and I have seen them together several times. Not only
that, Croke was at the church the evening Rachel died. Kirk
was there too, and saw Croke speaking with her. Kirk was the
father of her child, or so he believes.'

'So it was Croke,' Blount grunted. His face almost relaxed
into a smile. 'This fellow decided to murder her.' Then he
frowned. 'Why? Rachel wouldn't have told him about going
to France.'

'No. She was far too clever for that,' I said.

His eyes now were just as I'd imagine the devil's to be: red
and fiery with the gleam of red-hot coals glittering in their
depths. 'Then what?'

'Gerald Marbod allowed the news to get to Croke – and to
his Spanish friend.'

'You're saying Sir Gerald is a traitor?'

I waved my hand airily. It was rather pleasant to have Blount on a knife-edge for once. 'I said nothing of the sort.'

'You said . . .' He tried to lean forward threateningly, but the action unbalanced his dagger. He gave a short exclamation, and I was delighted to see the blood spring from his fingertip. He thrust it into his mouth, glaring at me, as I continued.

'I said that Sir Gerald allowed the news to get out. I didn't say he did it deliberately. Croke's Spanish friend has a keen interest in young ladies. Especially a certain maidservant of Sir Gerald Marbod. I saw her only yesterday meeting the Spaniard and relaying news to him. I expect that Sir Gerald discussed Rachel's plans with her in front of the maid, and Moll hurried to take the information to the Spaniard. However, when Rachel decided to leave for France, she also wanted to speak with her lover. She sent a message to him to tell him to meet her at the church, perhaps with a view to a fond farewell. I don't know, and I suppose we never will. But she went to the church, she met her lover, spoke, perhaps with Croke, and then continued into the church and there she was murdered.'

'You think Croke killed her? Or this lover?'

'Not her lover, Kirk, no. He was madly in love with her. It was the first time, I imagine, that he had felt like that in many a long year. I think he and she parted outside the church, and he hurried to the Green Dragon, where he drank away the rest of the evening, while Rachel hurried inside the church, where she met her killer. I expect it was the Spaniard, seeking to prevent Lady Elizabeth's escape.'

He sat staring at me for a long moment, sucking reflectively on his finger. 'So what now?' he said.

'I think the important thing is to find the Spaniard, if possible, and ensure that he never commits murder again in England. And while you do that, I shall visit the Marbod's maidservant. She should be arrested too, since her spying caused Rachel's death.'

No, I know what you will be thinking: why bother to go and capture the maid, when the Spaniard was plainly the man who was most guilty? And you would usually be quite right, but I had another reason for wanting to talk to Moll, and it was all because of that dreadful head which I had suffered from on the day after Rachel's death.

Yes, I know. At the time I had merely thought it was the result of my concerns mingled with, admittedly, rather a lot of wine. But it was far too painful for it to be only that. And Moll had, almost as soon as I arrived, disappeared to hunt about the house. I hadn't given her much thought at the time, obviously, what with Rachel's news and the thought of the journey to come, but now it was clear that Moll must have set out that jug of wine in such a tempting fashion to ensure that I was would drink it.

The more I thought about it, the sudden disappearance of the little minx could only mean one thing: that this most capable spy had deliberately poisoned me. She had drawn off a jug of wine for me, as though it had been set out by Raphe, and added something toxic to it, leaving it for me to consume once she and her mistress had left. And then I remembered that Rachel was suspicious of someone listening at the keyhole. I had thought it demonstrated a great intelligence on her part, because she had realized that my servant was not the most reliable of fellows and might not be averse to listening to matters that didn't concern him. Now I was forced to realize that Rachel may well have been alert to the dangers of her own maid. Perhaps she held suspicions against Moll, and that throwing open the door against eavesdroppers was a proof of her awareness of Moll's untrustworthiness.

For many people I daresay that her attempt would have succeeded, but she was not expecting a man with the constitution of a boar.

It was the main point that remained uppermost in my mind as I trudged back to the Marbod house, Ned the Gorilla behind me. Blount had offered Ned or someone else, but I have to confess, there was something deeply comforting about the gorilla now that I had grown accustomed to his presence; this was intimidating to those who didn't know him, but for me it was now a proof of my own security. I had little doubt that

Ned would be more than adequate against almost any assault on my person.

Knocking at the Marbod hall, I was soon in Sir Gerald's hall. I didn't need Ned's assistance to capture a young maid, so I left him outside.

The chamber had grown to be quite familiar now, and that itself made my task just a little easier. It's troublesome to walk into a place in which a fellow is unknown, and to start casting allegations around. Knowing the room as I did made me feel just a little more confidence than I otherwise might. And of course there was the fact that Marbod was a loyal servant to Lady Elizabeth.

He was not there, and after some minutes of waiting, the bottler reappeared, asking me to follow him. He was one of the two who had escorted Rachel to church and back, and I followed him without the slightest suspicion. What should I have suspected? I knew that the Spaniard was the guilty party, and that Moll was his enthusiastic servant, but I also knew, so I thought, that Marbod was himself an ally. I had nothing to suspect.

Sir Gerald Marbod was in an office at the rear of the house. He had a great steel chest, fitted with many locks and devices, in which was his fortune, and I confess it rather took my attention. There is something about the sight of little sacks of gold that always appeals to me.

'Well, Master Blackjack?' he demanded. He was a little short in his manner. 'I understand you wish to see me? As you can see, I am very busy, so if we could quickly attend to the matter, I would be grateful.'

'Yes, of course,' I said in my most haughty manner. 'I am here to arrest your maid, Moll.'

'Eh?' Marbod blinked furiously, then glanced helplessly at the bottler as though seeking inspiration. 'What for? What are you talking about? Moll, you say? What has she done?'

I turned and gazed at the bottler, expecting that Marbod would take the hint as he had on the first couple of meetings, but he was having none of that today. 'Come, Master Blackjack. I don't have time today. State your piece and be quick about it!'

'It would be best to speak in private,' I said. 'However, I would like to speak with Moll.'

'Oh, very well!' Marbod waved his hand and the bottler nodded to us both and left the room, pulling the door closed quietly behind him. 'Well?'

'It is very simple, and yet it's shocking,' I said, and began to explain.

'She did *what*?' he exploded. 'Listened to my conversations with my wife, you say? Passed them to a damned Spaniard? And this fellow murdered poor Rachel?'

'Yes. Croke was at the church to meet her, and she walked inside to her doom after giving him her farewell. I assume Moll professes to the Catholic faith?'

'Of course she does. All our servants do – any man who admitted to following King Henry's church would be a source of danger to a household like ours, and so all have been persuaded to pretend to the pope's faith. It is not easy for them, but one must try to demonstrate fidelity to the queen, naturally.'

'Perhaps she does more than merely profess allegiance,' I suggested. 'It is perfectly possible that the child is a Catholic by conviction, and when she heard about Rachel, and perhaps overheard conversations between you and her, or you and your wife, she realized that it was information that would be useful to someone in Queen Mary's household. She contacted this Spaniard, and has been giving information to him ever since.'

'I find it hard to believe,' Marbod said. 'She always seemed such a meek, pleasant young maid.'

'But one with loyalties elsewhere,' I said.

'Where is she?' Marbod muttered suddenly. 'The fellow should have found her and brought her to me by now.'

'Perhaps we should seek him,' I said. 'If she has fled already, our lives could be—'

I need not continue. The door was suddenly flung open, and Moll was thrown in by the bottler, who walked in after her. She fell to the floor, tear-streaks running down both cheeks. 'Master, please, don't let them hurt me! I've done nothing to harm you, *nothing*!'

'And you will be safe if that is true,' Marbod said, but his tone was not the genial, mild cooing of the turtle dove intended to calm the troubled maid's breast. Rather, it was the stern delivery of a judge who has already heard the allegations and has noted the jury's *veredictum*. 'Tell me all.'

'I don't know what I can tell you, sir!'

'First you can tell me about this Spaniard,' he said.

'But, what can I tell you?'

'You refuse to speak?' The tone had sunk to the one in which he pronounced the sentence involving the Tyburn tree.

'I can't!'

'The girl is quite right, too, Gerald.'

To my surprise, Sir Gerald's wife, Eleanor, slipped past the bottler, who remained in the doorway. She stood looking at Moll for a moment or two, before fixing her glittering, rather pig-like (so I thought now) eyes upon me. In them there was none of that amiable companionship which a man might hope to see in a friend's. No, rather than that, her expression held only contempt and loathing, which I thought was a little rich, bearing in mind I was the main victim here. Well, other than Rachel, of course. If you ignore her, people had tried to accuse me of murder, they'd poisoned me, they'd assaulted me – honestly, to look on me as she might on a slug discovered on her plate of lettuce was more than a little thick.

'My dear, what do you mean? Who . . .?'

This last was uttered as the familiar figure of the Spaniard sidled in, looking as smug and confident as only a Spaniard can, on finding himself in a room of Englishmen who were unable to assault him.

Eleanor Marbod continued calmly, 'I have instructed her to keep all her dealings with Señor Diego and me entirely private.'

Marbod wore a perplexed frown, which he shared with me. 'I don't understand.'

'No, dear. You never did. You married me, thinking that I was a loyal servant to your Lady Elizabeth. You assumed that I was a follower of your ridiculous religion, and you assumed my devotion to any cause you might espouse. You never cared to ask me what I thought of things, did you?'

'Of course not! You are my wife,' he said.

'And I have been a good wife to you. However I am also a loyal subject to my queen.'

You may not understand this, but I had a sudden intuition. 'You mean, it wasn't Moll listening at keyholes and giving messages to the Spanish? It was you as well?'

'How dare you, you ridiculous little man!' she snapped. '*I* do not listen at keyholes! What do you take me for? I don't need to. My husband discusses his affairs with me, naturally. And then I would send Moll to Diego, and he would pass on the news to his colleagues.'

'So all the news about Rachel's journey, that was passed on to this Spaniard?' Marbod exploded. 'Woman, you have committed petty treason against your own husband!'

'Better that, husband, than committing grand treason against your queen and the Holy Catholic Church,' she retorted.

'You swore an oath to honour and obey me!'

'You swore an oath to honour and obey your queen!'

'Um . . .' I was reluctant to get between the two warring parties, especially since as any man knows, it is always dangerous to enter the lists when the contenders are a married couple. 'What will you do?'

Marbod looked at me with a frown. 'We shall have to tell the authorities what has—'

'No, husband. You shall not. *We* shall. We will send a message to the proper authorities describing the events here at St Helen's. I fear Master Blackjack here will go and be entertained by the queen's inquisitors in the Tower. It may not be the style of comfort to which he is used, but it will be a matter of comfort to know that it will not be for long. Moll, if she keeps quiet, can remain with us. As can you, if you swear to keep our secret and help uncover more heretics.'

I wanted to protest at that. It was, of course, entirely unreasonable that I should be forced to take the responsibility for all that had happened. It was nothing to do with me that Rachel had decided to undertake a journey to France to negotiate the safe passage of Lady Elizabeth; it was not my fault that Rachel had been lured into the church and murdered; I had done nothing, other than try to learn who had killed Rachel.

However, in order to protest, first a man must speak up, and just now, I could not.

Oh, it probably sounds amusing to put it like this, but as soon as Eleanor Marbod had mentioned the Tower, my mind had filled with pictures of pincers, tongs, fires, hooks and racks, and my tongue was cloven to the roof of my mouth. I made certain noises, but they were not speech.

'Stop whimpering!' Eleanor snapped. She really was a deeply unsympathetic soul. Although I was determined to appeal to her better nature, I was not sure that she had one. Meanwhile the Spaniard sniggered. I tried to give him an appealing look, but the man had no fellow-feeling. He curled his lip.

It was Moll who now took the centre of attention. She burst into tears. 'I'm sorry, Master Blackjack, I did try to warn you away from me. I tried to make you see that there was nothing to learn from me, but you would keep asking me questions.'

'You tried to poison me.' My voice returned in time to rediscover sarcasm.

She looked at me with confusion. 'Poison?'

'And you didn't want to find the messenger boy because there was none, was there?' I said bitterly. 'It was a message given to you by Madam Marbod, telling Rachel to meet me at the church.'

'I didn't know Rachel was going to be murdered. I liked her! She spoke to me and wanted to take me away from here.'

'But you still took messages to her murderer,' I said.

'What do you mean?' Moll turned her face to me.

It was a face devastated by misery, all broken and red and weeping, and in the normal run of things I would have liked to console her, but I couldn't. The thought of the poison in my wine was still in the forefront of my mind, up there with the idea of tongs, fires, pincers and so on.

'I mean, you still took messages to the Spaniard, this Diego, didn't you? And he was the man who slaughtered Rachel.'

Moll gaped, and then turned to stare at the Spaniard next to Madam Marbod, who peered at me rather like a physician discovering a new form of cancer, and said, 'You really think so?'

'You warned him about Rachel travelling to France so that he could murder her. You pretended there was a message for her, and sent her off to the church where he could ambush her and cut her throat.'

'Oh, dear. You really do seem to have worked it all out,' she said, although there was a nasty, sarcastic edge to her voice.

I was about to respond, when her husband stood. He looked as if the last five minutes had aged him ten years. He tottered, and looked like a man would, I suppose, who'd just learned that the wife he had lived with for years was in fact a snake who had betrayed everything he believed in. 'You arranged for Rachel's death?'

'Yes, happily. I could see the hold she had over you, and I wasn't going to let her get away with her treachery to the queen.'

'She was pregnant. You saw to her death and that of her child.'

'You think I didn't know of the child in her womb? I knew of your infidelity before she began to show. You betrayed my trust when you decided to part the legs of a guest here in my own house!'

'*My* infidelity? I did nothing with her!'

'Enough of this! Come, we have to go and deliver this Blackjack to the queen's officers. Husband, you will confirm everything I say to them. The alternative will be to confess that you have been colluding with the queen's enemies, including her half-sister. If you do so, you will join Master Blackjack in the Tower.'

'What of Moll?' Marbod demanded.

'She will keep her mouth shut, unless she wants to learn what the Tower is like as well. As things stand, she has acted faithfully on behalf of the queen.'

I know you will have thought of this already, but I swear I had forgotten that I had one means of escape ready to hand.

As I stood, I pulled out my pistol and pointed it at the Spaniard. He took one look at the enormous bore of the gun and quailed. It was a really rather lovely sight. I thought he might even wet his cods.

'You wouldn't dare,' Eleanor Marbod said. She turned to face me full-on, her eyebrow lifted cynically as she took in my appearance again, with a show of contempt. 'If you fire that weapon, you might kill Diego or Edmond here, but you won't be able to kill us all.' She put her hand to her belt and drew out a long-bladed knife. 'And I will kill you.'

'You can't kill a man,' I said. I was keeping my eyes on Diego and her bottler, Edmond. He was moving carefully to remain behind the shield that was his mistress.

'I've done it before,' she purred. 'There was a man on the committee of the Lord Mayor, who was an incompetent and devious thief. I cut his throat for him.'

Her husband was startled into a gasp. 'You killed Adam?'

'No,' I said, 'wait! The man who killed Bonner was surely Kirk? It was Kirk who benefitted and won a seat on the council.'

'Bonner was a fool and a danger,' Eleanor said. 'He was involved in activities that threatened my husband's business, and he had to be removed. It was fortunate that the committee decided to elevate Kirk in his place, since he is more congenial to our tastes, but Kirk could not have killed him. That insipid ingrate? He barely dares tie his codpiece without his wife's permission. He could never commit murder once, let alone twice.'

'What do you mean, twice?' her husband asked sharply.

'I didn't send a message to Diego to tell him to kill Rachel, dear husband. I sent a note to tell him the problem was resolved. And I went to the church with Edmond here, and set a trap for her. When she walked through the door, I took hold of her and cut her throat then and there. And I told her it was punishment for her treachery, but also for tempting you.'

'What do you mean, "tempting me"?'

'*Don't* try my intelligence! I know she was bearing your child!' his wife spat at him.

'But . . .' Marbod was dumbfounded, and for once it was I who could answer for him.

'The father wasn't Sir Gerald. The father was William Kirk.'

'Don't be ridiculous!'

'That was why I set guards about her,' Marbod said. 'I knew

she had been having an affair, and I sought to prevent it. I didn't want her to feel any divided loyalties because of an affair of the heart.'

'Nonsense! It was because you were trying to protect her and your child in her belly!' Eleanor shouted. Well, to be honest, she screamed it. And as she did, she sprang forward.

Now, if you are in an enclosed space, and someone with a knife in her hand leaps in your general direction, the first thing a fellow does is flinch and try to beat away the threat. Which is what I tried, and for the second time in a week, the gun fired.

If you have a smoking fire, it can be unpleasant in a room. The smoke builds, and after a while the coughing inhabitants are forced to wipe their eyes and open the windows and doors, because the atmosphere becomes intolerable.

With a gun, it is different, because the discharge fills the room instantly with a thick, oily, blue/black fog. Immediately I fired the pistol, I tried to dart away, and barked my shins on a chair. It made me howl, and I was forced to hobble away before Madam Marbod could reach me with that blasted knife of hers.

However I need not have worried. Sir Gerald's wife tried to get to me but, forgetting her maid had been thrown to the floor in front of her, she tripped over. She gave a hiccup as she fell, which I heard quite distinctly, but just then I was trying to press myself as close against the wall as I could, in case someone else came to try to stab me. In any case, I couldn't see her. The room was filled so thickly with the foul, suffocating fumes of burned brimstone, and all vision was defeated.

I could hear a moaning and coughing, but although I waved my hand before my face, it did nothing to clear the fog. I thrust my pistol back into its place in my belt and placed my hand on my sword hilt.

And that was when I heard with relief the sound of knuckles dragging on the floor as the smoke swirled and started to clear.

Ned heard the shot, apparently, and realized at once that it was probably heralding some kind of trouble for me. I was surprised by this. Ned has never before indicated any great reasoning ability, after all, but that day he heard the explosion and immediately rushed the door (which was fortunately not barred), and followed the smell of rotten eggs to the room.

Edmond the bottler was standing outside the room with his back to Ned. It was the work of a moment for Ned to club him over the head, and Edmond collapsed into an untidy heap, sitting with his back to the wall. He looked up at Ned in something like horror, before slowly sliding sideways. Inside the doorway was the Spaniard. My shot had punctured his forehead, and Ned did not concern himself with the fellow.

'Ned,' I coughed as he walked in. 'Don't let her get away,' I gasped, pointing to Madam Marbod.

It was a pointless command.

Sir Gerald was on his knees before his wife, his features contorted with grief and shock. I didn't understand at first, but then I saw that his wife had fallen on to the knife she had been holding. I suppose she dropped it to break her fall, but it fell with the blade uppermost somehow, and since it had a sharp point, her weight drove it in deep into her breast. Sir Gerald covered his face and wept, while Moll struggled desperately to free herself from the woman's body. In the end it required Ned grabbing hold of Eleanor's shoulders and lifting the body from her before Moll could scurry away, fretfully tearing at her clothes, which were liberally smothered in Eleanor's blood.

'Moll, calm yourself,' I said, and it was then that she looked at me with a tragic expression, her eyes rolled up, and she collapsed beside Eleanor.

NINE

I stretched luxuriously.

There are mornings when waking is merely refreshing a nightmare, and then there were those mornings like this, when waking was a pure joy.

In the last week I had been advised that I was to undertake a perilous journey, been accused of murder, threatened with robbery and violence, with castration, and finally with exposure to the queen as being a heretic and traitor. And by some miracle, I had confounded all my enemies and was now, on a fine morning, listening to the birds making a racket outside my window, considering the alternative pleasures of a trip over the river to the Cardinal's Hat to be entertained by the floozies there, or perhaps a visit to the Green Dragon to see if there were any games of skittles or cock fighting where I could chance my luck with a little gambling. The options felt endless.

The main thing was, I had survived. It was ironic that my shot had slain the Spaniard. He would have been a sore embarrassment, had he survived, and the death of Eleanor Marbod, falling on her own dagger like that, was also fortuitous. Either of them, had they lived, could have been difficult to deal with. As it was, there was only the bottler to deal with, and since Marbod had a position in the law, he was quickly bustled away to Newgate, where he would find it enormously difficult to make any allegations that would stick, whereas the fabrication that he had been found trying to rob Eleanor Marbod's jewellery box, and murdered her when she discovered him, and the fact that these were all stated by Marbod, and confirmed by me, would tend to ensure that he would be sentenced to a Tyburn Trot before long. And that, having seen him try to help capture and kill me, was a very satisfying conclusion to the entire affair.

As it was, we had a new tale to tell: the Spaniard had broken into Sir Gerald's house to rob him, and had actually stabbed Eleanor Marbod, but I had been in his office and shot the murderer. It was a deeply satisfying story.

I was soon dressed, and while downstairs, I demanded a light breakfast and a thin ale. Cecily seemed fairly pleased with herself on hearing this, as if my sudden return to Lenten habits was in some way her own doing, but I ignored her.

After breaking my fast, I decided to go outside and took the sun as I walked about the parish, finally returning to the church, which had been reconsecrated the previous Friday, I now learned. However Peter was not in attendance. Instead there was a youth who must have been fresh from university, from the look of his pimples and nervousness. At least he was too young and inexperienced to rail against the parishioners for any perceived lasciviousness. It all made for a more relaxing service than those over which Peter had officiated.

The main aspect, I reflected later, walking from the church while carefully avoiding Gawtheren, who was trying to catch my eye, no doubt with a view to continuing our dialogue from the inn, was that my reputation was secure, and now I could consider returning my life to a moderately even keel.

I walked up the close to Bishopsgate, turned right and headed to my favourite pie maker's. With a good coffin of meat and peas with thick gravy inside me, I sighed contentedly, leaning against the shop's trestle.

And while I was there, I saw the apothecary idling his way along the road. I hailed him, and enquired after his patient.

'Him? Oh, he is well, master. I shall submit my fee shortly. He said that you would reimburse me for the full amount.'

I felt my mouth fall open at that. So the foul tavern keeper Pudge was going to try to impose another bill on me? When I had saved his life, sending for the physician so swiftly. No doubt without his ministrations, Pudge would have died on the floor of my parlour, shot by his own henchman.

The man had already moved on, and feeling weak and out of sorts, I decided I would return to my house and rest. I should spend more time there, ensuring that Raphe and Cecily did not get up to any more playing of the beast with two backs.

After the stern example given by Rachel and Croke, I thought I should spend more time in the house acting as a principled barrier to their further enjoyment of the natural pleasures. If there was one thing I did not want in my house, it was the sound of a squalling child.

Once inside, a grumpy Raphe brought me a fresh thin ale as I sat in my parlour, and I was just finishing that when there came a loud rapping at the door. Shortly afterwards Raphe brought in John Blount. His henchmen, I understood, were waiting outside in the street.

'Master Blount, I am glad to see you. I hope I find you well?'

'I am content, let us say. It is a shameful matter, and sad to see how Sir Gerald has become a widower, but the affair has at least been tidied up.'

'By which I take it you mean to thank me for resolving things.'

'I am content that my incentive worked.'

'Incentive?'

'I thought it convenient to suggest that you might be considered as the murderer. It gave you the spur to try to discover the true culprit,' he said with a dry grin tugging at his mouth as though this were the most splendid joke, and we must shortly fall about in great amusement. I felt a different cast of mind.

'You allowed me to believe that you were going to report me to Lady Elizabeth as responsible for slaughtering her favoured ambassador,' I said, and no, there was no answering smile on my face. No, I was angry. All that pain, all the anguish and terror, the fear that I must leave London and flee to some godforsaken peasant hamlet far away, was enough almost to make me shout and curse, but so many words vied for expression that I found myself unable to speak for a while.

In the meantime, this obnoxious scoundrel continued speaking as if chatting about the price of sack or bread.

'Yes, I knew you had the sly intellect to work out the truth of this matter, were I to give you just the baldest hints that you must seek the murderer. It was, so I believed, one of the men in the parish, although it did not occur to me that it could be the wife of Sir Gerald. Indeed, I had always taken his assurances of his loyalty and that of his entire household as being utterly convincing. It only goes to show that, no matter how determined a man might be, his own home could be the source of trouble.'

'I could have been killed.'

'Yes, but fortunately you are a most competent man at living, aren't you? I suppose it is a function of your job as an assassin, that you can move from one death to another without allowing it to affect you, and similarly you can cope with others trying to kill you. Your constitution must be robust.'

The door opened, and Raphe walked in with a jug of wine and two cups. He set it down and poured. 'Not for me, Raphe,' I said. 'Bring me more thin ale.'

He nodded and left the room, and Blount sipped the wine. 'A little sharper than I would have expected,' he said, smacking his lips in a vulgar fashion, 'but acceptable.'

'Would you have informed Lady Elizabeth that I was the suspect in Rachel's death?'

He finished his cup and refilled it. Raphe entered with my ale, and left quietly. Blount stared into the cup thoughtfully. 'Only if you were unable to resolve the murder yourself. She was demanding results, as you can imagine, thinking that the murder of Rachel meant that her attempt at exile was already thwarted. After all, if the queen and her husband heard of the lady's planned escape, the chances of her succeeding in leaving the country would be significantly reduced. She would almost certainly be captured before making it to the coast, and that would mean a protracted rest in the Tower at the queen's leisure. Better for her to remain at one of her own manors than incarcerated. As it is, we do not know whether Diego de Toledo managed to pass news of her planned escape to anyone in Queen Mary's court. I believe that Elizabeth cannot make the attempt now, even were the French king to agree to it.'

'So Lady Elizabeth must marry this Emmanuel Philibert?'

'Possibly, possibly not. I would not make any rash assumptions about the lady's ability to confound her enemies. As one escape has been blocked, no doubt she is already looking for a second and perhaps even a third. She is a most determined lady. One setback will not discourage her. It merely reinforces her resolution.'

He drank again. 'And now I must go and speak with Sir Gerald again, and ensure that all is well with him and his affairs. It has been a terrible time for him.'

Setting the cup down once more, he took his leave, and I was tormented with the thought of the knowledge that the entire matter had been an exercise in deception. All my concerns, the fear of being held in the Tower, the worry that I might be convicted of murder, or worse, were a fiction invented by my master. I was prepared to be enraged, but in truth, I was happy. It felt as though a vast weight was lifted from my shoulders.

When Raphe entered, he saw that my cup of wine had not been drunk, and eyed it covetously. 'You have it,' I said magnanimously, and he drank it off without hesitation. Then he refilled the cup with the last of the jug and dashed that off too.

The day stretched before me, and I considered that I might go and walk a little. Some exercise would be enjoyable. And if I were to pass by Marbod's house, I could enquire after young Moll. After all, the silly chit had been through much, and she would surely appreciate the offer of a new position in a household where there were fewer excitements. She was an appealing little wench, and with Eleanor Marbod gone, perhaps she would be a pleasant addition to my household? And then I quashed the idea. The fact was, that she had surely tried to poison me. I would never feel safe drinking a cup of wine or brandy, were she in the house.

It was interesting, because she had been so convincing in her denial of attempting to poison me. It was nonsense, of course, because no one else could have had access to my wine, and she had the time to make the attempt when she was left alone in the house while I spoke to Rachel on that fateful Sunday. No one else could have done it, I was thinking – and as I did so, I was rudely interrupted.

It was, as so often, Raphe.

He suddenly burst back into my room, alarmed, his hair standing up, his eyes round as his mouth moved several times without making a sound.

'What is it, Raphe?' I demanded somewhat acerbically. I was not in the mood for his foolishness.

He was pale and somewhat incoherent. 'She done it! It was her!'

'What?'

As he spoke, Cecily entered. She had a chaste appearance, her hands clasped before her, and yet she glared with all the venom of a Medusa.

'It was me.'

'What was?'

'I put powders in your wine.'

I gaped. Yes, I was shocked, and if this was not the height of betrayal, I don't know what is. 'You put poison in my wine last week?'

'Yes. Last Sunday. It was for your own good,' she asserted.

'How is killing me good for me?'

'I wasn't going to kill you. It was just to put you off wine over Lent,' she said, and suddenly it all became clear. Her grumpiness over Lent when I asked for wine and food; her sudden alarm when the effect on me became obvious. This cook was a regular tartar when it came to religious festivals, yet she did not intend to kill me, only to make me regret my lack of religious fervour.

'She put more powder in your wine today,' Raphe expostulated. He was all but tearing his hair out, his finger pointing shakily at her. 'I'm going to die! She poisoned me!'

'Shut up, Raphe,' I said, and suddenly my anger was dissipated. It was like gunsmoke. It was thick and cloying, but as Raphe spoke, it was as if a window had opened, and suddenly the fumes were released, and all I knew was a certain beatific contentment. 'Cecily, did you put more powder into the wine today as Raphe says?'

'Yes.'

'As much as last week?'

'I wanted to make you realize you shouldn't go drinking and eating all through Lent,' she said without remorse. There was no contrition in her attitude, only a steely determination, rather like a martyr confessing.

'I cannot have a cook working for me who will willingly poison me or my servant,' I said severely.

'No, master.'

'I want your solemn promise, on your faith, that you will never do this again. You will not add dangerous substances to my wine or food. Is that clear?'

She became sulky at that, but after a little prodding, she agreed.

'And I'll take the rest of the powder now,' I said.

She went to fetch it, while Raphe stood writhing somewhat. I was a little short with him, pointing out that whatever he was suffering, it was nothing compared to what I had endured a week since. After all, I had consumed an entire jugful of wine. Raphe had only drunk two cups.

But what was most pleasant to consider was, that John Blount, my master, the man who had led me such a prolonged and unpleasant week, was just now perhaps beginning to show the effects of the powder. He would be, if I recalled correctly, slurring, and perhaps dribbling slightly, and trying to make his mouth function properly while interrogating Sir Gerald Marbod. And tomorrow, he would wake with the most foul head he had ever experienced.

I sat back with a broad smile on my face as Raphe left me.

This, I felt, was true justice.